OPERATION
SISTERHOOD

SISTERHOOD

OLUGBEMISOLA
RHUDAY-PERKOVICH

CROWN BOOKS FOR YOUNG READERS

NEW YORK

Text copyright © 2022 by Olugbemisola Rhuday-Perkovich
Jacket and interior illustrations copyright © 2022 by Brittney Bond

Visit us on the Web! rhcbooks.com

Educators and librarians, for a variety of teaching tools, visit us at RHTeachersLibrarians.com

Library of Congress Cataloging-in-Publication Data
Names: Rhuday-Perkovich, Olugbemisola, author.
Title: Operation sisterhood / Olugbemisola Rhuday-Perkovich.
Description: First edition. | New York: Crown Books for Young Readers, [2022] | Audience: Ages 8–12. | Audience: Grades 4–6. | Summary: Eleven-year-old Bo is used to it being just her and her mom in their cozy New York apartment, but when her mom gets married, Bo must adjust to her new sisters and a music-minded blended family that is much larger, louder, and more complex than she ever imagined.
Identifiers: LCCN 2021037989 (print) | LCCN 2021037990 (ebook) | ISBN 978-0-593-37989-9 (hardcover) | ISBN 978-0-593-37990-5 (library binding) | ISBN 978-0-593-37991-2 (ebook)
Subjects: CYAC: Sisters—Fiction. | African Americans—Fiction. | Family life—New York (State)—Harlem—Fiction. | Music—Fiction. | Harlem (New York, N.Y.)—Fiction.
Classification: LCC PZ7.R3478 Op 2022 (print) | LCC PZ7.R3478 (ebook) | DDC [Fic]—dc23

The text of this book is set in 11.75-point Adobe Jensen Pro.
Interior design by Katrina Damkoehler

Printed in the United States of America
10 9 8 7 6 5 4 3 2 1
First Edition

Random House Children's Books supports the First Amendment and celebrates the right to read.

To the kids of New York City—

ALL OF YOUR STORIES MATTER.

OPERATION
SISTERHOOD

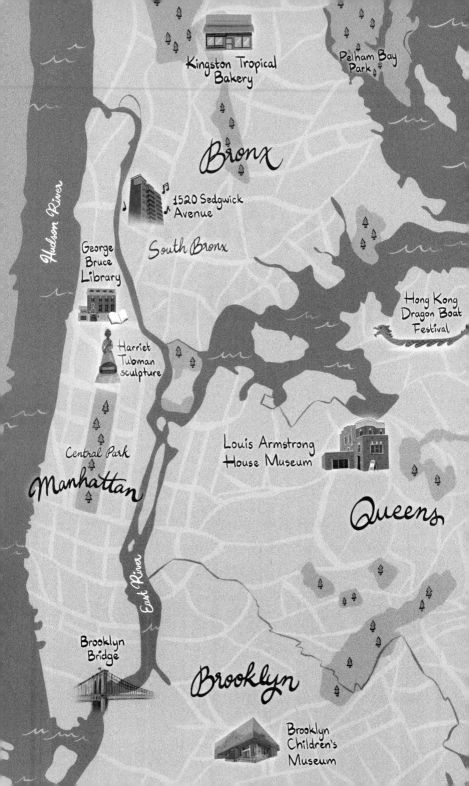

SO IT REALLY WAS a dark and stormy night, and it figured, thought Bo. *Of course* it was a dark and stormy night. Of course it was.

Okay, so it wasn't actually night, technically. It was afternoon, and Bo sat on her bed, looking through the iron child-safety bars of her bedroom window, listening to the rain *thunk*ing against the metal fire escape outside. Still, dark and stormy afternoon was close enough. And on the same day that her teacher had made the whole class enter an annoying writing contest where the prize went to the worst writing possible. School was almost over, and instead of just letting Bo hang out in the band room with the monster drum set, Ms. Phillip expected her "to spend the time productively." On a writing contest that didn't matter. What sense did that make? Ms. Phillip said the contest was inspired by some guy who'd started his book with "It was a dark and stormy night," which apparently was the worst writing ever, even if it didn't seem so bad to Bo. Certainly not as bad as spending an ENTIRE PERIOD trying YOUR BEST to write YOUR WORST. At SCHOOL. She was sure Mary Church Terrell would not be happy to have her name on a school that did things like that. And she was sure because she'd won the award for the best Mary Church Terrell speech last year. She'd always had the best teachers—she made cards and cookies for them every winter break. Until Ms. Phillip. She was the kind of teacher who kept changing due dates after you already turned the assignment in. Bo had just given her a card she bought at CVS—and she'd signed it "Best," which Mum had told her was petty-polite. Still, Mum had let it slide. She was cool like that, like a swing cymbal beat.

Thunder clapped, and Bo jumped. She heard her mum laugh down the hall. Bill must be telling one of his corny jokes again. Since neither of them had normal jobs, Bill and her mum had developed an afternoon tea routine that Bo had to admit was pretty cute. When he'd arrived today, shaking his wet umbrella all over the floor, he'd said, "If anyone needs an ark, I happen to NOAH guy!" and Mum had actually for-real laughed! Bo had laughed too, mostly because it was such a bad joke that you couldn't do anything else. And because she liked Bill and his corny jokes. And because he'd winked at her; he'd known it was bad, but he'd said it anyway, and there was something good about that. Bo liked Bill a lot. But now that he had his own key to their apartment and felt comfortable enough to be shaking his umbrella all over the place . . . it made Bo a tiny bit itchy.

BOOM! Thunder again. It was so dark. Looked like it was going to be a dark and stormy night for real, and there was no need to say it some other, prettier way. Sometimes it was good to just see and speak things as they were. Like: her mum and Bill were serious. Real serious. They'd probably get married, and Bill would be telling jokes all day long, and Bo would have to hurry up in the bathroom even though she was just getting to the age where she was supposed to spend all of her time in there, looking at herself in the mirror and figuring out her best selfie angles.

Even though she never took selfies and kind of liked Bill's jokes and loved hearing Mum laugh . . . the idea of Bill as her . . . stepdad(?) needed some time to settle. She and Mum had been a team of two for all of Bo's life, and it worked. Bill was clearly becoming essential to Mum, and Bo was used to being "all I need to get by," as Mum would sing when they baked together.

As lightning flashed and the rain continued to thud against the window, Mum called, "Sweetie pie, Bill's leaving!"

"Don't come out. I'll see you soon," yelled Bill. "Just saying bye. I'm heading home before it starts raining chickens and ducks, because then it would be real FOWL weather!" He laughed, Mum laughed, and Bo had to laugh again too, even as she rolled her eyes.

"Bye, Bill!" she said, sticking her head out of her door. "See you soon." She really did like him. She closed the door so she wouldn't have to hear goodbye smooching, and went to her desk.

She pulled an overstuffed folder that said BO'S BAKES on the front from the middle of a precariously placed tower of books. Mum had started collecting and creating special "mother-daughter" recipes when she was pregnant with Bo, and as soon as she could sit in a little vibrating baby chair on the table while Mum baked, Bo had been her "special helper" for weekly baking dates. They hadn't baked together in a while; Mum had been working a lot, teaching cooking in schools and community centers. And spending time with Bill.

As she slid out the folder, the entire tower toppled over.

"Of course," muttered Bo. "Blast!" As she bent to pick up the books, she thought about adding "Blast!" to her Bad Writing contest entry but then decided against it. She liked that word.

"You are not normal," Celia Whitlock had said to her earlier that day. Celia had been dipping orange slices in ketchup at the time, so Bo wondered who the abnormal one really was, but okay. Celia was her best frenemy; she made pronouncements like that often, like when Bo had asked why they had to be extra nice to Amber White when Amber was extra mean to almost everyone else.

"*That's* why," Celia had said with a sigh. "So she won't be so mean to us. We don't want to be targets!"

"But I don't even talk to Amber," Bo had said.

"Exactly! So that makes you a target already. You act like you don't care if she likes you."

"I don't."

"Exactly," Celia had said again as she helped herself to some of Bo's homemade apple ginger mini doughnut holes. "Mmmm, these are like . . . cake candy."

Now, picking up the books, Bo shook her head and jumped a little as the thunder roared again. As she shoved the books back onto her already overfull bookshelves, a half sheet of paper fluttered to the floor. She picked it up and immediately recognized Mum's handwriting.

SUNSHINE SURPRISE SMILECAKE

A recipe she'd never seen before! Smilecake? The recipe was clearly unfinished, with crossed-out words, question marks, and phrases like: "How much cinnamon?" and "Almond extract or anise?" in the margins. Despite herself, Bo smiled. Unlike Bo, Mum loved surprises. Which made it surprising in itself that Mum would be planning a surprise cake for Bo. But then again, it was cake, and Mum was always trying to get Bo to try new flavors, so what better way than in cake? Parents.

Bo looked up, realizing that the storm had stopped outside. Birds were chirping, and the sun was pushing out from behind the clouds. It was suddenly a sunny, smiley afternoon. She looked back at the piece of paper in her hand. SUNSHINE SURPRISE SMILECAKE.

She smiled again. Even with anise, she'd play it off. Mum had a little surprise for her, and she wasn't going to spoil it. Bill or no Bill, nothing was going to change. She was going to stay in charge of making her mother happy. "Mum!" she called, rushing out of her bedroom. "Mum!"

2

BO LOCKED HER APARTMENT door and double-checked both locks. She could smell garlic in the hallway; Mr. Korin was cooking again.

"Where you goin'?" said a little voice a few doors down. Bo didn't have to look up to know it was Dougie. That was one of his favorite questions, next to "What you doin'?" and "Snacks?"

"Somewhere where I mind my business," said Bo gently. Now that Mum had finally agreed to let her bake when she was alone in the house, she was going to test bake the Sunshine Surprise Smilecake. But first she had to finish the recipe herself. She had some ingredient ideas, like caramel extract instead of vanilla, and of course Mum had given her a scroll-long list of other things to pick up at the store.

"Where's that?" asked Dougie. Bo had tried to teach him the difference between good questions and bad questions. "No questions" was not an option.

Bo sighed. "Nowhere you know," she said. The problem was now that he was in kindergarten, Dougie was always telling her that "Teacher Jessie" always said that "curiosity is cool." Teacher Jessie seemed kind of annoying to Bo. "Try telling that to a cat," Bill had joked when she'd told her mum and Bill about Teacher Jessie's bad advice. But when she'd said "Curiosity killed the cat" to Dougie, he'd replied that Teacher Jessie always said that satisfaction brought it back, and also, was she saying that his cat was going to die? So even though she apologized right away, Mum had made her babysit him for free every afternoon for a week. Which was fine; Dougie was a pest, but cute.

"Can I come with you, though?" asked Dougie.

Bo sighed again, but she followed up quickly with a grin, nodding. Despite the questions, Dougie was good company. His mother called Bo "Big Sis," and Bo loved that. "Let me ask your mom," she said, helping him pick up the Legos on the floor in front of his apartment door. "What are you making?"

"A water park for Dinobotland!" Dougie answered. "I just started it, though," he added quickly. "I want us to finish it together."

"Okay, I got you," said Bo. "We're still finishing the pizza factory too, remember? I got a bunch of red and yellow pieces from the flea market near the museum."

Dougie cheered and Bo joined him in a happy dance. They'd been working on Dinobotland ever since Bo had started babysitting him a year ago. It was getting so big that they had to store it in sections in their respective apartments. "Your own collection of 'tinker tools' is already too big for this place," Mum was always saying.

"You are such a natural, Big Sis," Dougie's mom said to Bo every time she came over. "Dougie actually asks me to go out sometimes just so you can be his babysitter!"

Now Bo stuck her head through the doorway of Dougie's apartment. Old-school hip-hop music was playing in the kitchen. Dougie's mom called it "classic hip-hop" and never left off a mention that her uncle "used to run with KRS-One and them back in the day." "Um, Mrs. Dougie? I'm running some errands for my mum. Can Dougie come with me?" Bo was six years old before she realized that Dougie's last name was Douglas; his name was actually Douglas Douglas. She loved Mrs. Dougie, but . . . really? Douglas Douglas? And people thought kids were the silly ones.

"Bo, you can call me Dawn," said Mrs. Dougie. "Dougie, are you bothering Bo?"

"Yes, but she doesn't mind," said Dougie confidently.

Bo laughed. "It's fine, Mrs. . . . um . . . well, yeah, it's fine." No way was she gonna say "Dawn." Her mum's Supersonic Bad Manners Hearing would probably be instantly activated. Adults were always *Auntie, Uncle, Miss, Mr.* . . . they had to have a title. Bo thought that was good. It reminded them to be adults, the ones who had things under control.

"Your mother told me that Bill has a bookstore, that's

wonderful," said Mrs. Dougie. "It is so nice to see us owning businesses in our own communities." Bo nodded politely. Mostly Bill talked about needing more "traffic" in the store and "commercial rent crisis." None of it sounded that nice. Also, she'd gone a few times; he had only one shelf of kids' books, and they looked like they were there to teach her a lesson.

Mrs. Dougie went on. "And she said Bill and them bought that building from Sunflower Rogers! Rogers' Secret Spice Mix is my absolute favorite! Her grandmother made some magic right there. Since she lives right next door to them, you'll probably be cooking and baking up a storm, getting tips and tricks from Black culinary royalty. . . ."

Bo nodded some more while Mrs. Dougie talked about "descending from Kings and Queens." Bill had told her about his neighbor who had inherited a spice empire. "She's young but she's got real heart," he had said, as though people had fake ones until they got old.

Mrs. Dougie was still talking. "We've got to preserve our stories! I've been trying to get our building association together— this building has a history and we need to claim it! But everybody's too busy."

Last year, Bo had asked why there was a plaque with DJ Kool Herc's name on it when Kool Herc hadn't even lived in the building, but Mrs. Dougie had told her to hush because she had been "down with him back in the day," and a friend of his cousin's had lived in the building, and that was enough to claim that they lived in "the heart of hip-hop history." Bo had been thinking about this, since:

1) Mrs. Dougie always said she had been "tight with" every famous person in New York City, even though none of them ever seemed to come visit her or anything;

2) Even if this cousin's friend existed, she could never remember the cousin's friend's name, when they'd lived there, or how she'd gotten that convenient tidbit of information; and

3) That was a real shaky connection to "hip-hop history" anyway.

4) So, basically: no.

But Bo just kept smiling and nodding as Mrs. Dougie continued. "They called my auntie Trace-Ski-Rock back in the day, you don't even know, y'all think you invented Adidas, but what you know about fat laces? And I still have my cousin's white bomber jacket, like new condition," which she always said. Mrs. Dougie worked at the hospital, but she also had a side hustle; somehow she never ran out of family hip-hop heirlooms to sell.

Mrs. Dougie did have a point about holding on to stories, even the ones you made up for yourself, like that you were perfectly happy being by yourself most of the time. Bo understood the power of the past. You could get a lot of comfort from the things you knew; better than worrying about the future, like middle school. From what Bo had gathered about "Bill and them," they were overly concerned with "the possibilities" instead of staying safe in what they already knew. Why else would they have left Brooklyn, where they had lived for more than ten years? Bill talked like he was so excited about having his bookstore in Harlem now, but the fact that he could close his store and come over for tea almost every day meant that "the possibilities" didn't mean a whole lot of customers.

"I think that if you announce a 'Back-in-the-Day Gathering,' instead of a meeting, people will come," Bo said. "All the adults I know complain about meetings. They like gatherings because it sounds almost like a party. And you can say that classic hip-hop will be played. It'll sound fun. And Mum and I will bake a toto cake. We made one for Old Mrs. Higgins and she spoke to us in the elevator after that."

"I'll be the DJ," said Dougie. "And also in the video."

"What video?" said his mother, laughing. "Bo, that's a really good idea. I like that—'Peace! Unity! Love! And having fun!' What y'all know about that? Anyway, Bo, you're always coming up with things like that, making just hanging out into something special. My sister still talks about that little tea party you set up for my birthday. That chocolate cake—whew! And if one of your cakes got Ol' Hige to talk, well . . . that's something!" She raised an eyebrow. "You and your mom could go into business together.

How cute would that be? You plan the parties, your mom feeds the people." She tapped her forehead as Bo smiled awkwardly. "Think about it. Our people need to think of doing for ourselves, building our own economy."

Uh-oh. Bo could tell Mrs. Dougie was about to go off on one of her empowerment speeches. If Bo didn't escape soon, Mrs. Dougie would make her and Dougie recite the principles of Kwanzaa. Bo pulled the Velcro on Dougie's sneakers tight, took the bananas Mrs. Dougie offered them both, and set off with her "building little brother."

She held Dougie's hand as they crossed West Tremont Avenue. For some reason his hands were always sweaty, and he gripped hard. He never said it, but Bo knew he was still a little scared of crossing their busy streets. Bo used to wonder if it was the fact that New York City wasn't supposed to be a big car city that made people drive like they were in a bad action movie. She squeezed his hand gently, and he relaxed.

It did make Bo feel good, knowing that Dougie wanted her around and that his mom wanted her around him too—usually you got one or the other; it wasn't easy to be cool with both kids and adults. But it was the same at school, where Bo managed to glide between the boundaries of cliques, groups, trios, and clubs, never getting deep enough into any to need to pledge allegiance. It was sometimes kind of lonely, but she avoided a lot of drama. Bo did not want drama.

They walked to the West African market first. Bo had decided against telling Mum about the cake recipe; she'd ended up just pretending to be excited about finding an old book on her shelves. When Mum "surprised" her with it, it would be good and special and like the sun coming out after a storm. Even if it wasn't chocolate, which Mum knew was her favorite.

In the shop she picked up the spices and palm oil and then a couple of packets of tiny dried, smoked whole fish. From the looks of Mum's list, she was making egusi soup soon. They'd been trying Nigerian recipes in preparation for a trip to Lagos that summer. Bo was already a chin chin–making expert.

"Will those fish come back to life if you put them in a fish tank?" asked Dougie as they waited at the counter while Mama Fatou rang up the items. Mama Fatou smiled at Bo.

"Uh . . . no," said Bo. She had to be careful after the whole cat-curiosity situation. "These fish are kind of already cooked, so they are, uh, ready to be eaten. They won't come back to life."

"Except in Heaven," said Mrs. Atta, who sat on a folding chair by the entrance, as she did every day, chatting with Mama Fatou and listening to what Bo called "Jesus radio." Sometimes Bo wondered if they slept there. "We are all given new life in Heaven!" Her voice rose on "life" and "Heaven" in a way that made Dougie's eyes widen. Bo squeezed his hand again and smiled politely at Mrs. Atta.

"Stop talking that nonsense!" Mama Fatou said, sucking her teeth. She handed Bo her change. "Animals don't go to Heaven!"

Bo mumbled thanks and hurried out, pulling Dougie along with her.

"Animals don't go to Heaven?" asked Dougie, his eyes dangerously watery. "Not even cats?"

Bo hesitated. This was definitely an adult question, but she also definitely wasn't going to take him back to the store where those aunties would probably make them both sit and listen to a radio preacher right then and there.

"It's hard for me to know about Heaven exactly, because I've never been there," she started slowly. "But your momma says your dad is there, right?"

Dougie nodded.

"And that it's a place that means love, no matter what, right?"

More nods.

"So, my mum says that when we love, we can take part in Heaven's love light and shine it wherever we want."

"Yay!" yelled Dougie, jumping over a raised crack in the sidewalk. Bo jumped after him.

"So I think that anyone or anything we love can be a part of Heaven in a way." She looked up for lightning bolts and, seeing none, kept going, even though Dougie seemed to be more interested in the Icee cart up ahead. "But we don't have to talk about that with those aunties, okay?"

Dougie nodded. "Yeah. I like talking to *you*." He began to sing. "'You're alllll . . . I need . . . to get byyyyyy!'"

Bo echoed him, smiling. "You remember our lesson! Do you remember who sang that?"

"Marvin Gaye and Tammi 'Rell one time," he said. "And Diana Ross another time."

"Very good," said Bo, nodding. "And don't forget Mary J. Blige and Method Man, because the beat on that is—" She stopped, hearing her name.

"BO! Hey, Bo, it's us!" Celia, Amber, and another girl named Katrina were sitting together on a large rock in the park. Celia was waving her over, so enthusiastic that she almost fell off of the rock. The other two girls laughed as they pulled her back up. They looked like friends in movies who had sleepovers and shared lockers. Bo squeezed Dougie's hand and slowly walked over. She wanted to try with Celia. She wanted a friend to sit on a rock with. Maybe she could be more like these girls and giggle her way into their world.

"Hey," she said, looking down at the ants walking toward part of a Snickers wrapper. She looked up. Amber was still finishing her Snickers. Amber caught Bo's eye and held it; after a moment, she shrugged.

"You dropped something," said Bo. Celia giggled. No one else said anything.

"I'll get it! *I'm not a quitter when it comes to litter!*" sang Dougie, reaching down. "I remember when you taught me that song too, Bo."

"No!" yelled Bo.

Dougie froze. "Yes, you did. And why are you using your big voice? Even though we're outside, you don't have to use your outside voice." His lip trembled and Bo heard an ominous sniffle.

"Dougie, I just meant . . ." She looked up at Amber, who was making her patented "stank face."

"I was trying to be a good stew!" he cried, picking up the wrapper. Celia laughed, and Amber and Katrina immediately joined in.

"Yeah, Bo," said Amber. "He was being a good *stew*." She yawned. "Oh my goodness, New York City is so boring. I can't wait till we're all at the Vineyard, right?" Bo watched Celia and Katrina nod. Celia avoided her eyes. "We're all going to the Vineyard together."

Bo shrugged, and Dougie sniffed loudly, still clutching the wrapper. "You *are* a very good steward," she said softly. Bo took the wrapper from him and walked it to the trash can a few feet away. She heard the muffled whispers and giggling as soon as her back was turned.

When she returned to the group, she focused on Dougie. "I'm sorry I used my *outside* outside voice. I just meant that that wrapper was . . . dirty," she said, hugging his shoulder.

"Whatever." Amber rolled her eyes. "You're cute," she said to Dougie.

"Bo's my best friend," said Dougie. "I know she's sorry."

"She sure is," muttered Katrina, and the girls laughed again. Celia was the loudest. Bo glared at her, and she laughed louder.

"You really put the *fr* in *frenemy*," said Bo, looking directly at Celia, who glanced at Amber before she stopped laughing.

Celia looked back at Bo as she spoke. "Amber, I can't wait to get there either." Then she slowly and deliberately turned away. "It's gonna be so much fun—best friends at the Vineyard!" Celia, Amber, and Katrina fell into a conversation about waves and beach picnics as though Bo and Dougie weren't there. Celia leaned into Amber and Katrina as though she and Bo hadn't been clinging to each other in the cafeteria wilderness just a few days ago. As though Celia hadn't been the one who invited Bo to join them.

Bo grabbed Dougie's hand again and left without saying goodbye. The giggles and whispers got louder as they moved away. And Bo realized that that was why Celia had called her over in the first place.

"Were those your school friends?" asked Dougie as they got back on the sidewalk and she sprayed his hands with hand sanitizer.

"I don't have any school friends," said Bo. "But I have a best friend—that's you." She hoped Dougie didn't notice her voice breaking. "And I'm sorry again I yelled. But she should have picked up her own trash."

"Yeah," said Dougie. "But sometimes you have to help people be better." He shook his head. "I don't know if it worked, though."

Bo wasn't sure if she could still hear them laughing or if it was just in her mind. It didn't really matter. She shook her head. "I don't know either."

Dougie peered at her. "Are you okay?"

"Yep!" Bo said brightly, forcing a smile. "Now. 'You're All I Need to Get By.' There's a hip-hop version too, but, uh, that's for when you're older."

"My mom always says that. Older is a long time away!"

"Not as long as it seems," said Bo, swinging his arm. "My mum says life comes at you fast."

"What does that mean?"

Bo shrugged. She'd already handled cats and fish in Heaven; that was enough for today. "I guess we'll find out."

3

"THE ORGAN WAS SOMETHING else today, huh?" said
Mum.

Bo shrugged. "It sounded like an organ."

Mum smiled one of her frustrating smiles at Bill. "Bo adores
the organ. It's how we started coming here."

Bill nudged his daughter, Sunday, who was standing next to
him, looking like she liked herself a lot. "Hear that, Sunshine?
Another thing you girls have in common." He looked over at Bo.
"Sunday plays piano."

"I don't play the piano," said Bo. "I'm a drummer. Percus-
sionist." In her opinion, if your name was already Sunday, your
dad probably shouldn't nickname you "Sunshine." Even if you did
seem to smile a lot.

"Bill meant that you're both musicians, honey," said Mum,
elbowing Bo gently.

"Oh. Yeah. I guess we are."

"And keyboards," said Sunday. "I'm on the keys."

"Aren't pianos keyboards?" asked Bo. And who says they're "on the keys"? Sunday didn't talk like she was eleven.

"Yeah, I just meant I play the regular piano and electronic," Sunday said, smiling bigger. Bo had vowed not to like this girl, but all of that smiling threatened to loosen the knot in the pit of her stomach.

"The organ too?" asked Bo.

"No, but I bet I could," said Sunday. "It's in the family, you know?"

Bo was silent as they left the Cathedral, with one of the usual tour groups filing out after them. Sometimes all the tourists made it feel a little less churchy, but sometimes it also made it easier to hold whatever all this churchy stuff meant inside of herself, because no one was looking at her when they were gawping at the stained glass and art exhibits.

The sun was still bright. One thing about it almost being summer was that even though the Evensong service was the last one of the day, it felt like there was still a lot of day left. The casual service was her favorite: low-key, lots of music, no swinging ball of incense that made her cough. She didn't know how she felt about sharing it with Bill and his daughter, though. So far Sunday seemed okay. SEEMED.

"Do you like pepperoni? I do, so I hope we get that," said Sunday to Bo as they were seated at V&T, the cozy Italian restaurant across from the Cathedral. Bo and her mum had been eating there weekly since before Bo was born—literally. She'd seen photographs of Mum and her dad here, laughing as they tried to balance a pizza box on her mother's very pregnant belly.

"Yeah—yes, I do," said Bo. "Actually—"

"I knew it! I knew we'd like the same thing," said Sunday. "I'm good at predicting. And deducing—did I tell you I'm working on a series of detective novels? The main character is sort of based on me. . . ."

Bo was going to say that she'd read pepperoni was the most popular pizza topping in the United States, so it wasn't exactly a thing that needed detecting. But she just smiled because it was easier. And because everyone else at the table was smiling, and it seemed super important to everyone else that she have things in common with Sunday.

"Do you want to get penne?" Mum whispered to Bo. "Even if we get a pepperoni pie, I'll split it with you. We've got a long subway ride home—we should fuel up." She winked.

Bo nodded. Mum still had her back. For a fleeting moment, she thought about asking Mum to come to the bathroom with her so she could spill it all—the whole story of the cake recipe, asking Mum what this dinner with Bill's daughter really meant, and maybe just bursting into tears because even though she wasn't exactly sad, she needed a good cry. And a big hug.

Then Mum hugged Bo's shoulders and smiled at Sunday, saying out loud, "Bo and I are going to order penne vodka too, if anyone wants to taste. It's one of their best dishes."

And as they shared Caesar salads and mozzarella sticks and smiles and stories of all the things that Bo and Sunday had in common, Bo wondered what it would be like the next time she and Mum came to V&T on their own, or if they ever would again. Or would she have to share everything, even her secrets?

4

"LEMON ZEST OR OIL?" Bo squinted as she read the hand-written notes in the margin of the recipe. Since she didn't like surprises, she'd decided that she was going to make sure she didn't get one, even a cake one. She didn't have a whole lot of time. Mum had only gone to Boogie Down Grind with her friend Lauryn; that gave her about an hour and a half. It had taken quite a bit of work to get Mum to agree to home-alone cooking, and even though it made her feel very grown-up, it also made a lump form in her throat. When she was little, it had been so much fun to whip up little floury clouds and laugh and laugh. Now she took things more seriously. Bo had had to take a kitchen-safety course at Uptown Community Center—and she'd aced it, of course. Not one spill, and she'd been named the youngest winner of the Most Careful Cook Award. Then she'd had Mum's personal cooking-safety course, which was twice as long and ten times harder, and didn't come with a certificate or party when it was over—just a list of warnings and conditions. Technically it was over, but Mum still gave her pop quizzes and made her do routine reviews every night while they did the dishes together.

As she poured the last two capfuls of caramel extract in with the eggs, their yolks warm and golden, she made a mental note to add coconut extract to her next shopping list. She poured the wet ingredients into the dry. Sunshine Surprise Smilecake. She still had the tiny aluminum cake pan from her Little La Belle Bakery Kit. Mum had tried to get her to give it to Rachel, who lived on the first floor and wanted everything anyone else had, but Bo had held firm. You never knew when you'd need things, and she just pretended she didn't hear Mum sigh the way she always did over her collections. But since Bo kept everything in order and out of the way, even in their small apartment, Mum couldn't force her to get rid of anything until she was good and ready. Anyway, Rachel's frequent whining and constant tantrums did not make her a worthy recipient of even the empty gummy bear bag that Bo was saving from last year's Sunday school Easter party. She wasn't sure why she was saving it, but she knew it wasn't for a pain in the butt like Rachel.

About five minutes after she put the tiny cake in the oven, Bo's phone rang. She looked over at it: Dougie. She sighed, but she couldn't leave him hanging.

"HELLO!" He always yelled on the phone. Bo could hear his mom in the background whispering, "Inside voice, bunny."

"Hi, Dougie, what's up," she said, trying to keep the smile in her voice.

"Hi, Bo! I thought that maybe you were making treats. We were walking past your door and I smelled something good, and then I heard dishes, and remember how we played Detective the last time you came over? I deducted that you were making treats. Can I come help?"

Bo tried to smile. "I'm sorry, buddy," she said slowly. "Not today."

"You're not making treats?"

Bo never lied to Dougie. "Well, sort of. But this is . . . special."

"Aren't we special friends?" Dougie sounded more confused than anything else.

"We are, but this is . . . something I have to do all by myself." There was a long pause. Bo looked at her timer. "I'm sorry, Dougie."

"But we're a team!" said Dougie, and Bo could hear the tears gearing up. "Teamwork makes the dream work, remember? That's how you helped me with my bad dreams! You said we were a team!"

Bo's heart sank. It wasn't Dougie's fault he didn't understand. He was still a baby, in kindergarten, where learning meant fun, and read-alouds happened every day. She offered a few more weak words of apology and hung up quickly, promising an extended game of Pretend Superstore soon.

Forty-five minutes later, she was smiling again. The cake had been perfect, like being filled up with sunshine from inside. As she wiped the counter clean, the doorbell rang. Bo ignored it. After a couple of minutes, she heard the key in the lock, just as she expected: Mum. Another test, and she'd aced it.

"Good job, sweetie pie," said Mum, kissing her forehead and sniffing. "Never answer the door when you're home alone." She sniffed again. "What did you bake? And more importantly, where is it? Bill's going to pop by. He'd love a treat."

"Oh, uh . . . it was nothing. I was just . . . experimenting, and . . . you wouldn't have liked it," said Bo quickly. "Waaay too sweet." She opened the refrigerator. "I made a fruit salad for dessert, though!"

"Well, all right, then!" said Mum, rubbing her hands together. "Dessert for dinner!"

Bo breathed a sigh of relief. She didn't want to hurt her mother's feelings when she was so happy about Bill and wanting Bo to be best friends with Bill's talky daughter. Talking about all the things they used to do Before Bill was probably the kind of thing that would make Mum sad.

After the fruit salad (along with some homemade vanilla whipped cream) was finished, though Bo had homework to do (because Ms. Phillip was the kind of teacher who gave homework until the very last second of school), they settled in the living room for a game of dominoes before bed. Bo wanted to draw the easy laughter and deep joy of the day out even longer. It seemed like the magic of the cake had enveloped the whole evening.

"Domino!" called out Mum. Bo didn't mind losing; she was happy anytime Mum could play something with her. Dougie's game skills only went so far. They snuggled together on the couch with an issue of *Cherry Bombe* magazine that Mum had been saving; Bo learned about Chef Edna Lewis and how she understood that food had a story. Mum was hoping to teach her own "culinary tales" workshops one day, and she was thinking of writing a book about the history of different foods across the African diaspora. Bo loved the word *diaspora*—it felt wide and deep. Every time they did a little more research for their upcoming trips to Paris and Lagos, she'd whisper it to herself.

Bo pictured another day like this, not too far in the future, when she and Mum would laugh together about the story of the Sunshine Surprise Smilecake—maybe they'd even put the recipe in their own cookbook!

With her head and heart full of ideas, and her stomach full of good food, Bo didn't protest too much when it was time for her to "go to bed." She finished her homework by flashlight after Mum's last tuck in, just as Bill's signature quick double doorbell ring sounded. She folded the recipe carefully and stuck it under her pillow. Magic was real, and just like in a fairy tale, if she was good, maybe it would last forever.

5

BO HAD DECIDED THAT there were fifty-two ways this could go, and she'd glued each one of them onto a playing card, these really ugly ones that Auntie Fola had gotten at a real estate conference. Making this First Meeting like an art project had helped. A little.

As she and Mum stood on the steps of this giant, old red-brick brownstone, Bo was thinking that maybe she'd start another project right away: a scrapbook of their old life, since it was going, going, gone. She snuck a piece of the Cadbury Dairy Milk bar that Mum had surprised her with before they'd left their apartment. A *real* one; Mum had gone all the way down to Myers of Keswick to get it, along with some Cornish pasties for later.

Mum caught her eye and grinned, all glowy and shiny. She'd been this way for weeks. What else could Bo do but smile back? Mum was too excited to see that it wasn't a real smile.

But Bo noticed that Mum hadn't actually rung the doorbell

yet. They'd been standing on this step for a while now. There was a ramp round the side that curved and wound its way to the same door; it was slightly newer-looking than the rest of this brick . . . well, Bo didn't even know what to call this place. It was somewhere between magnificent and *eccentric*, which was a word she'd heard Auntie Fola use after she'd met the rest of Bill's house family. It looked like something out of a book, with bright curtains in every window and plants on the steps, on the windowsills. There was a poster of a raised fist and the words NO JUSTICE, NO PEACE! underneath in one window, and a painting with fancy lettering that read LET US THEREFORE MAKE EVERY EFFORT TO DO WHAT LEADS TO PEACE AND TO MUTUAL EDIFICATION, which Bo thought sounded churchy and also not easy to do. A jet-black cat peered down at her from one of the highest windows. Cats always looked like they had an attitude, which probably should have meant that Bo felt a bond with them, but she never did. She glanced over at Mum, who was still just standing there.

Bo pulled from her pocket a card labeled THE HOUSE FAMILY. When her mum had first explained it to her, it sounded like one of those books she loved, about a warm and wacky family where everyone got over arguments quickly and had ice cream for breakfast on Saturday mornings. But that was books. In real life, this was just confusing. Of course there was Bill's daughter, Sunday, who had, along with Bill, become a regular at Evensong and more awkward but tasty pasta dinners at V&T. Mum and Bill had talked so much that first day that Sunday and Bo had mostly just looked at each other and answered their respective parents' questions. Sunday hadn't asked for anchovies or extra onions or anything weird on the pizza, at least. Yet.

So there were the Twins, Lil and Lee. And they were *identical*. What if they tried to trick her? She'd have to figure out subtle ways to tell them apart right away. Then there were the Twins' parents, Hope and Charles. Mr. and Mrs. Dwyer. Or was she supposed to say "Auntie Hope" and "Uncle Charles"? She'd just say "Hi." Hope, Charles, Lil, Lee. Got it. And she couldn't forget Auntie Sunflower, who technically lived next door but was so much "part of the family" that after she sold them the house, she had taken the fence between their backyards down so they'd have one big yard ("enough room for Rubia, and Barbara and Shirley's chicken mansion," Sunday had told Bo, as though that explained everything). But Sunflower Rogers was an impressive name. Apparently she could build just about anything, and even though she was really, really rich, Bill said she was "good people," and that counted for a lot.

Bo looked up at the roof of this massive brownstone. This house could hold a whole village. Bo had grown up in what Auntie Fola called "the boogie down birthplace of hip-hop" when she was talking in real estate agent talk and not just saying "the Bronx." Bo and Mum's tiny one-bedroom apartment was "cozy," another word for "small." Their building did have an elevator, which was good for Bill's wheelchair when he came over. It wasn't so good when the elevator was out of service. Bo and Dougie had climbed those six flights of stairs together many times. That's how it was when your building was just plain old *old*, not "historic," like this place. This place looked like a mansion, or even a castle. It was definitely a step up. Maybe even a whole flight up, judging by the fancy door knocker and the flower boxes in the windows. Flowers were nice.

Maybe this wouldn't be so bad after all.

Bo smoothed her T-shirt, forgetting about the chocolate on her hands until she saw it smeared across her front. So much for first impressions. A dog barked from somewhere nearby. Mum had said that the family had a dog, two cats, a bearded dragon(?), a turtle, and some "other household friends." Once she thought Mum had mentioned chickens, but she must have heard wrong. Anyway, it sounded like a lot of animals. Why did Mum have to fall in love with a man who clearly lived in a zoo?

Maybe this was going to be terrible.

Yikes, Twins. She hadn't met them yet, but Bo already thought of them with a capital *T*. They probably finished each other's sentences, just like in a movie. She wondered if they dressed alike even though they were eleven years old, just like Bo (and Sunday), and matchy-matchiness seemed a little, well, *juvenile*. Were Bo and Sunday supposed to dress alike too? What if Sunday was actually not that nice when there wasn't pizza around to be happy about? What kind of name was *Sunday* anyway? It might be worse than *Bo*, because at least *Bo* was short for something. She could put on her full name, *TOKUNBO*, at any moment, like a royal robe or an invisibility cloak.

More barking. More Mum not ringing the bell. Bo sent secret daughter brainwaves. *We can just turn back now, Mum! Auntie
Fola will find us a new place, and we can go back to no animals and
no Twins and no days of the week for names, just you and me sticking
together no matter what!*

Bo squeezed her mother's hand and took a deep breath.

"Mum? Want me to ring the bell?"

ARGH!! That was NOT what she meant to say! Whywhywhy
did her mouth always do that?

Because she knew her mum wanted this more than anything.
Parents thought they were hiding their feelings when really they
told you everything with just a look.

Bill had appeared like a Prince Sorta Charming (with corny
jokes and a people-filled brownstone and a daughter and apparently a zoo), and Mum said sometimes you just have to go for it,
and here they were, not ringing the doorbell yet. Mum wanted
"Community and Stability and Like Sisters for You, Honey," and
the thing was, Bo felt you either had sisters or you didn't. Bo
didn't, and that was fine. Anyway, they *had* a community. They
had Dougie and Mr. Korin and the West African aunties with
a Jesus radio soundtrack. Their lives were as stable as Nana's
old table, which was so heavy it took both of them to move on
cleaning days. What did "like sisters" mean anyway? Bo had always known what she wanted. Why did she need something she'd
never asked for?

Mum squeezed her hand back and rang the bell.

The barking got louder, and what sounded like a herd of horses thundered toward the door. Voices, excited and maybe a little squabbly, got closer. Bo looked down at the chocolate smear on her shirt and tried to fold her arms across it in a way that looked totally natural.

The door opened, and a panther cub sprang out.

Okay, so it turned out to be just a cat, apparently the one that had been giving her side-eye from the window. She'd had no idea that a cat that big could move so fast.

Also, it LEAPED at her and Mum, and when they jumped back, it ran outside and down the stairs. A girl with a short afro and a white T-shirt that said **SAVE THE WHALES (and all the other animals too)** in thick black lettering pushed past Bo to chase the cat out onto the sidewalk, turning back and yelling "WELCOME! I'm Lee!" She swooped onto the giant cat. "NOOOO, MR. BULTITUDE!"

Another girl, who looked like an anime version of the first one, with her long hair up in two high buns that cascaded down into long two-strand twists, waved and yelled, "WELCOME! Hi, I'm Lil!" and then turned and ran up the flight of stairs.

A turtle sauntered into view, looking around like, *Hey, what's all this?*

Bo wondered the same thing.

There was one girl left, and Bo knew her, but she was still surprised when Sunday grabbed her into a big hug. "WELCOME! I'm Sunday, remember?! Of course you remember, that's silly, we see each other all the time!" While Bo caught her breath, she wondered if she'd ever heard the word *welcome* so many times in one day. And if five pizza dates really counted as "all the time."

And then she felt bad for wondering that.

Lee came rushing back inside with the cat, who was holding itself all floppy and limp, just like Dougie when he'd stage his silent protests against bath time. Would she ever get to babysit Dougie again? Lee plopped the giant cat onto Bill's lap, and it immediately began to clean itself as though it had been there all afternoon. Lil came back down the stairs, looking like Dougie after he'd eaten all the frosting out of the Oreos and then put the empty, licked-clean halves back in the package for his mother to discover. Sunday grabbed Bo's hand, and everyone stood and smiled in the doorway.

Mum cleared her throat and said, "Uh, can we come in?"

Then, a flurry of apology and more "Welcome!"s from Bill and a woman who picked up the turtle with one hand and held a dripping paintbrush in the other. Bo figured she must be Lil and Lee's mother, "Mama Hope," the mapmaker, and wondered if she was about to paint a map on the turtle's ample back. And if she was, why? Five minutes and there was already a lot to wonder about. The panther cat jumped from Bill's lap and stood in front of Bo, side-eyeing again.

Bill moved his wheelchair backward, and everyone shuffled into the living room.

"Mama, you're dripping," said Lil.

"Oops, let me go finish up . . . ," the Twins' mom trailed off, and she left the room, setting the turtle down gently on the coffee table. Bo thought she heard her mutter something about checking on the chickens.

Oh-kay.

Bo noticed two things: that Mum's eyes were sparkling, and that something smelled . . . burnt.

"Uh, are you cooking something?" she asked.

"Oh NOOOO!" Sunday wailed. Everyone rushed into the kitchen. Mum took a peek into the oven and turned it off.

"Well, it looks like these . . . interesting-looking baked goods might be ready!" she said, and pulled out the muffin tray.

"It smells like they were ready last week," said the Twin called Lil. She coughed and coughed, and just when Bo thought she was overdoing it, Bill gave Lil the universal *Stop Now or You Won't Like the Consequences* parent face.

"Happens to us all the time, right, honey?" Mum turned to Bo, who did a kind of nod/shrug thing. Bo wasn't sure what to say or do or *anything*. Also, that tray of blackened, smelly blobs did *not* happen to them. Not ever.

Now everyone stood looking at the muffin tray. Sunday pried out one of the smoky blobs, and it plopped onto the plate like a mini-asteroid. Bo heard the front door open, and a very tall man swept into the kitchen. Bo guessed it was mostly the cape he wore that made him sweep instead of just walk. She also guessed he was the Twins' dad, "Papa Charles," because she'd heard he was an actor, and this was a pretty dramatic entrance.

"So sorry I'm late, we had a feline emergency on set," he boomed, grabbing both Mum and Bo into a quick double hug. "Welcome!" (*Six*, Bo thought. She couldn't help it.) He eyed the still-smoking tray. "Science experiment?" he asked, giving Sunday a forehead kiss. "Looks very authentic!"

Sunday sighed, and Lil giggled.

Papa Charles glanced over at Bill. "Closed the shop early again?"

Bill nodded. "Yep, I'll probably just change the hours." His smile didn't quite reach his eyes. "More time to be home with my beautiful family!"

"What kind of feline emergency, Pops?" asked Lee.

"Nothing dire, just living out the diva cat stereotype," said Papa Charles, untying his cape and hanging it on a hook over a bright yellow apron. Bo wondered if he had a regular coat or just wore a cape every day, as though at some moment he might need to become a superhero. He reached down and scratched the black cat, Mr. Bultitude. "This guy would have been too frisky, but Mrs. Pilkington probably should have auditioned." Right on cue, another cat, tan and floofy, strolled into the kitchen; Bo figured this was Mrs. Pilkington. Bill had told her that Papa Charles was the host of a local public television show called *Urban Wildlife*, which was about, well, urban animals. It turned out that there was a lot of wildlife in New York City. Now Bo wondered if it had all come from this apartment. "We're doing an episode on bodega cats, and the cat treats we brought from Mr. Bultitude's stash weren't the ones they liked."

Hearing his name, Mr. Bultitude stalked to the middle of the kitchen and flopped over on his back. Mrs. Pilkington meowed and stomped out and up a flight of stairs. Attitude. Bo almost smiled. She could work with that.

"How many cats do you have?" she asked. It felt like more than two.

"Only two," said Lee. "*So* not fair."

"But Mr. Bultitude thinks he's not just a cat," said Lil. "Neither does Mrs. Pilkington, that's who went upstairs. Are you allergic?" she asked Bo, looking hopeful. Lee shot her twin a look.

"No," said Bo. "He's just . . . kind of . . ."

"Large?" said Lil. Bo nodded.

"He's just healthy," said Lee quickly, bending down to scratch his belly. "Aren't you a healthy cat?" Mr. Bultitude rolled around a bit more and then got up and sniffed Bo and Mum before he walked out of the kitchen with his butt very high.

"I think he was mad that you were talking about other cats," said Lee to her father as Mama Hope wandered back in. "And he doesn't like the *B* word."

"*Bodega?*" asked Bo.

"Yeah," said Sunday, rolling her eyes. "Our cats are so bougie."

"Oh! It's almost dinnertime! Whose turn was it? I hope

not mine." Mama Hope sniffed, and her face fell. "Is that what I smelled?"

"It's MUFFINS," Sunday said loudly. "WELCOME MUFFINS, not SCIENCE, not dinner."

"Not edible," muttered Lil, and Lee nudged her. Bo directed a small smile around the room, to look like she wasn't taking a side.

"OW!" yelled Lil. "You are all witnesses! She just totally flicked me! This better be up for Table Talk tonight!"

"I didn't see anything," said Sunday. "My name's Bennett. Not in it."

"What's Table Talk?" asked Bo. Suddenly she wanted to take a nap.

"Your name is literally Saunders," muttered Lil. "So . . . no."

"Sometimes we sort of set discussion topics for dinner," said Sunday, dumping her muffins into the trash can. "And we can submit them in advance if we want."

"Sweetie pie, go with the girls. They can show you around this beautiful old house," said Mum.

Sunday grabbed Bo by one hand, Lil took the other, and they dragged her out of the kitchen. Mr. Bultitude marched behind them, and Lee scooped up the turtle and brought up the rear. Bo turned to look back at Mum, but she was heading into the living room with the other parents, smiling even wider than before.

6

"LET'S GO STRAIGHT TO YOUR ROOM," said Lil to Sunday, who frowned and said "*I know*," and led Bo down the hallway to a big, messy bedroom with a constellation mural on the ceiling. Bo tripped over some books and clothes on her way in.

"I spent all day cleaning up," said Sunday. "I really wanted you to feel welcome. I deduced that you might be into order and method. I'm kind of like the Black Hercule Poirot."

"That's . . . really not true," said Lil. "But there should be a famous Black detective. *I* should be a famous Black detective!"

"I literally just said—" huffed Sunday. She stopped and looked at Bo. "We're not always like this." She glared at Lil. "And this is not how I expected to welcome you!"

Nine, thought Bo. *That's nine welcomes.* Between the "muffins" and this "cleaned-up" room, she wondered if this was supposed to be a giant joke. If they were just having her on, like in one of those movies where the family bands together against the Outsider. Bo narrowed her eyes and didn't say a word.

"Bo is a really nice name," continued Sunday.

"My full name is Tokunbo," Bo said. "But you probably can't say that."

"Tokunbo! It's beautiful! It's Yoruba, right?" asked Lee.

Bo's eyes widened. "How did you know?"

"We did a study of Nigeria last year," Sunday answered. "We learned a little Yoruba too when my dad and your mom . . . got more . . . serious." She pointed Bo to the big pillows on the floor. Lil was sprawled out on two of them, and Bo pretended not to see Lee give her twin a *look* before Lil moved over to make room for Bo.

"Oh, wait—you go to real school now. That's good. I thought you guys, like, didn't believe in school or something." Bo was relieved. Even with its Celias and oral reports and bleach-scented cafeteria food, there had been bird-watching trips to Pelham Bay Park with Mr. Delgado and lunch in the library with Ms. St. Hubert. Bo still believed in school.

Lil looked like she wanted to pull the pillows out from under Bo. Sunday cleared her throat. "Um, so. We believe in Education for Living," she said, sounding just a little speechy. "We're lifelong learners. We aren't limited by the confines of the school building or some state-sanctioned curriculum, we—"

Lee broke in. "But we totally don't have anything against traditional school—we're just doing the freeschooling thing. Kind of like homeschooling, but we just . . . have a special name for it. We, um, do a lot of projects and writing and stuff. We go out a lot too. The Parents want us to take advantage of living in New York City."

"'*Concrete jungle where dreams are made of, there's nothing you can't do!*'" Sunday sang, almost in tune. "You're making it sound boring!" She turned back to Bo. "It's exploratory learning. Or expeditionary learning. Or—"

"Extra-long explanation learning," cut in Lil. "It's fun, it's interesting, it's what we do. End of story." There was an awkward silence. Bo kept her eyes on the ceiling. Ursa Major looked unfriendly.

She heard a muffled thumping sound. "Um, okay. . . ." She heard muffled barking and looked around. "Do you hear that?"

"Hear what?" asked Sunday. Bo didn't think her detecting career was off to a good start; the thumps were pretty loud.

"No," said Lil.

"Why would we hear anything?" said Lee, looking miserable.

Now Bo heard little yelps from somewhere outside of the room and looked around at the girls again. "Okay, you guys. Is this another joke? Because I . . ." Lee made a move toward the door, but Sunday stopped her with a warning look.

"What do you mean, *another* joke?" asked Sunday.

"Hey!" Lil yelled. "Do you play an instrument?" She made little yelps, imitating the sounds Bo was hearing. "*Oooooooooh,*" she sang, super loud and not exactly on key. "Sunday probably told you we all play something. I play electric guitar, because I'm awesome; Lee's on bass, and she thinks she can sing; and Sunday's always banging on the keyboard. We all might try out for the Young

People's Chorus of New York City next year. Did you know that's where Adedayo and Airi got their start?"

At the mention of music, Bo forgot the yelps. "I'm a drummer, actually," she said. "But . . . I didn't realize that *all* of you are into music."

"I told you that already, remember?" said Sunday. "Didn't I? I mean, *I* found out ages ago." She looked from Lil to Bo. "I mean, not you, Bo, because you didn't know, like you just said. But I told *them* about the drums. I think it's so cool! Can you imagine what it's going to be like when we're all practicing? Old cranky Ms. Tyler already knocks on the door so much we were kind of pretending she was a drummer. Now we know an actual drummer! Maybe you can teach me one day! I mean . . . if you want to, or . . ." She trailed off.

Awkward. Didn't parents realize that they created all sorts of awkward situations? Suddenly Bo was angry. The yelping got louder. Then she heard barking. "I thought your dog was in the backyard? This sounds like it's coming from somewhere close by."

"Oh, Rubia, she's so loud!" said Lee quickly. "She's outside with the hens, you can't miss her, she's a Great Pyrenees, you don't see many around here, she'll probably come in to say hi in a minute, or maybe we should go out and say hi to her, yes that would be fun, her doghouse is almost as big as this room, and did you know our yard is part of Auntie Sunflower's yard next door, so it means we really have one big, giant yard for her to play in—" She paused to take a breath, and Lil handed her a glass of water.

"I mean, like, really *inside* the house," Bo said.

"We want to hear more about your drumming!" said Sunday, jumping up. "Like, djembe? Or conga?" As the barking got louder, Lil started pounding the dresser really hard. "I play keyboard, which is kind of percussive," said Sunday. "I'd love to learn more about *skins*."

Bo raised an eyebrow. Because she wasn't sure if this was still part of a big joke, and if *percussive* was actually a word or just something that these freeschooling, joke-playing sisters made up. Did they even know claves from castanets? And she did it just to show that she could, because single-eyebrow raising is always impressive. "I play all kinds of drums. And I don't really call them skins. Seriously, do you have a dog in here?"

More barking. "You mean, do we technically own a dog?" asked Lil. "Because technically—"

"I can't take it anymore," cried Lee. She raced out of Sunday's room, and Sunday and Lil followed. After a second, Bo did too. They went to another bedroom, Lee opened a closet door, and a tiny, fluffy brown dog leaped up into her arms.

"I thought so," said Bo. "Why are you keeping a dog in the closet?" *And why are you holding it like a baby?* she wanted to ask.

"It's a long story," Lee said.

Bo got the feeling that this family was made up entirely of long stories. "Were you going to play some kind of joke on me?" Bo crossed her arms. "Because if you think I like jokes, you're barking up the wrong—"

"Hey, *barking up the wrong tree*," said Lil, grinning. "Get it?"

"I *told* you, Lee," said Sunday, scowling, "it doesn't take a detective to figure out that this was a terrible—"

"No! I promise, no jokes!" Lee bundled the dog back into the closet with a few hugs and pats. "It's just—I volunteer at this animal shelter, and someone abandoned this dog, and he looked so sad, I uh—"

"Literally smuggled him out like a *dog pirate*," said Sunday.

Lee ignored her. "We didn't have time to talk to the Parents about it yet, but we will, and don't be scared of him, he's the sweetest, but, um, can you keep this a secret for now?"

Lee, Lil, and Sunday looked at Bo.

Bo looked back, her arms still crossed. The eyebrow went back up.

"Can you teach me that?" asked Sunday.

"Not the time, Sunday," said Lil.

"So . . . please?" asked Lee. "Just until we . . . have a plan."

Bo lowered her eyebrow.

"Girls, dinner!" called Bill from downstairs.

"Woof!"

"Okay . . . ," she said, just as her mother's voice rang out, echoing Bill's call.

"Thank you," whispered Lee, studiously ignoring Sunday's glare. A look passed among them all. The three sisters smiled at Bo, and Bo smiled a small smile back; something was sealed. Then Mrs. Pilkington led the way downstairs.

7

"MAMA HOPE, WHAT'D YOU MAKE?" asked Sunday as they walked into the kitchen.

"It's not finished yet," the Twins' mom replied cheerfully. She was huddled over a large casserole dish. Bo wondered why Sunday and the Twins exchanged a look.

"Can we help, Mama?" asked Lee gently.

"Like by ordering takeout?" asked Lil hopefully. "Didn't I hear something about Charles?"

"What about me?" asked her father, who now, without his cape and clearing the table, looked very much like a regular dad. "Did you hear something good? I'm sure you didn't hear anything that meant you could call me by my first name."

Lil groaned. "Haha, I meant Charles' Chicken," said Lil.

"Not so loud," said Lee. "I don't want Barbara and Shirley to hear."

"The best fried chicken ever," whispered Sunday to Bo. "We

used to hardly ever get it because it was too far away, but now it's right here in Harlem! Correction, *we're* right here in Harlem!"

"Who are Barbara and Shirley?" Bo whispered back. "And I know Charles'. I go there a lot." *A lot* was an exaggeration, but still.

"Oh, the hens, but I keep telling Lee that's different." Sunday waved her hand.

Bo wondered how it worked to have your own chickens and still eat their ... cousins?

Sunday might have read her mind, because she added, "They're not like the chickens you eat. They're like family."

Lee looked like she wasn't having it. Bo might ask Sunday about that later. But then again, she might not want to think about it too much herself.

Bill handed Lil a stack of plates. "I think you heard that from *you*," he said. He turned to Mama Hope. "I'm excited to see what Hope's cooked up for us today!"

"I hope it's cooked," muttered Lil.

Mama Hope looked over as she dipped a fork into the dish. "Uh, funny you should mention that," she started slowly. "I was going for a layered effect, and, uh, it seems that some of the layers didn't make it through the process." She lifted the fork, pulling up what looked like raw, white dough.

Mum cleared her throat. "Uh, that looks interesting! What exactly is it?" she asked.

"I call it the Seven Layers of the Earth," said Mama Hope. "It's my own geology-inspired invented recipe. But I think the mantle and the asthenosphere needed a little more time in the oven." She waved Bo's mother closer. "Lola, you're an expert . . . what do you think?"

Mum poked at the casserole with the fork. "It looks very . . . creative," she started carefully, lifting up the dish.

Just then something small and barky and already familiar to Bo streaked into the kitchen and through Bo's legs and over to Mum, who dropped the casserole dish in surprise. The "casserole" popped out in one piece and rolled under the table. Mr. Bultitude, apparently an expert at detecting food-on-the-floor moments, sidled in, sniffed at the blob, and then backed away, hissing. Everyone stared at the tiny dog cowering at Mum's feet.

"Oh!" Mum cried.

"Did Lil finally get her Incredible Shrinking Machine to work, or am I right in deducting that this dog is *not* our own Rubia?" asked Papa Charles, scooping the food back into the dish, which was miraculously unbroken.

"Rubia?" Bo looked at Sunday, who sighed.

"Oh, you'll meet Rubia, you can't miss her. She's the Great Pyrenees, the very big *actual* dog who already lives here," she said, rolling her eyes. "Very funny, Papa Charles." She shot a pointed glance at Lee.

"So what had happened was . . . ," started Lee, "as I mentioned last week, the abandoned animal crisis in New York City has risen to unprecedented—"

"Nope, nope, nope," said Mama Hope. "We are not getting another dog."

"Looks like we already got one," said Lil. "But what we don't have is dinner."

"But," said Lee, "with Auntie Sunflower's yard plus ours, we have plenty of room! And Rubia probably needs help guarding Barbara and Shirley."

"Nope, nope, nope," said Mama Hope. Papa Charles shook his head vigorously.

Mum looked over at Mama Hope. "Hope, I'm so sorry, I was just startled, and—"

"Are you kidding?" Mama Hope hugged her. "You saved us all! I'm not too proud to admit that that was a . . . a . . ." She shook her head. "I don't even know what to call that mess." The little dog licked her foot. They all laughed, and Bo realized that it was her first good laugh of the day.

Maybe this wouldn't be so bad after all.

Lee scooped up the pup and slipped out of the kitchen, but Hope and Charles were right behind her. Lil raised her eyebrows and shrugged.

"I *told* her," said Sunday.

"You all know what I'm thinking," said Bill, smiling at Bo, and even though Bo had no idea, she nodded. "I've got backup chili in the freezer!" He held his arms up in a big victory V.

"Woo . . . hoo?" said Mum.

"You always have backup chili in the freezer, Pop," said Sunday. "It's good, but . . ." She looked at Lil.

"It's scrumptious." Lil nodded. "Remember that time we had it with stew peas from Islands? Something about the two together . . ." She looked at Sunday.

"Uh, made them both even better!" finished Sunday.

"I remember that we got so full on Islands that we didn't even get to the chili," said Charles. "And no, as much as we all love Islands, we're not going to Brooklyn tonight."

Bill laughed. "I get it, I get it." He sighed and looked at the other parents, who nodded. "Looks like it's Billy's Chili and Charles' Chicken tonight!"

"Yes!" whooped Lil, holding up her hands and running victory laps around the kitchen. After a beat, Sunday joined her, gesturing to Bo to join in. Bo looked at Mum, who was smiling again. Then she jogged behind the other two girls. It *was* weird. But it wasn't *bad*.

Lee returned, sad eyed, with her parents, and the four girls finished cleaning up in the kitchen while Bill and Papa Charles went to get the takeout and Mama Hope and Mum defrosted chili and talked casserole recipes.

"Do people call your dad *Billy*?" Bo asked Sunday.

"He's the only one who keeps trying to make *Billy* happen, and only on chili days," said Sunday, adding, "which is kind of every time it's his turn to make dinner."

"Billy's Chili does have a ring to it," said Lil.

"We're not usually bad cooks," Sunday whispered to Bo.

"Well . . . ," said Lil, leaning over, "my mom usually is."

"Mama's just creative!" whispered Lee.

"My muffins really were Welcome Muffins," said Sunday sadly.

"That could have doubled as a science project," said Lil. "That's actually a good thing. We have two more projects to do this summer. I was going to do some math knitting for Dwayne Wayne, maybe a Klein bottle hat."

"What happened with the dog?" Bo asked Lee.

"He's in the workroom for now, but I have to take him back to the shelter where I volunteer," said Lee. "I had to call over there and tell Dr. Coleman the truth. It . . . wasn't good. I *might* have led her to believe that the Parents had already said yes to bringing him here."

"And . . . Dwayne Wayne?" Bo was almost afraid to ask.

"He's our bearded dragon. His tank is in Mama Hope's basement studio, with Urkel the Turtle's," said Sunday. "He loves hats."

Bo resisted the urge to hold her head even though she felt like it was going to explode. Just then the biggest, shaggiest dog she had ever seen came trotting to the kitchen entryway.

"Oh, Rubia, you know you'll always be the big dog around here . . . literally and figuratively," murmured Lee, walking over to the yeti-sized beast, nudging her out.

"No dogs in the kitchen," Sunday explained to Bo. "It's supposed to be no pets at all, but the cats don't think the rules apply to them."

Bo stared. "Whoa!" The dog looked back at her as if to say, *Yes, I am magnificent. You may pet me now.* Bo shuffled a few steps back.

"Ugh, what a mess, Lee! I *told* you," started Sunday, then she stopped and hugged Lee. "Sorry." Lil joined the hug, and Bo stood and looked away, shifting from one foot to the other.

"Living room?" Mama Hope asked, and Sunday and the Twins cheered.

Bo wondered what the workroom was, but before she had a chance to ask, Sunday grabbed her hand again. "Let's get the games," said Sunday.

"Games?"

"Whenever we have takeout in the living room, we sit on the floor—"

"And play board games," added Lil. "Like Monopoly."

"We played that last time," said Lee. "How about Scattergories?" Lil and Sunday groaned, and Bo let herself be led out to the living room, where a cat, a turtle, a hat-wearing bearded dragon (which was a thing she hadn't known existed), and who knew what else awaited.

8

AFTER A DELICIOUS DINNER of perfectly crispy fried chicken (for most of them—Bo noticed that Lee didn't eat any even if the chicken was "different") and potato salad that tasted auntie-made, along with the crunchy and spicy cabbage that Mum and Bill cooked together and a very enthusiastic game of charades that nobody won, the sisters draped themselves on various giant cushiony pillows around the living room. Bo tried to perch carefully on a beanbag and immediately tipped over. Everyone, including Bo, laughed, and she stayed on the floor, leaning her head against the beanbag.

"What are we listening to?" asked Bill. "My soca party playlist?" Without waiting for an answer, he turned up the volume on "Give Me Soca," and the adults started snapping and wiggling. Bo looked away.

Lil groaned. "I love soca, but can we listen to music from this century? And every song on there is Byron Lee. It's not like a real playlist anyway."

"Byron Lee is all you need," said Charles, high-fiving Bill and switching to a standard Uncle two-step dance.

"This is Saturday morning cleaning music," said Sunday.

"She's not wrong," said Hope, nodding.

"The whole family cleans together! To a playlist!" whispered Mum to Bo, like she was telling Bo that they'd just won a million dollars. Bo just nodded and smiled back. She decided that it was Charles' Chicken that had put something warm and cozy inside of her; she wanted to let it grow for a little while.

"Oooh, we should play Spontuneous!" yelled Sunday.

"Only if it's our own version," said Lil. "All those rules make it boring. There should be a rule getting rid of rules."

"That's called cheating," said Lee.

"It's literally not," retorted Lil.

"It's not exactly cheating," said Sunday to Lee, "but on the other hand"—she looked at Lil—"if you change the rules, everyone has to agree on the new ones."

Bo thought Sunday must have to do a lot of "on the other hand"ing between the Twins.

"Girls," their mother murmured half-heartedly from the couch as "Ragga Ragga" came on, and they all got distracted by singing *"ragga ragga ragga ragga"* at the top of their lungs. By the time "Tiney Winey" started playing, even Bo was up and dancing.

"You see what I'm saying?" said Charles as the song ended. "Byron Lee is all you need."

"On that note," said Hope. "Did I mention that we have coconut drops for dessert?" She started to leave the room, but Bill waved her back.

"I can get them," he said, smiling at Mum, who was already on her way over to him.

Hope cleared her throat. "And before anyone asks, no, they're not homemade. I got them at Trixie's in the Bronx."

"Yay!" yelled Lee and Lil. "No offense, Mama," Lee added quickly.

"None taken," said Hope cheerfully, and Bill and Mum danced out of the room.

"You see how you all were dancing? Even you young'uns can't help but move. Once again, Jamaica: we likkle but we tallawah!"

"Technically," said Lil, "soca music has roots in Trinidad and Tobago."

"But technically," added Sunday, "Byron Lee's music is also Jamaican ska, so we should allow it, right, Bo?"

Technically, Bo didn't really know exactly what tallawah meant, but just by the way Charles puffed up his chest when he said it, she knew what it meant.

Mum shrieked from the kitchen, and everyone looked up. Sunday jumped up and gave Bo a thumbs-up. "Detective Sunday on the case!" She ran toward the kitchen.

"Sunday, I don't think . . . ," Mama Hope called after her, but Sunday was gone.

"You *sure* you didn't make the coconut drops?" said Charles to Hope. "That scream sounded like the time my mother tasted your rum cake."

"I didn't," said Hope, batting him with a small pillow. "Very funny. And I stand by the kiwi slices. They were pretty."

Sunday came running out, yelling loud enough to elicit a cacophony of protest from the animals, indoors and out. "AHHHH THEY'RE GETTING MARRIED I SAW THE RING AND EVERYTHING!"

Mum and Bill rushed into the living room, without dessert. Bo's eyes widened when she saw the giant smile on Mum's face, and the tears in her eyes.

"Sunday," said Bill quickly, "we just . . . we weren't planning to announce tonight, I . . ."

Mum walked over to Bo and hugged her. "Uh, this isn't how we meant to tell everyone. . . ."

Bo couldn't speak; the rest of the family crowded around, creating a big group hug before she could hug Mum back.

"Congratulations," Bo said, because Sunday was jumping up and down, and that's what everybody else was saying. She tried to keep her smile big and wide too, because she was happy for Mum and she liked Bill; this was just . . . a lot.

"Where's the candy?" asked Lil when everyone settled down a little. Lee shushed her.

Mum pulled Bo aside and hugged her again. "I'm sure you guessed this was coming, but we didn't exactly plan for it to happen this way." She looked over at Sunday, who was still jumping. "I'm so relieved that she's happy with the idea of me as a second mum. When Bill and I get married, it'll already be like we're a family." She kissed Bo on her forehead and laughed. "You'll put in a good word for me, yes? I'm using you as my reference." She jumped up and started dancing over to Bill as "Is This Love" started playing.

Bo's eyes widened. Mum hadn't said *Bill asked me to marry him*, which she'd been expecting for a while. She'd planned to nod solemnly when Mum first brought her the news, then lay out a list of pros and cons with her mum before offering her real, but still slightly solemn, blessing. She liked Bill. A lot. But . . . they'd already decided. Her mum had said "when Bill and I get married," like it was a done deal, all set, no discussion necessary. Mum didn't say anything about being relieved on Bo's behalf. Like she was in a dream, Bo got up and joined the dance party. Someone turned up the music, and the animals even came in to join the celebration. As that giant tan cat plopped itself right next to her, Bo thought about how she and Mum had always had discussions. Talked things through before taking action. Those were the rules. But as Bo looked up at her mum's happy tears, she knew that the rules had already changed, even though she hadn't had a chance to agree on the new ones. She turned her head to catch the other monster cat giving her side-eye like he knew what she was thinking.

Mum leaned down and whispered in her ear, "This is . . . not quite how I thought I'd tell you, hunbun. I know this is a lot. But I hope . . . a lot of good?"

Bo looked back at Mum. The hope and happiness was radiating out of her so brightly that Bo wanted to shield her eyes for a moment. "Congratulations, Mum," she whispered back after a pause. "I love you." She gave Mum the secret double-cheek "kiss" that they used to do at bedtime; they hadn't done it in a while, but she knew Mum would get it. She'd cheek "kiss" back two times. It had been a ritual ever since the night of Bo's fifth birthday.

But Mum pulled Bo and Sunday into a big group hug, which was not at all the right response. "We'll talk later," Mum mouthed. She hugged Bo again, hard, and Bo knew she meant it; this was supposed to be a new and wonderful adventure. Sunday started crowing about how they might redecorate "their" bedroom, and Bo slid into the nearest love seat. One of the cats promptly jumped up on her lap.

"Back off, cat," she murmured. What was her name? Milkington? The cat moved closer and started to purr. "I am not now, nor will I ever be, a cat person," Bo whispered, "so don't even try it. I'm not even going to think about where your litter box is, because no matter how many weddings happen, you and your litter will have nothing to do with me."

Bo took a tiny bit of comfort in knowing that one thing was for sure: in a house this big, she could stay far away from these funky felines. Far, far away. No matter what.

9

WATER EVERYWHERE! Bo's shirt was completely and thoroughly wet, even though this cat she was hugged up on seemed to be remarkably dry. She was holding Mr. Bultitude down in a tin tub while Lee gave him his sponge bath.

"Awww, he loves this so much," murmured Lee.

Mr. Bultitude, who they'd had to drag out from under Bo's bed (why did the animals all sleep under her bed?), gave Bo a look that actually seemed to say *Can you believe this?* Bo closed her eyes. She was not going to get sucked into becoming a Dolittle just because she now lived in a menagerie. Three weeks after the Welcome Muffins and that big announcement, the whole family had trooped down to city hall to make it official and then hopped the subway to Queens for a soup dumpling feast at Shanghai You Garden. Fun, and festive in a way, but still . . .

"Too boring," the girls, even Bo, had complained. Plus, they'd all gotten fancy new outfits for the occasion, and they, especially

Lil, wanted an audience. But even though Bill and Mum were In Love, they said they were also Practical and On a Budget, so it was city hall and a train ride to show off their wedding clothes.

Even though they still had a lot of stuff to move out of their old home, Bo and Mum had pretty much settled into the brownstone. Mum was loving it; now that they were in Harlem so much, she was always hanging out at Cake Lords for long talks about butter and frosting techniques. The animals all acted like they'd been waiting to glom on to Bo for their entire little lives. Even that miniature hatted dinosaur turned up in her things as though they went way back, which, Bo told him, they most certainly did not. *Again, no talking to the animals!*

Lee thought Bo's "bonding" was wonderful, just like she thought the cats loved these backyard baths. Mr. Bultitude was glaring and yowling furiously. He didn't seem like he loved it at all. Bo leaned back as he shook himself vigorously. And apparently he wasn't all that dry.

"Are we done?" Bo asked. It was a beautiful day to be in the backyard, and it had turned out that the hens were the least bothersome pets in this menagerie. They stayed out there, near the bright yellow coop, laying lovely brown eggs that she could bake with, coming over to say hello respectfully, not shedding fur on her. Bo really liked the hens. Once she found herself singing "Who Fed the Chickens?" along with Lee.

"Wait, let me get the towel, and you have to put the mei tai wrap on," said Lee, who could be pretty bossy when it came to her four-legged friends.

"Aren't those for babies?"

"Yeah," Lil said, coming out to join them. "It used to be, but we use it for Mr. Bultitude's baths so we can get him inside the house without freaking out the chickens." It turned out that, unlike the cats on her old block, these cats were very much indoor cats; in fact, any hope that the animals would spend most of their time outdoors had been dashed the night of Bo's first sleepover. Rubia came in and out as she pleased, giving Bo a *Who gon' check me, boo?* look every time she used her giant paws to push open the special door that Auntie Sunflower had built for her. But she wasn't all up in Bo's face, like Mr. Bultitude and Mrs. Pilkington were. That very first night, Bo had woken up to a face full of cat fur. And it hadn't stopped, no matter how much side-eye Bo gave those funky felines. Only the hens, Barbara and Shirley, lived outside. She really loved those hens.

Sunday, who had just finished feeding Barbara and Shirley (Bo now knew they were Sussex hens), ran over to Lil, who had a plateful of Bo's cookies in her hands. "Let me help you with that," she said, grinning.

Mr. Bultitude meowed.

"I know a cat who hangs out on Grand Concourse who could take you," Bo whispered. Mr. Bultitude meowed loudly in response, sidled closer to Bo, and shook harder. "Argh, cat fur water in my eye!" He purred and gave her arm a lick.

"Next up!" said Lee as she brought Mrs. Pilkington over to Bo. Barbara and Shirley clucked in a way that sounded suspiciously like laughter.

After she'd dried off and changed, Bo rearranged her precious stones on the bright yellow bookshelf that now held her treasured collections. She definitely had space for everything now, but her new shared bedroom wasn't exactly Bo's idea of a showcase space.

Sunday was fun in a lot of ways—she made anything into a story—but when it came to that "order and method" she talked about, she was clueless. Right now, there were pages of her "book" everywhere and three pairs of balled-up tights on the floor. Why were tights even out in July? Mum called Sunday's half of the room the "Hurricane" and told Bo to be patient.

Bo had lived in the house for two weeks, and it was still weird.

But it could also be kind of fun.

Sometimes, when she relaxed for a few minutes, Bo really felt like she'd stepped into magic. Sometimes she pinched herself (not too hard, because duh).

Other times Bo just needed to take a breath. Sometimes that could mean a bubble bath in the third-floor bathroom with the old-timey claw-foot bathtub, or sitting in the big bay window in the second-floor room that Lil insisted on calling the parlor, which was always bathed in light and full of plants that took almost thirty minutes to water. And, joy upon joy, in this *splendiferous* house, she could grab a few moments in the in-house elevator, built specifically for Bill's wheelchair but open to all.

Mum was kind of fun now too. Her new live-in-the-moment attitude had gotten all mixed in with "Community and Stability," and she sang while she cooked and even made jokes cornier than Bill's. Bo had vague memories of life before kindergarten when, instead of preschool, Bo had had "kitchen table school," where Bo would practice clapping out sounds and letters with Teacher Mum and cooking with Cafeteria Mum. Now, in freeschool, Mum still sang and had the same "you can do it" attitude, but they didn't sit, just the two of them, with mugs of ginger tea and digestive biscuits at the end of the day.

She returned to the backyard, where her sisters (sisters!) were chowing down on the cookies. She had to admit, it felt good every time they were wowed by her baking skills. And how cool was it that baking could be a science and math assignment! She'd come a long way from the bad writing contests and fill-in-the-bubble tests that had snatched most of the joy of school from her. Mum said she'd escaped just in time; right before the year ended, they'd found out that the increase in bubble tests was because Terrell had been taken over by a bank that was turning it into a Scholar Achievement charter school. The teachers had protested on the last day of school, with the notable exception of Ms. Phillip, who'd told the whole class that she was "looking forward to the introduction of the discipline of discipline" with the takeover.

Now Bo and her sisters had finished their academic work for

the day, and a whole glorious afternoon lay ahead. They spread a soft, blue flannel blanket on a patch of grass near the high fence. Leaves and branches from the adjoining yard reached over, waving slightly in the light breeze.

"I still can't believe you thought Mr. Bultitude was, like, an actual panther!" Lee squealed for maybe the 117th time. She giggled, but stopped when she caught Bo's glare. "I mean, it's kind of cool, that you thought we would have a panther, because, um . . ." She trailed off as Bo gave her a look.

"I mean, that doesn't even make sense," added Lil, leaning back and dropping another cookie into her mouth. "Plus, it would be *weird*."

Yeah, okay. Like a "patchwork-quilted" family that "free-schooled" instead of homeschooled wasn't weird. And backyard hens in New York City. Not to mention that Rubia was basically the size of a tiger! Bo had never even heard of a Great Pyrenees before, but Rubia was basically the definition of the term *Big Dog*.

And even though she rarely saw him, Bo couldn't leave out the bearded dragon that seemed to actually like the little hats her sisters put on his head. *That* wasn't weird?

"That cat really *is* freakishly huge," said Bo. "And hello, Rubia?" She balanced the plate of cookies in her arms as they moved inside; Sunday grabbed another one as they walked. It looked like Bo's idea of adding coconut cream to the batter had been a good one. Technically, the rule was no eating in the bedrooms, so Lil had declared it the practice room for today. Lil was also keeping lookout for parents because they might not understand the distinction. "Plus, Mum had already told me about the chickens, so a panther didn't seem that preposterous."

"Oooh, *preposterous*—nice!" cried Sunday. The family list of "good words" in many languages constantly filled the chalkboard-painted wall in the first-floor hallway. Since each of the girls had Skype language lessons in the language of their choice, the list included words like deggeh deggeh, tòlótòló, gingembre, and chingu-deul. The girls got bonus points for using good words in everyday conversation. But it had to be natural, not something awkward like "That was indubitably erroneous," which Lil had tried a couple of days ago.

Now, all together under one (pretty sweet but slightly leaky) roof, her new sisters called Mum *Mum* too, and Bo had started calling the Twins' parents *Papa Charles* and *Mama Hope*. She was supposed to call Bill *Pop*, but she was mostly not calling him anything yet.

A lot had changed.

Bo and Mum didn't eat on the futon anymore, plates propped on folding, fake wooden tables. The whole family ate their meals around a big, solid, heavy wooden table, which teetered a little every time they sat down because the floors were uneven. Now there were other kids to take turns with when it was time to say grace, even though it sometimes seemed that Lil didn't take her turn as much as she was supposed to.

Bo shared a room with Sunday now, instead of feeling guilty

about taking the only bedroom while Mum slept on the sofa bed. But Sunday's relentless friendliness gave Bo other things to feel guilty about. Bo had lived a whole eleven years as a happy only child. It was much easier to be considerate of others when there weren't actually any others around. This togetherness thing . . . was kind of hard.

"Ooh, this is pretty!" Sunday had said when she'd seen the line of washi tape that Bo had placed down the middle of their room as a not-so-subtle hint to her sister to keep her chaos on her side of the room. "You collect that tape too? You have so many cool collections!" Then Sunday had proceeded to use the rest of the tape roll to decorate one of her many notebooks. Sunday had shown great appreciation for Bo's collections as Bo had slowly and meticulously unpacked, and Sunday seemed to have a lot of random "stuff" that she seemed eager to share with Bo's well-organized side of their room, whether Bo wanted to or not.

These past few weeks of sibling life, not to mention the animals, meant a lot of Mum whispering "flexible and creative!" in Bo's ear every time Bo was smacked by another "Dwyer-Saunders" tradition. Some of them were great, like classes at Harlem School of the Arts and then getting Mikey Likes It ice cream (Brady Bunch was Bo's favorite flavor). Others were . . . questionable, like "community historian" assignments where Bo had to talk to people she didn't know. Which was basically everyone.

Yeah, a lot had changed. And that meant a lot more could change. The summer was going by so quickly, and Bo's old life was fading fast. Instead of cozy kitchen table dates with Mum, freeschooling meant four girls crowding around the sink to chop peppers and radishes for salad when only one of them (Bo) really knew proper knife technique, or having breakfast on the steps of the Metropolitan Museum of Art before it opened for the day, free tea and a biscuit at the Seward Park Library during a study break, and going on a graffiti scavenger hunt before dinner. Which was almost as cool as spending the night in the museum like those kids in that book.

"Ahem." Lil cleared her throat and pointed to the clock. She was timekeeper this week, and as usual, she tended to be choosy about which activities she kept time for. She always managed to forget when it was time to clean the chicken coop. Lee, on the other hand, sang lullabies to the chickens every evening, when she was supposed to be writing in her journal. Bo kept it secret, but sometimes she tested out a few beats on the cats when they curled up on one of the beanbags next to her newly acquired drum set that Bill's old friend "Uncle Winston" had dropped off for her. Bill had been so excited to unveil it; he'd invited her down to the book-store, which was as empty as it always seemed to be except for this glittery gold drum set, complete with snare, bass, tom-toms, and cymbals, in the middle of the store. Bo hadn't had to pretend to be happy at all, and her thank-you hug had been very real, even though she'd pretended not to see Bill wipe a tear from his eyes.

Practice time. All of the instruments were in this big room next to Mama Hope's studio, so they usually took turns for practice; Bo had made a plan for that. "I was thinking we could both warm up on piano," Sunday said to Bo. Sunday was the pianist. Lil played guitar, and Lee said she mainly played bass, but she took vocal lessons and had an amazing voice. And one thing that Bo was REALLY glad to have in her new life was the space to play the drums. She could shred as much as she wanted to, and she always wanted to.

"I'm good," Bo said to Sunday. "I've got some rhythm exercises I need to work on after you're done." Bo was pretty proud of the rotating practice schedule she'd created for them; everyone said that it had cut down on the Ms. Tyler noise-control knocks by at least 40 percent already. Sunday frowned and turned away.

If anything was genuinely weird, it was Sunday's attitude. One minute she didn't seem to understand the concept of personal space; the next, she was sulky. Bo thought that even though people used to call her moody, she was at least consistent. They didn't have much in common. Sunday was loud, and Bo was only loud when she played. Sunday seemed to say whatever was on her mind; Bo thought that was what journals were for. Sunday loved anything new—ideas, experiences, people. Sometimes Bo wondered what garlicky dish Mr. Korin was making that day, or how long she could convince Dougie to freeze Dinobotland operations without her.

"Why don't we do one warm-up together?" suggested Lee. "I wouldn't mind waiting a few minutes before I go back to my essay draft. And then I have to talk to the animals." Every day, Lee met with all of the household pets. According to Sunday, it was the key to keeping the peace across species lines. Papa Charles sometimes joined her in order to get tips for his show. Lil thought that Lee should charge him for that, because Lil thought that there was a way to charge for everything.

"Did I mention that I went up two levels at New York Math Circle? I'm supposed to make some new logic puzzles for you guys," said Lil. "I don't mind putting it off a little. It's hard to create things that have to be so simple." She ducked as Sunday and Lee threw popcorn at her. "Kidding! Kidding!"

"You're cleaning that up," said Bo. And Lil, smiling, cleaned up the popcorn, then put on her guitar.

"'ABC's'?" said Sunday, who had already moved to the keyboard.

"Not *that* easy," retorted Bo, grabbing her brand-new black Zildjian drumsticks. Sunday shrugged, frowning. Oops, there . . . she'd done it again, hurt Sunday's feelings.

"How about 'Mary Had a Little Lamb'?" said Lil. "We can jazz it up and riff off of the original melody and rhythm."

Everyone agreed that that was a good idea, and Bo mumbled, "I'm surprised there's not one in this house already. Probably a matter of time."

"One what?" asked Lee.

"Duh . . . lamb!" shouted Sunday, smiling again, right along with Bo. And they all laughed until Bo took a deep breath, started a 12/8 groove, and called out "One, two . . . one, two, three, four!"

And to Bo's surprise, they sounded pretty good. Like magic.

10

BO HAD TO ADMIT, she could fit three of her old kitchens into this one. She and Mum still had two big boxes of kitchen stuff to unpack, but she was sure everything would fit (once they did a teensy bit of organizing—how was the cinnamon next to the rosemary???). It was frustrating to be in this half-in-half-out stage of moving. She'd been almost expecting Mum to spring the Smilecake on her before they'd moved, but . . . nothing. Bo had even practiced her surprised, sunshiny smile for that moment. And she hoped that Mum had ditched both the almond extract and anise. Then she thought that maybe it was going to be like a housewarming gift for her, and they'd sit in the sun-drenched living room and have a casual conversation about doing a Vietnamese versus Indonesian cinnamon challenge one day when they had the house to themselves, and it was just the two of them, like it used to be . . . but no Sunshine Surprise Smilecake, and definitely no house to themselves.

Mr. Bultitude strolled over to Bo, with Mrs. Pilkington at his heels. The two of them stopped in front of Bo and stared.

"What do you want?" Bo asked in a not unfriendly voice. She'd never admit it, but she was beginning to think these cats got her in a way that her sisters didn't yet. That made her feel a little lonely and a lot surprised. *Bo Parker and cats,* she thought, rubbing Mr. Bultitude's belly. *Who woulda thought?* "No animals when I'm baking," she said to them, pointing toward the living room. "Out." Surprisingly they listened, though Mr. Bultitude's butt was high, which Bo had learned was a sign of his disapproval.

Bo had also learned that a big, "historic" brownstone didn't necessarily mean the people inside were rich. Well, "rich in spirit," (Pop) Bill was always saying, which was another reason why it was no surprise that Mum had married him. It did mean that sometimes at night there were a lot of creaky and mysterious sounds Bo didn't necessarily *enjoy,* but she wasn't exactly *scared* of them either. Except there was that one closet door that never fully shut and swung open at unexpected times—*that* was creepy. And also they couldn't use the washing machine or the dishwasher when it rained, but the dishwasher usually didn't work anyway. And having a washing machine was pretty awesome itself. No more fighting for a dryer or running out of quarters for the large-load washers.

"Whatcha making?" asked Sunday. "How about a baking lesson?"

Bo bit back a sigh and turned around and smiled. "It's kind of funny that with all of the freeschooling, you all haven't done much in the culinary arts department."

"I guess we seemed pretty weird to you," said Sunday.

It's mostly a good weird, Bo thought. She had dropped into true Black magic here, and she didn't want to mess it all up. But with so many changes, it was hard to know what the new rules were. She waved Sunday in. "I was just looking around. I didn't have a plan."

"Sounds like it's time to improvise!" said Sunday, rubbing her hands together. "Woot!" She started pulling items from the pantry.

"Okay, the thing is," said Bo, "it's cool to improvise, but you have to know what flavors will go together." Bo raised an eyebrow as Sunday grabbed a few jars from the nearest cabinet. So, um . . . mustard powder and vanilla, that's probably not going to work." Bo gently removed them from Sunday's grip. It would be going so much faster if she was alone.

"But what if it does?" asked Sunday, wiggling her eyebrows. "We won't know unless we take the risk."

Bo just gave her a look, and Sunday turned to mixing the ingredients that were already in the bowl.

"The snickerdoodle is a delicate cookie," said Bo in her TV-chef voice. "The flavors must be . . . *subtle.*" The girls giggled. Bo shaped the dough into balls, and they rolled them in cinnamon sugar before they plopped them on the cookie sheet and slid it into the oven.

"If we do broil instead of three hundred fifty degrees, won't they be ready faster?" asked Sunday. "Papa Charles made his blackened salmon on broil, and there was smoke everywhere."

"Um." Bo guessed the Twins' parents were a real match in the kitchen.

"Okay, okay. . . ." They sat at the kitchen table in awkward silence. "It smells good already," began Sunday. "Did your mom teach you to bake?"

Bo nodded. She suddenly wanted to cry. Sometimes the sadness sort of jumped out from behind a rock and scared her. "Yeah. Mum told me my, um, father taught her all his best recipes. Almost all the baking stuff we brought was his. Or his parents'. My grandparents'. They owned a bakery."

"Ooh, so it's in your genes!" Sunday said. She pointed to the oven. "And soon those'll be in mine."

"Huh?"

"*Genes, jeans,* get it?" She made a sweeping gesture at her light- and dark-blue patchwork jeans.

Bo groaned. But she was glad to move on from talking about her father. "Your dad—I mean, um, he's a good cook too."

"Especially if you like chili," Sunday said, grinning.

Bo had realized quickly that Bill/Pop had two specialties: meat chili and veggie chili. And since he often did the cooking, the family ate a lot of chili.

"As long as there's one of something in a patchwork family, we're good," Sunday went on. "And you and Mum could have your own cooking show, so we are in so much luck!"

"Why do you guys say 'patchwork'?" Bo asked. "In my old school we learned to say 'blended family.' Which kind of sounds like a smoothie, but . . ."

Sunday smiled. "After me and Pop moved in, the Parents would say it's like we're stitched together with a lot of love, but each of us is still totally our own self, like a patchwork quilt."

Bo forgot that Sunday had been new once too. "It's funny. Lil and Lee are really different, but sometimes they kind of seem like one person, you know?" Bo shrugged. "I guess it's a twin thing."

"I KNOW!" said Sunday eagerly. "That's why I was hoping—" The oven timer beeped, and Bo removed the cookie sheet from the oven. They stood and took a deep breath, both taking in the buttery, cinnamony aroma. Bo realized that, in her old life, this was when Dougie would have knocked.

Was baking really in her genes? And if it was, how would she keep it there without it getting crowded out by all the "new" she had to adjust to? And with all of the adjusting, would she end up moving her old self out of the way?

"Let's work in the living room," said Sunday. "I can go get our books, and we can have tea while we read."

"I . . . think I'll just wait till later. To eat the cookies, I mean." Maybe Mum would have time later.

Sunday's face fell. "Okay, I guess I can wait too . . . but should we taste one, just, you know, to make sure?"

Bo lifted her head. "Make sure of what? They're always perfect. Me and Mum have been making those since I was three."

"Oh, of course!" Sunday put a hand on Bo's arm, and Bo held still so that she wouldn't shake it off. She knew Sunday meant well. But sometimes meaning well didn't matter. Sunday was still talking. "I was kidding, because I can tell how good they are, and—"

Bo turned to head up the creaky steps. "I'm going to practice," she said. "You don't have to wait for me. You guys can go ahead and eat or have tea or whatever." She'd wait for Mum to get home, and maybe they could spend a few moments together, just the two of them, munching and giggling the way they used to.

"We'll wait for you," said Sunday sadly. "After all, you made them. We should enjoy them together."

Bo couldn't say that sometimes there was too much togetherness these days. She could feel Sunday's eyes follow her up the stairs, but she didn't know what to say, so she just kept walking. Even though it wasn't scheduled, she was going to practice. She could play hard and fast and drum it all out like Nandi Bushell. She'd figure things out in the music.

"THANK YOU FOR DOING THIS, BO," said Mrs. Dougie. "It's so sweet of you. Isn't it, Dougie?" She looked at Dougie, who was staring at the floor with his mouth turned down. "Isn't it, Dougie?" The look got harder, and Dougie looked up but didn't speak.

"It's okay," Bo said, hugging him. "You know I'm not going to be far, right? Just a few train stops away!"

"If you have to get on the bus or the train, it's far," said Dougie. Your neighborhood is West Harlem, so it *is* like another country."

Bo had to laugh even though he looked fierce enough to fight. "Harlem is in Manhattan. Right next door to the Bronx. Remember when we made the map of the five boroughs? They're all part of New York City."

"Well, you know, Staten Island got issues, but they also got Wu-Tang, so . . . ," muttered Mrs. Dougie.

"Thanks for making me smile, Dougie," Bo went on. "Because

I do feel sad that I won't be right down the hall from my best little buddy anymore." Dougie sniffed. "But," Bo quickly went on, "I am so glad that we'll be best buddies no matter where I am, even Harlem."

"And we'll go visit Bo on her new block," said Mrs. Dougie.

Bo thought about Mr. Bultitude, the chickens, Mama Hope's mystery meals, and Lee's tendency to let Dwayne Wayne the bearded dragon roam around the house. "Uh, yeah, you'll love it," she said.

"Do you love it?" asked Dougie suddenly, narrowing his eyes.

"Of course she does," Mrs. Dougie answered. "It's her new family, and we're happy for Bo."

"We're never gonna finish Dinobotland now," said Dougie.

"Of course we will," said Bo. "Don't do anything without me, okay? We'll finish it together, just like we planned. Now, come on." Bo grabbed Dougie's arm. "Let's go. Ice cream awaits. And guess what—there's TWO ice cream places in my new neighborhood. One's called Mikey Likes It and the other is Sugar Hill Creamery!"

"A whole hill of sugar!" said Dougie. "I want to move to Harlem. ICE CREAM! Dougie likes it!" he yelled.

"ICE CREEEEAMMM!" Bo yelled back, using her outside voice just this once. Just because.

After a whirlwind morning of Dougie time, which included a visit to Mr. Korin for some garlic-laden wild rice and mushrooms and the West African ladies, who gave them each a mini Bible and a can of Milo, Bo returned to their apartment, sweaty and triumphant, to find Mum just as sweaty and . . . way more grumpy. They were finally getting the last of their things from the old apartment. Bo's official goodbye to the Bronx was well underway.

"Why is there still so much to pack?" Mum asked, clearly not expecting an answer. "Whyyyyyyyy do we have so much stuff?" She plopped down on a large box, sinking into it before she popped up again.

"I'm sorry, Mum, I should've stayed home to help finish," Bo said, offering her mother the water bottle that sat on the floor nearby. "I didn't realize how long the goodbyes would take."

"Oh, honey, don't apologize! We just have to hurry to Lee Lee's for the sweets. I wanted you to be able to say proper farewells—but remember they're more like 'see you again's, because you will."

"Au revoirs," said Bo.

"À bientôts," Mum replied.

"O daabos," they both said together, high-fiving. Auntie Fola had helped Bo learn all of the different Yoruba greetings and salutations as a birthday surprise to Mum a few months earlier. (Bo couldn't wait to finally go to Nigeria to meet her family there.)

"Speaking of à tout à l'heures and o dun mi," said Bo, "we'll learn some more when we do our Black Paris tour on the way to Lagos this summer, right?" They had already gotten matching T-shirts that said **Paris Noir** and had a picture of a chic lady in a headwrap and big hoop earrings on the front. She looked just the way Bo imagined herself when she grew up.

Mum stood up and gave her the kind of burrito-wrap hug that Bo would never, ever get tired of.

"Bo, nothing's changing—I mean, okay, a lot's changing, but you and I are still us, okay? Our lives are getting . . . *more*. Nothing's being taken away."

"Mmmmffiggle," said Bo, still trapped in the hug.

Mum loosened her arms and kissed Bo's forehead. "Let's get ourselves to the park," she said. "I hope the B is running well today, or it will take forever. Isn't it great that one of their favorite spots is also one of ours? So much serendipity!" Bo nodded. She had many favorite places in Central Park, but there was something extra magical about the area around the Great Hill, with the 110th Street Bridge to the north and the Glen Span Arch to the south, that always made her feel like she was in a fairy tale. It had turned out that the Dwyer-Saunders household often joined a New York City homeschoolers group that went there for not-last-day-of-school and not-back-to-school picnics.

Bo looked around the apartment. It looked a little sad, with everything boxed up and off the walls. She could still see faint traces of the time she'd written *TokunDo* in purple crayon on the off-white kitchen wall. The Dwyer-Saunders brownstone exploded with color and was easily the brightest house on their block. It seemed to be alive and bursting at the seams, with yellow curtains and hot-pink window boxes, and thick ivy clinging to its corners. Sunday had been hinting that they had welcome gifts ready for Bo's arrival; she hoped they weren't more muffins or anything like the gecko that Bo had "discovered" in a hall closet during a game of hide-and-seek. Another one of Lee's animal shelter "guests." Bo wasn't sure how she felt about geckos in general—the funny one in the TV commercials was cool—but she knew for sure that surprise ones were not her cup of tea.

Every day of Dwyer-Saunders life meant Bo discovered something new, like she was on an unexpected scavenger hunt. Sometimes it was cool, like the wooden platform in the backyard that Papa Charles would jump on after dinner while reciting silly verses from the children's play he was writing, and other times it was . . . interesting, like the chicken mansion (they didn't call it a coop) and the visiting cats that Lee said were Mr. Bultitude's former best friends "from his lean days." Bo didn't think they looked that friendly, and something told her the chickens agreed.

"Should we bake Welcome Muffins for the new tenants?" she asked sweetly, keeping her face blank.

"Oh, that's a lovely idea, hon," Mum started, then she frowned a little, but her mouth twitched. "Tokunbo Marshall, don't be funny. . . . Your . . . Sunday tried, poor thing." She giggled. "They really were awful-looking, weren't they? Bill said he was afraid I'd turn down his proposal after the way that evening went off." She smiled, one of those secret ones that she smiled a lot lately that felt very far away from Bo.

"You're so smiley lately, Mum," Bo said.

"I'm so excited for us, I can't help it! I know it's a lot for you to take in. I mean, under typical circumstances it would be a lot, and I know that the Dwyer-Saunders crew is definitely not typical circumstances. . . . You haven't even met Sunflower yet. . . ."

"Does she have animals too?" demanded Bo. "Because there are *laws*, Mum."

Mum smiled again. "No, she's a real jet-setter; she travels a lot. But when she's home, Bill says she's like a member of the family, real down-to-earth even though she's probably a gajillionaire. She's involved with the Studio Museum, the National Black Theatre, the National Jazz Museum, and of course the Apollo—a real Harlem heavy hitter. And she works with her hands—Bill says she can build or fix whatever you throw at her! They all think of her more like family than anything else. What a family we'll be!" She pointed to a small laundry basket. "Do you want to take one last look at the giveaways before we . . . give them away?" It had taken Bo weeks just to pull that small collection together. Mum didn't seem to understand that there was no such thing as "things you don't need anymore." Maybe "things you aren't using at the moment but might any day now." But she'd finally parted ways with some things, like book fair books where the pretty sister always had blond curls.

As Bo carefully placed the last of her belongings into boxes, she wanted to ask her mum if she was really supposed to fold into this new family situation like egg whites into batter, because every new thing she learned made that sound really unlikely. At least their new house was way bigger than this apartment; it meant that Bo didn't have to give up her stamp collection, her seashell collection, her tiny toy collection, her stuffed sloth collection, or her button collection. There would be space for everything, Mum had promised.

"I collect pens!" Sunday had said the night before, from across the room, after lights-out-for-real, which meant no flashlights either. Bo resisted the urge to frown. Now she couldn't even be the only collector? Still, pens, she had to admit, were a pretty good thing to collect.

"Let's go, Mum," Bo said. "Lee Lee's, remember?"

"Maybe we should have made the rugelach ourselves," said Mum, looking worried. A bead of sweat escaped her headwrap and trailed down the side of her face.

Bo patted her mother's shoulder like she was the parent. "Don't forget it's part of the Black Business Challenge! Now the whole building's doing it with us. Mr. Korin even posted a list of Black businesses in the lobby, and Mrs. Dougie said it was our legacy. Plus, even we can't make rugelach like Lee Lee's. Well"— she smiled—"maybe *I* can."

Mum laughed and jumped up. "You're right. All this packing is making me loopy. And I love that we're leaving a legacy. Mr. Korin said that you were the genius behind the Back-in-the-Day Gatherings they're going to have every month. It's nice to leave a place better off than you found it."

"We're lifetime residents. That's what Mr. José and Mr. Lenny said," added Bo. The supers had even given her a button that said so. "We can come back for every gathering."

Mum didn't answer as she stared at the boxes. "There are lots of Black businesses to support in our new neighborhood too. I have to remember that we have a whole lifetime to bake for and with our new family. What would I do without you?"

Bo kept the smile on her face, even though she wondered why, if she was so great, she hadn't been enough.

She hugged the box of apricot and raspberry rugelach to her chest as they walked down Frederick Douglass Boulevard to Central Park. The sun shone bright, but it was comfortably hot, not summer-in-the-city hot, so outdoor restaurant tables were full and buzzing with laughter and clinking silverware. People waited patiently in a long line at one coffee shop while another right across the street sat empty.

Bo had to jog a little to keep up with Mum, and she thanked herself for being smart enough to plan on two braided buns for picnic day. When they were a block away from the Great Hill, she smiled, already hearing the sounds of the Harlem Homeschool picnic. Serendipity, Mum was always saying these days. So even though they weren't homeschoolers, they had (well, Mum had) connected with this Harlem Homeschoolers group in the park one day when Bo was too little to explain that she preferred to be alone. Mum was the one who was always talking to Auntie Fola about "only-child syndrome." Mum had basically forced her way into this group, and they'd been invited to their picnics and kickball games and fencing and whatever ever since. But Mum couldn't force Bo to participate, and so Bo had stayed carefully and safely on the fringes, occasionally being a scorekeeper or a tiebreak judge but never really joining in. So now they *were* going to be homeschoolers (or "freeschoolers," whatever), and Mum thought they already had people. Mum believed in having people. Bo liked to say she believed in being her own person.

Every time Bo went to Central Park, she found something new to love. Her mum's sour-faced cousin (like, third or fourth cousin, so she barely counted) used to constantly FaceTime them from her house in New Jersey to ask why they chose to live in "that dirty, ugly, scary city." After they'd had a lot of good laughs about what Mum called "the sheer, sad ignorance," Bo and Mum had had a lot of fun sending Cousin Yemi postcards of New York City every day for a year until she stopped.

Mum's friend Gustavo led tours of the park and knew all of its secrets, from the strange, like the fact that the zoo kind of started when someone in the olden days just left a bear in the park, to the sublime, like the Whisper Bench. Bo had cried when Gustavo told her about the community of formerly enslaved people who had built a whole neighborhood called Seneca Village in an area where she and so many kids now ran and jumped and played.

"Basically, a multiracial community was mowed down so that rich people could have a playground," Gustavo had said before Mum could stop him. Sometimes when Bo was in one of the playgrounds there, waiting for a swing, she thought about how Mum had always said that she should never be afraid to "take up space," which was a way of being that Bo didn't quite get, because didn't everyone take up space? But whenever someone called out "Next!" in the store, and a white woman would answer as though Bo and Mum were not right there, and Mum would have to *let them know*, Bo understood what taking up space meant. Whenever she was in the park, she said a silent prayer of thanks to the Seneca Village community, and tried to take up space herself in their honor when bullies were hogging the swings or not saying "Excuse me" when they should.

That was the thing about living in New York City. There were stories upon stories upon stories. Mum always said there was no place else like it for "everyday magic," available to rich, poor, or somewhere in between, like them. Bo did agree, even though sometimes she thought that probably the people who were living along the path next to the Hudson River might want to be in a more comfortable and hotter place in the winter. And now Mum kept talking about how one of the many perks of being free-schooled with Sunday, Lil, and Lee would be "the city as a classroom" blah, blah, blah.

But still, this was one of her favorite places to be. It was like playing a light swing, or a one drop rhythm, easy-feeling but way more complex than it seemed.

"There you are!" Bo heard Sunday's voice and looked up to see the trio of sisters waving frantically. Mum's pace quickened, and Bill and the girls moved forward to meet them. Sunday was carrying a huge, old-fashioned picnic basket, and Bo hoped she hadn't prepared whatever was inside. Nor Mama Hope for that matter. For a family with such hearty and enthusiastic appetites, they weren't exactly kitchen whizzes.

Sunday was wearing leggings that said **Black Girl Magic** in gold letters down the side, and an oversized purple tank top; Lil was wearing denim shorts overalls with circles embroidered all over—Bo wondered if she'd done that herself. She also had on a denim visor that somehow did not look silly. Lee was wearing a yellow one-shoulder top that might have been a bathing suit and a puffy green skirt. She looked like a flower, but in a good way.

Sunday got to them first and wrapped Bo in a big hug. "We are going to have so much fun today—I brought cards, Boggle, chess, and dominoes!"

"It's a real party," said Lil as she and Lee made it over. "Boggle. Whoop. Whoop."

Lee looked around. "Who wants to go to the North Woods with me later for bird-watching?"

"Not Sunday," said Lil, and Bo laughed before she noticed Sunday's frown. "Kidding," said Lil. "But kind of not. You know you're too loud for bird-watching. I am too. Maybe Bo will be your buddy for that boring stuff now, Lee. Thank goodness. Bo, you may go on snail-watching expeditions next. Welcome to our world."

"I can be quiet when I need to," muttered Sunday.

"Remember the first time you came over, and we were saying 'Welcome,' like, a million times because we were so nervous?" asked Lee.

Bo raised an eyebrow. "No," she started, but she had to cough to keep from letting a smile break out. The looks on the other three's faces told her that they didn't think it was funny.

"Reese Cruz does that fake cough laugh all the time," said Lil. "Do you know her or something?"

"Uh, who's Reese Cruz?" asked Bo, looking around. "Is she here?"

"Perish the thought!" said Sunday, lifting her hand to her forehead and swooning, which helped to lighten the mood.

"She's our block frenemy," explained Lee. "Kind of a sore subject for Lil, especially."

"There's no *fr*!" said Lil.

"And I can't stand her either!" said Sunday. "She's the kind of fake that ends up being meaner than someone who's just up-front mean."

Bo nodded. "I get it, an Amber type." And she told them about Amber and Celia, and they nodded and made indignant sounds at all the right moments.

Some of the Harlem Homeschoolers ran toward them. Bo started to make introductions, but Sunday, Lil, and Lee fit right in, Bo noticed, and not just because they were extreme homeschoolers too. It was like they glowed, and even though Bo usually *wanted* to be invisible, this felt a little itchy.

"Your sisters are so much fun," said a girl named Mallika. "What's your name again? I know I've seen you around."

"I'm Tokunbo," said Bo, and she smiled even though she really didn't want to. It was like everyone agreed that she was "new and improved" with her new family around.

After they'd eaten cold jerk chicken; warm fried chicken; potato salad; watermelon-and-feta salad; "salad salad," as Bo used to call it when she was little; still-warm rice and peas; and more food than Bo could have ever imagined eating, Bill and Mum wandered off to the duck pond while the Dwyer parents joined a spirited game of spades.

The girls brought a soft blue blanket and the box of rugelach over to a thick patch of grass under a tree.

"Has your mom talked to you about the wedding party?" asked Sunday.

"Like, about her dress?" asked Lil. "Is she looking for a designer?"

"Uh, yeah, a little," said Bo. "Not about her dress, sorry, Lil, but mostly she just keeps saying they don't want a big fuss."

Lil threw up her hands and flopped dramatically to the blanket. "Ow," she mumbled.

"I know!" said Sunday. "It's a WEDDING! I mean, you're, like, legally obligated to fuss!"

Lil and Lee nodded, so Bo did too. Sunday went on. "At least they agreed to do *something*. For a minute there, city hall was going to be it. We shouldn't let them make their wedding just be, like . . . grocery shopping or something."

She looked at Bo. "Unless you think it should?"

"I mean, grocery shopping at Wegmans is kind of an event,"

started Bo, "but yeah, I know what you mean." The image of a wedding ceremony in the Wegmans bakery aisle flashed in her mind's eye.

"We need some serious Secret Table Talk time," said Lil. "That's with snacks on a tray and without Parents," she added.

"Yeah, I guessed that," said Bo. "And we did that when I slept over the first time, remember?"

The adults started dividing up for games of spades.

"You know they'll start 'fussing,' as Pops says," said Lil as they scooted away, "and then they'll make us each perform or recite a Claude McKay poem or something."

"Aren't you guys used to that?" asked Bo. She'd spent enough time at the house to see that the family was constantly playing music; writing plays; arguing about parts; playing charades; and with the exception of Papa Charles, whose job it was to be dramatic, all being just a little extra.

"Yes, but it's always different when they try to make us," said Lee. "And we have to prepare. Or at least I have to. I get too nervous."

"And our outfits have to be on point," said Lil. "*Mine* always are, but we all need to look good, or else it brings the others down."

Bo wasn't sure how to respond to that, so she held up the box of rugelach.

"Now, that's what I'm talking about!" the other three shouted at the same time, then they all laughed.

They spread out on the blanket under a tree, and Bo passed around the still-warm box.

"Mmmm, buttery, sugary goodness," said Lee. "These are delicious."

"Lee Lee's is pretty legendary," said Bo. "Even though I bake, I go there all the time. We know all the good bakes in the city. Do you like Taipan in Chinatown? Those buns with the cream inside—I've got to learn how to do that. Susan's bakery is great too. It's not far from here. Mum and Susan even exchange recipes sometimes. She says Ms. Berlin is one of the best bakers she knows—next to me."

"This neighborhood has a lot of good food, and you know about it," said Sunday, popping a whole rugelach into her mouth. "Our family is perfect now."

Something warm and buttery and sweet rose up in Bo after that, and she told herself to hold on to it.

"So," said Lil. "This non-wedding thing. I think we have a situation on our hands."

"Really unromantic," said Sunday. "Maybe Famous Sichuan, I heard Pop say. Nothing against Famous Sichuan, but we should at least be going to Flushing Chinatown since it's a special occasion!"

"The Parents did more when I passed my Shark-level swim test," said Lee.

"I guess Mum did throw a whole party when I finished third grade," mused Bo. "I got a crown and everything."

There was a silence. Bo could hear the faint strains of Stevie Wonder playing over by the spades groups.

"Do you think it's because they don't want to celebrate?" asked Lil.

"Absolutely not," said Sunday quickly. "Pop is so happy. . . ." She trailed off, looking at Bo.

"Mum is really happy too," Bo said. "Like *really*, really. I think it's . . . Mum is always working hard to be all reassuring. It's that they want to keep everything 'normal.'" Which made no sense, because nothing was "normal" anymore, she thought.

"They're probably also stressed out and tired," said Lee, who had already made a dandelion crown and placed it gently on her head.

"They're parents; they're used to being stressed and tired," said Lil. "The thing is, what do we do now?"

"I have an idea," said Sunday slowly. Bo had already learned that Sunday always had an idea.

"Does it involve me designing bridesmaid dresses for us?" Lil asked.

"And a new dog to be the ring bearer?" asked Lee, sitting up so fast her crown fell off.

"See what I put up with on the daily?" Sunday said to Bo, who laughed. "You're laughing now, but just you wait. . . . Anyway, here's my idea—drumroll please!"

Without thinking, Bo automatically tapped out a rhythm on her book, and Sunday squealed.

"It's so good to have an actual drummer as a sister," she said, which made Bo all flustery and fluttery, and she stopped drumming.

"Ahem. So. Here's my idea," said Sunday. "We make it a project!"

"Huh?" asked Bo.

"Everything we do is a project," said Lil in a bored voice.

"Exactly," said Sunday. "So this wedding party could be too!"

"Ohhh, I get it," said Lee. "We throw the party for Pop and Mum—" She stopped and looked at Bo. "It's okay if I call her that?"

Bo shrugged. "Uh-huh. I just have to . . . get used to it." She cleared her throat. "Anyway, what do you mean?" she asked Sunday.

"She means," answered Lil before Sunday could speak, "we make the wedding celebration a summer freeschooling project. We plan the whole thing, we present the idea to the Parents, they say yes, then I get to design dresses for us all!"

Sunday rolled her eyes. "Yeah, what she said, sort of. Basically, if we make it a project, they'll know we're serious and let us handle everything!"

"That sounds like a lot of work," said Bo slowly. But it also sounded like . . . fun?

"What could be more fun than planning a party?" asked Sunday. "Think about it. You could be in charge of the cake, obviously. I'll direct—"

"It's a party, not a movie," said Lil.

"You're right," said Sunday. "I'll direct and produce!" Bo and Lee laughed.

"It could be fun," said Bo. "Mum loves parties, but she's always too busy to go out. She'd *have* to go to her own wedding party." And Bo could plan the whole thing!

"Mr. Bultitude could be best cat!" said Lee.

"Okay, so what's next, besides pretending you didn't just say that?" said Lil.

"Uh, so . . . there's just one thing," started Bo slowly, hoping she wasn't about to ruin everything, especially the sunshiny mood.

"What?" asked Sunday. "Speak up! Feel free! Pontificate! Elaborate! Cogitate!"

"That's not—" started Lil, and Sunday shushed her. "No hating on my vocabulating. I'm on a roll."

"It's just that . . . this will probably require some real organization and careful planning," she said slowly, the words putting a song in her heart. This was where she felt comfortable. "And, um, maybe that's not totally your, uh, forte?" She grimaced, waiting for the barrage of denial and many more indignant sounds.

Sunday shrugged. "No lies detected."

Lil and Lee spoke simultaneously. "FACTS." Then they glared at each other. "Stop copying me!"

"Decided. We're not good at that, but you are. Like, really good," said Sunday.

The Twins nodded. "The way you set up the spice cabinet?" said Lil. "Even our mom can't mess up now. Mostly."

"You produce, Bo. You help us make our plan, all those pesky details that we might, er, overlook, and we'll follow your lead," said Sunday. They looked at Bo expectantly.

"I mean, I could sort of just . . . keep us on track . . . ," said Bo slowly.

"Done! You'll be in charge of us all coming up with a presentation," said Sunday. "Tomorrow morning we work on it. Tonight"—she looked at Bo—"secret sleepover celebration!"

"How is it a secret?" asked Bo. "I'm pretty sure we all know it's happening."

And I live with you for real now; it's not a sleepover, she wanted to add.

"You know, all of us in one room, the flashlights, the snacks in the bedroom . . . the good stuff," said Sunday. "It's a celebration!" She hugged Bo, and this time when Bo hugged back, she meant it. If she felt a twinge of something like fear mixed with sadness mixed with confusion, she shoved it to a place far from her heart. This new life just might work—if she made it work. And that was going to mean leaving a lot of her old self behind.

"Welcome!" said Lil and Lee, and Bo laughed out loud from deep inside, and it felt good.

12

Okay, this is harder than I thought it would be. If we're really freeschooling, can't I be free to choose worksheets? I don't miss Ms. Phillip's yelling or Mike Miller's stank breath or bubble tests, but I wouldn't mind some more directions to follow. How do I know if I'm getting it wrong, if I don't know how to get it right?

BO KNEW SHE COULDN'T REALLY TURN THAT IN for her daily journal entry, but it felt good to write the words down. Because along with the goodness, like someone to whisper with after lights-out and adults who brought home props and costumes, her new life also meant daily reading journal entries and weekly project plans.

Blergh.

Now that she didn't have to go to school anymore, it seemed like she had to go more places and work harder than ever. When

Mum had first told her that the Dwyer-Saunders clan were free-schoolers, Bo hadn't paid much attention because *what was that even*. She hadn't known that it was going to be so *serious*.

But now here she was, "taking charge of her own education and following her passions to new academic heights while developing critical-thinking and creative skills in an unstructured but supportive environment." At least, that's what the "Freeschoolers' Manifesto" on the refrigerator said. Bo thought that Ms. Phillip would have hated the manifesto. And she probably would have loved the weekly trips to the Schomburg, the Museum of the City of New York, and the New-York Historical Society, but not the letter campaign they'd started for permanent Black Lives Matter collections at every museum in the city. For "extra credit," which in this family meant just because, Sunday had turned Bo's BLM poem into a song, a joint project that had made it easier to study a hard subject. Bo had to admit it turned out beautiful.

But it was *work*. The Parents were still *parents*, which meant that they talked a good game about freedom and *self-directed learning* and all that, but they were still in charge and setting "guidelines" that were really rules. Like daily reading journaling.

> I started out strong, with the Pie Pockets and all. I could tell everyone loved them. But it's hard to keep up with things here. Whenever I used to hear "It's a fluid situation," that usually meant that things weren't going so well.

But in this family it's supposed to be kind of a good thing, like part of going with the flow. But I know that that flow can turn into a waterfall—a DELUGE (yes, vocab!) quick fast, and I'm not trying to get caught out there. I know Bill/Pop loves my mum, a whole lot, but what if something happens to him? Something already did, right? Nobody was prepared for that. Even though it's cool that he pops wheelies with his chair, and the whole downstairs of the house is tricked out to be super-accessible, I'm still worried. Something always happens.

"Blergh!" Bo said, this time out loud, tearing the sheet of paper from her journal into small pieces.

"Shhh," whispered Sunday lazily, not looking up from *The Boys in the Back Row*. "I'm right before a good part."

"How do you know? Are you rereading?" Bo asked. "Can you count that for your journal?"

"I can just tell," answered Sunday. "So shh."

Bo stood and yawned, a little loudly on purpose, but didn't say any more. She liked sharing a room with her new (not-so-neat) sister most of the time, and they'd made a pact to respect each other and the space at all times. Like, a real pact, all written down and everything. Bo had learned very quickly that this family was all about writing things down. Which reminded Bo that she needed to write her reader response for *Some Places More Than Others*, which she loved so much she didn't want to ruin it by *writing* about it. Stalling, she took out her planner, where she'd been collecting ideas for the Block Party wedding celebration. She was going to share it with her sisters tonight; she'd been making notes (and collecting Sunday's ideas) for days, and she really wanted to impress them. She sighed. She wasn't feeling too impressive lately. Mostly confused and out of place.

Sunday closed her book and sat up on her bed. "Still getting used to us, huh?" she said. "I know how it is." True. Before Bo and Mum had moved in, Sunday had been the new girl. Late one night, over flashlights and out of earshot, Sunday had told Bo a few stories about being the single joining a family with twins. But Bo knew she was just trying to make her feel better. Sunday was always trying.

"I just thought the whole freeschooling thing would be . . . different," said Bo. "Sleeping late."

"Reading all day," continued Sunday, nodding. "With snacks like caramel popcorn anytime you want. And no homework, since you're kind of already home."

"No nasty school lunches—well, that part's true," said Bo.

"Yeah, and now you're here making all of these cool bakes!" added Sunday. "That's awesome. Better than caramel popcorn. Even though you can probably make that awesomely too."

Bo nodded and smiled. For the most part, this new way of learning was pretty sweet so far. They did get to sleep later than other kids who went to school, and they had a lot more independent reading time too. Bo knew she'd probably realize how fun it was after it was too late, because that's what always happened. It was hard to appreciate life when it was happening, because there was so much life constantly happening! Especially now. There was a lot to get used to, like calling Bill *Pop*. She still stumbled a little on that when she spoke to Bill.

Now three other girls—her *sisters*—called out "Mum" just like Bo when they wanted to speak to Mum. It was a lot to remember. Bo was not fond of change. At least this change brought more people into her life. Most of the time she wanted to keep them there.

Still, it wasn't easy getting used to all of this. No more coming home from school to Mum waiting just for her with flour on her nose and an apron over her jeans. Bo wished she had written things down in those days. Because now it was hard to remember if Mum had made the chocolate cake with butterscotch frosting for her kindergarten class or for first grade. And even though she remembered licking the spoons with Mum at the kitchen sink before Bo practiced for the sight-words spelling bee, she couldn't remember if it was the caramel cake or the sour cream pound cake batter they'd been pretending was "sweet soup."

She was forgetting. And she knew she was supposed to, but she wanted to hold on to one small part of before, something that was still hers and hers alone.

Before they'd moved into the brownstone, she'd tried her own version of the Sunshine Surprise Smilecake one more time, with lemon extract, a little cake for herself, on an afternoon when Mum and Bill had gone to the botanical garden. Her new sisters had been very impressed when they'd heard that she'd been allowed to use the oven by herself since her tenth birthday. She'd shown them a few recipes, but not that one. She was still waiting for Mum to officially show it to her.

"What is it?" Mum started down the hall toward Bo quickly. "Everything okay, honey?"

But as her mum got closer and Bo thought she could literally see Bill-shaped stars in her mother's eyes, she faltered. Mum wouldn't be in a mother-daughter mood. Quickly she slid the recipe paper onto her bookshelf.

"Uh, I, it's . . . I'm going to organize my books!" she finished weakly. "So . . . fun tea with Bill?"

Mum frowned and rubbed Bo's cheek. "Well, yes, but . . . I've never heard you so excited about book organizing," she said. "Are you sure everything's okay?"

Bo took a quick, deep breath and smiled. "Yep. And I'm glad you had a good tea. Did you leave me a scone?"

"We did," said her mum, holding out her hand. "And Bill left you some chocolate-covered gummy bears."

"He's a good guy, that Bill," Bo said, trying to keep the smile on her face. "I know he is."

"And you're the best daughter in the universe. I can't believe my good fortune! Sometimes I feel like there's a bit of magic that hangs around the corner of my life, ready to go into action just when I need it."

"Cake-type magic," Bo hinted. But Mum just hugged her more.

"Helloooooo." Sunday waved her book in front of Bo's face. "Are you okay?"

"Oops, sorry. Yeah, I'm fine. Is it time for *elevenses?*" Bo asked. By now she knew that her book-loving sisters would get a Paddington Bear reference.

Sunday closed her book and smiled. "It's always time for elevenses in my book." She held up her book. "*In my book*, get it?"

Bo groaned, but she agreed that it was a good time for a toast-and-marmalade type of snack. They walked down to the kitchen. The house was unusually quiet; Bill was at his bookshop, Mama Hope was in the basement working on a series of maps for a new fantasy novel, Papa Charles had auditions all day, Lee was at the shelter, and Lil was at her hip-hop dance class at the community center.

"Where's . . . uh, Mum?" asked Sunday. So it was hard for Sunday too, Bo noticed, saying new names for parents. Sunday's mom lived in London, but she called twice a week, and Sunday visited her every spring.

"At a school in Red Hook," answered Bo as they stood holding the refrigerator door open for a lot longer than they would have if any adults had been around. "It'll take forever for her to get back uptown. Then she's going to stop at your—um, Pop's store."

Sunday opened the cookie jar and looked inside. "Empty," she said. "Totally empty. I bet Lil ate the last ones." Bo had made Chocolate Butterscotch Rice Krispies Cakelets two days ago. "I can't hate, though," continued Sunday. "They were delicious."

"I can make more, easy peasy," said Bo. "Or . . ." She smiled. "I can make Welcome Muffins."

"Haha," said Sunday, and they giggled together. Now they could laugh about it. "Science experiment!" said Sunday with a snort. "I was doing something . . . 'slightly transformed, just a bit of a break from the norm . . .'"

Bo didn't miss a beat. "'Just a little somethin' to break the monotony'?" she rapped.

Sunday raised her eyebrows. "You know that song? I thought only Pop was obsessed with old-school hip-hop like that."

Bo laughed again. "My neighbor played that one all the time. She was kind of a hip-hop historian. She gave me a whole lesson on the 'boom BAP!' and I still don't know what it is, just that you say it loud. Right now she'd probably tell you about the time her auntie or cousin or somebody met DJ Jazzy Jeff at the Roots Picnic or something like that."

"Oooh, I'd love to meet her!" said Sunday. "She sounds amazing!" And the way she rubbed her hands together made Bo feel proud of Mrs. Dougie and protective at the same time.

Bo took out some butter and eggs. "If we have vanilla, we're in business. . . . Okay, we've definitely got the ingredients for snickerdoodles again, and those are easy. Can you go let . . . Mama Hope know that I'm about to use the oven? Then I'll get on it."

"Okay, but . . ." Sunday paused.

"What? You don't want snickerdoodles?"

"No, I mean yes . . . of course, I just want to . . . well, can I watch this time? You baking? I mean, can you *really* teach me?"

Bo looked up. "To make snickerdoodles? It's really not that hard. This recipe is practically foolproof."

Sunday gave her a look. "Remember who you're talking to, Bo."

"Uh . . . yeah, haha." Bo smiled, but it didn't reach her eyes. It was different doing the thing that made her feel most herself when she could never be *by* herself. "Maybe you could watch, but—"

"Woot! Okay, don't move until I come back. Seriously— I want to know every step!" Sunday raced out of the kitchen.

Bo suddenly remembered something Mum hadn't done in a long time. She used to wake Bo up every morning by saying, "It's morning! Time for the Happys!" Some days (okay, a lot of days) Bo would be tired and grumpy and say, "SADS!!!" until Mum tickled her to Happy. (Sometimes she'd just say it so that Mum would tickle her.) These days she didn't know what she would say. Bo didn't wake up in her old bed in a new house with the Happys or Sads anymore. Most of the time it felt like both.

13

SOMEHOW, IT SEEMED TO BO that having three sisters to share chores with meant that the Parents just kept adding on more chores. Cleaning Barbara and Shirley's chicken coop was her least favorite. She didn't understand how Lee was singing. Rubia sat nearby, watching in silence; Bo suspected that she was supervising.

"Rubia looks so judgy," Bo whispered to Sunday. "Should we do another round of vinegar wiping?"

"Just because we call it a chicken mansion doesn't mean we're like indentured poultry servants," said Sunday. "It is so clean." Right on cue, Rubia gave an approving bark; the hens clucked and slowly strolled back into their sparkling home.

"I think that means we're done," said Lil. "Let's get something to drink and collapse."

They had time for a short break before they needed to get ready for the wedding party presentation they'd planned for later that day; for a moment, Bo thought about making an excuse so she could work on the cupcake recipe in a rare few moments of solitude. But Sunday grabbed her hand before she could say anything, and after a quick washup, they all filled their water bottles with lemonade and sprawled out on the front stairs. Mr. Bultitude and Mrs. Pilkington sat in the living room window, dozing, even though the ice cream truck song rang out nearby. Two little kids were making a chalk drawing on the sidewalk out front, and they looked up when they saw the sisters.

"Do you know how to spell 'bighead bossyface'?" asked one of them.

"Can you get us an ice cream?" asked the other. They both sounded so Dougie-ish. Bo made a mental note to give him and Mrs. Dougie a call soon.

"Oooh, bighead bossyface, I like that," said Lil.

"What she means is," said Bo, going into automatic sitter mode, "it's inappropriate to call someone names, even yourself. 'Bighead bossyface' doesn't sound kind. Do you want to sound kind?"

The first kid pointed to Lee. "Why is she singing? Does *she* want to sound like that?"

"Am I singing?" asked Lee. "I didn't realize it. I was just kind of, you know, vibing."

"It's also inappropriate to ask strangers to buy things for you," continued Bo calmly. "Including ice cream."

"Are you a babysitter?" asked the second kid. "You talk like one."

"Or my mom. She says 'inappropriate' a lot," added the other. "Can you help me write that word here?" She pointed to the sidewalk.

Bo shrugged. "Sure. Why don't we draw some ice cream too?" She gestured to her sisters. "We can all draw. It'll be like a sidewalk mural!"

"Look at you, sounding like a real Dwyer-Saunders," said Sunday.

Bo wanted to ask if she'd sounded like a fake one before, but she was trying to set an example, so she didn't say anything, just handed her sisters some chalk.

"I thought we were resting," Lil protested feebly. But Bo knew she didn't mean it. Lee started a cat-themed freestyle, and they drew up and down the block and it was fun; the sisterhood in the sun felt so good that Bo didn't mind that she was sweating while the ice cream truck's song persisted nonstop, or that she was not only doing another project but had suggested it. She didn't even mind that Sunday seemed to be doing a lot of suggesting and pointing and not much drawing. For a few moments, Bo didn't mind anything, and it wasn't until much later that she realized that she hadn't even been baking. Just . . . vibing. It was a new feeling, and she liked it very much.

The sisters had kept the Parents out of the living room for most of the afternoon. Lee was hunched over the coffee table as she fiddled with the iPad.

"How did I get stuck with putting the slide show together?" she grumbled, reaching for a saltfish cake.

"Because I did the whiteboard sketches, Bo wrote the outline, and Sunday's doing the talking," answered Lil, batting Lee's hand away from the food platter. "You got off easy. And stop sampling the appetizers."

"You're right," Lee said. "It's the first time we've had an outline," she said to Bo.

Sunday was pacing back and forth near the fireplace, clutching a stack of index cards. "I think it's awesome! I'm worried I'll forget my lines."

"You never forget your lines," said Lil. "I don't understand why you have those cards anyway. You know what you're gonna say. They're just making you more nervous. Do what you always do. Wing it."

Sunday glanced at Bo before she spoke. "Well, because I want to make sure that I follow the outline. The awesome outline Bo made!"

"Um," started Bo, "I'm not trying to mess with your usual process." All this talk about how great her outline was made her feel extremely not great. "I just . . . like to use outlines."

"It's GREAT," Sunday said loudly. "I can't believe how organized we are."

"It's just different," said Lil, shrugging. "Different good."

Bo knew that different was never good; it was just different. She started to apologize, but she heard voices outside the door getting louder as they moved closer.

"Places, everyone!" said Lil, and Sunday stuck her tongue out at her. "I was supposed to say that."

"Oh, go ahead," said Lil, rolling her eyes.

Sunday gave a high clap, like a dancer. "Places, everyone!"

And they scrambled into position: Lee planted herself by the iPad, Bo by the door, Sunday in front of the fireplace, and Lil to her left, by the easel.

Bo dimmed the overhead lights and turned on the twinkling Christmas lights as the Parents peeked into the living room.

"This is exciting," Mama Hope murmured. Bo guided Mum and Bill to the "front" where the recliner was. Mum sank into it and Bill pulled his chair up next to her.

"Stellar production design, ladies," said Papa Charles, looking around at the streamers and tinsel draped on the furniture.

"Ahem!" said Sunday. She waved Bo over. "Family! Festivals! Freeschooling!" she said loudly. "The three pillars of our lives!"

"Festivals?" asked Bill.

"Oh, that reminds me, I heard about a Morningside Festival coming up in a few weeks," said Mum. "I thought I should get a table advertising my lunch-delivery business, if you all would help me staff it. It would be a good way to meet our neighbors."

"Great idea!" said Mama Hope. "We really haven't gotten to know anyone yet. There's a crafting group that's organizing maker meetups in Calabar Imports over on FDB—we used to go to their Brooklyn shop all the time—I'd love to join and finally finish my hexaflexagon cushion."

"Do you think there will be entertainment?" mused Papa Charles. "I'd be happy to donate my services."

"SO ANYWAY," Sunday raised her voice. "So, we believe that our new family deserves—no, WARRANTS, a real celebration. And we would like to present to you . . . Operation Wedding Reception Party! Hit it, Lee!" On cue, Lee started the slide show and Bo started playing her marimba softly, as background music.

"And, in conclusion," said Sunday, fifteen slides and a not-so-subtle *wrap it up* signal from Lil later, "funny you should mention getting to know our neighbors, because we thought it could be like a block party! With a potluck buffet and community talent show!" Bo ran over to her drum set and gave the bass an emphatic whack for dramatic effect.

"We are all in agreement that not celebrating this momentous occasion would be tragic," finished Sunday.

"And this plan offers many learning opportunities," added Lil. "We'll collaborate, budget . . . do other planning stuff that Bo knows about . . ."

"And it won't be extra work for you all. We'll handle the whole thing," added Lee.

"It will mark a new beginning," said Bo. "We know you're excited about that." She swallowed. "We are too."

"One, two, three," loud-whispered Sunday. And on three, the girls tossed up the handfuls of glittery confetti they'd hidden in their pockets.

The Parents clapped, and Bo ran over to hug her very teary Mum.

Lil took more bows than anyone else and then asked, "Well?"

Bill started. "It's a beautiful idea and a commendable plan." He paused and cleared his throat. "You girls are just great, you know that? Really great." He cleared his throat again and looked away in an I'm-not-crying-you're-crying way.

Mum put an arm around his shoulders and then everyone gathered around for a big, sloppy group hug. "This sounds incredibly fabulous, but . . . ," Mum began. Bo knew what was coming next. "It also sounds like a very ambitious project."

"We do big projects all the time," Sunday said, waving her hand. "It's kind of our MO."

"Bo is just getting started on the whole project-based-learning thing," said Mum, smiling. "I don't know if a wedding, um, block party, is, uh, beginner-level stuff."

"Bo's the one who keeps us organized," said Lee. "She's so good, she's made a huge difference already."

Bo stood up straighter and tried to keep her smile at proud but not show-offy. She really had revolutionized things in the freeschool arena, with her chart system backed up by individual planners, and a giant group planner that was cross-referenced and double-checked daily. Her sisters needed her; she was making a difference. She just had to keep it up. Rubia walked over and leaned against Bo. And even though she knew it meant basically a wig's worth of hair all over her clothes, Bo leaned, just a little, into Rubia.

Bill smiled. "I don't doubt it. But this is work that people are paid to do. They make careers out of it. Plus, a block party requires a permit and some complicated maneuvering of the city bureaucracy. And, um, we don't have a huge amount of time."

"What do you mean?" asked Sunday. "That's what's so perfect—we have the whole summer! I mean, outside of field trips, research papers, French, Patois, cooking, sewing, HSA summer session—"

"And *maneuver* is practically my middle name," interrupted Lil with another bow.

"Finally seeing what fancy Black people do in Martha's Vineyard," said Lee, "when we go stay with Cousin Stacey and volunteer at Dr. Coleman's friend's animal rescue."

Paris Noir and Lagos markets, thought Bo. *Just me and Mum.*

The Parents laughed awkwardly and exchanged looks. Uh-oh. Bo knew that when adults exchanged *looks*, it didn't mean anything good.

"Bo, can you help me bring out dinner?" said Mum. "And again, that presentation was so beautiful and phenomenal and wonderful!"

She clapped, and the other adults quickly joined in.

"But—" started Sunday.

"Sunday, let's go get the vacuum," said Bill. "Maybe the hand vac too."

"Argh, Mr. Bultitude hates the vacuum," said Lee. "Lil, let's do some preventive petting."

Bo followed Mum into the kitchen, where a large bowl of salad, cheery and green, yellow, orange, and red, sat on the table.

"We just have to add some feta cheese," said Mum. They crumbled cheese in silence for a few seconds, and Bo was reminded of their days in the tiny kitchen on Sedgwick Avenue.

"What's HSA summer?" she asked.

"Oh, Harlem School of the Arts is not far. Isn't that great? The girls take all kinds of classes there—painting, dance, and of course instruments. Their music department is amazing—my friend Yolanda runs it, you'll see. Oh, and Charles is hoping to be hired by their theater department."

Mum was talking real fast. "I guess they're used to fitting a lot of things into one summer, but it sounds like a lot to me," said Bo. "I still think we can have a party for your wedding. You love parties! And we can invite our friends from home, so we see them before the trip." She glanced up at Mum, who was suspiciously focused on the salad. Finally she looked Bo in the eye. "Honey, I'm so sorry, I should have said something earlier. We have to postpone our trip," she said softly. "Black Paris and Lagos will have to be in the fall, or winter. We just can't swing it right now. The truth is, I didn't have as many school contracts as I needed this past spring, and Bill's shop, well, it's taking a while to get situated in this new location." As Bo's eyes widened, Mum added, "But the great news is that because you're being homeschooled, we can reschedule easily. We can go any time of year now without worrying about absences!"

"It's freeschooled, not homeschooled," said Bo. "They don't call it that."

"Right. Sorry. So much to get used to, right?"

Bo stayed silent, keeping her eyes down.

"I'm sorry, sweetie pie," said Mum, sighing. "I was going to talk to you about it this weekend. It's been such a whirlwind of activity, and we haven't had any 'just us' time together . . ."

"That's one reason why the trip would have been nice," said Bo. *Together* meant a whole different thing these days, and the warm feelings Bo had been enjoying just a few minutes earlier hardened.

"I'm sorry, I really am," said Mum. "It's just that we're part of a family now, and I had to . . . reconfigure the budget. It didn't seem right for the two of us to go off on a vacation right now when the rest of the family can't."

"But . . ." *We were already a family.* "We've been planning this for a year, Mum!" Bo cried. "I don't understand why, um, Pop, uh, Bill—"

"Bill didn't agree with this at all," Mum said quickly. "He really wanted us to go. But it just didn't feel right to me. We have moving costs, and grown-up stuff that I don't want you to worry about. I'm sorry. It's not canceled. Just postponed a little?"

How was she not supposed to worry? Bo picked up the stack of colored plates and matching cloth napkins. "Yeah," she said, but she knew that something else would happen and they'd never go, because nothing was the same anymore, and it was the confusing mix of good and bad that made her just want to pull the covers over her head sometimes. But she wasn't going to be the one to ruin this night. "Yeah," she said again. "I understand." Worrying about money was one of those things that Bo was used to, even if Mum didn't realize it. Sometimes they had to put things back at the grocery store, things that Bo could tell Mum really wanted. And she'd said a million times how great it was that they'd be saving on rent now that they were living in the brownstone.

"Here's something positive about waiting: the girls all have italki tutors! Bill already found a Yoruba tutor for you, so when we do go—and I promise, we will—you'll be able to make conversation! Bill's been studying with him and says he's a great teacher."

"Why is Bill learning Yoruba?" asked Bo, narrowing her eyes.

Mum waved her hand. "Oh, he just wants to learn, because of us. . . . Isn't that nice?"

Hm. Bo folded and refolded some napkins.

"We'll talk more about this, I promise," said Mum. "Tonight, before bed."

"Maybe tomorrow," said Bo. "Tonight, we're working on a plan to help Lee—" She stopped. She couldn't very well tell Mum about Lee's plan to hold an animal adoption fair in their backyard. Especially when they were still hoping to talk her out of it.

"Tomorrow, then?"

Bo shrugged. "Come on. Everybody's waiting, Mum," she said.

"It really was a lovely presentation," said Mum. "I can tell that you did so much planning. It just sounds like a lot of expensive work."

Being a kid was a lot of work. Didn't Mum realize that? Bo was silent as they brought the food into the dining room to cheers and applause, but it already felt like being happy about some things meant that it cost a lot.

14

THE BLOCK PARTY RECEPTION PRESENTATION had been a big hit—the Parents kept saying so—but what should have meant a victory lap for the sisters instead meant hearing repeated, vague "We'll see"s. Topped off by the bad news about the trip, Bo was pretty low.

"Hey," said Sunday, nudging her softly one day as they shared the couch with the cats. "I'm excited about Mum's fish dinner tonight. Mama Hope tried to make escovitch for us one time, but she mixed it up with jerk, which she thought used the same ingredients as curry. Papa Charles said he was taking away her Jamaican card." Her laugh trailed off when Bo didn't join in. "You okay?"

"Yeah." Bo shrugged. "It's just . . . you know. Changes." Some of the changes were good; she looked over at her new electronic drum pad that hadn't yet summoned the wrath of Ms. "Supersonic Ears" Tyler. She'd wanted one for a long time. Bill's friend who ran a recording studio had given it to Bill when he'd heard a "real drummer" had joined the family. "Another benefit of becoming part of Bill's family!" Mum had said, hugging Bo and Bill together. "Bill benefits" were double-sided, though: now Bo had an electronic drum pad, but she also felt like she had to practice extra hard to show that she was grateful for it.

"You'll get used to us," said Sunday confidently as Rubia walked into the living room. "I mean, we're not going anywhere. And neither are you, I hope!" She stopped mid-giggle and clapped a hand over her mouth. "Oh, Bo! Your trip! I didn't mean . . ."

Bo was saved from answering when Rubia joined them on the couch, ignoring the clear disapproval of Mr. Bultitude and Mrs. Pilkington—and the fact that there really wasn't any room. It didn't matter what Sunday had meant. The fact was, after all that planning, it wasn't happening. All the work to make sure that nothing changed, and everything was changing. What was Bo doing wrong? Rubia's bottom intruded on her thoughts, and Bo nudged it away. "Personal space, dog," she said. Rubia gave her a look that Bo could only describe as *aggrieved*, and despite herself, she scratched under Rubia's chin in apology. "You're not even supposed to be on the couch," she muttered.

"I really didn't mean it like I'm happy you're missing your trip," said Sunday, not realizing that apologizing again made it worse.

The Twins came in as Sunday was speaking, Lee holding a board game and Lil with the "Skateboarder's Skort" she'd just finished sewing.

"I'm really, really sorry about your trip, Bo," said Lee softly, and Lil and Sunday made comforting sounds.

"Maybe we can all go together next summer," said Sunday tentatively. "I mean, if you want." Bo's throat filled up; she was grateful when Mrs. Pilkington jumped up on her lap and demanded a belly scratch.

"What do you think of this?" asked Lil, holding up the skort. "I can make you one too. I can take your measurements now and build a duct tape dummy you, then you'll be on your way to an entire Lil wardrobe."

"Or," said Sunday, "we could do a live reading of my latest novel. I need to know if the big reveal is too obvious."

"Latest and longest," muttered Lil. "And I'm sorry, sis, but the answer is probably yes."

"Uh, I was going to practice," said Bo, pointing to the calendar on the wall. "It's on the schedule."

"Schedule, schmedule," said Sunday. "You can practice with me in an hour. It'll be an awesome duet. I've been working on a piece that starts out with a simple C-major triad. You jamming on the clams, hitting that break beat on the one and three . . . we can really jam!"

Bo burst out laughing. "'Break beat on the one and three'? 'Clams'? Do you have any idea of what you're talking about?"

"Okay, no, but . . . I'm glad I made you laugh!"

They decided to go with Taboo, and with Sunday's overacting and Lil's competitive streak taking over, soon Bo was laughing from her belly with the rest of the sisters. Her sisters. Living with them was definitely an adventure. Not Black Paris, and definitely not Lagos, but as Sunday decided to accompany Lee's turn at Taboo on the keyboard while Lil danced to distract them both and somehow declared victory, Bo had to admit—this family was a trip.

Bo was sitting at the kitchen table reading Chef Eliana's cookbook when she looked up and saw a squirrel outside the kitchen window. It stood on its hind legs and stared in at her, nose quivering. She made a face, but quickly fixed it when Lee walked in.

"Here, kitty kitty," murmured Lee, making kissy sounds.

"Uh, they're not cats," said Lil, coming in behind her. Sunday, walking backward, brought up the rear.

Guess the gang's all here. Bo put a smile on.

"Yeah, they're practically rats," Sunday said. "Don't be fooled by the old bright-eyed bushy-tailed disguise." She tapped lightly on the window to shoo the squirrel away. It glared back at her with something like contempt, took a bite of the nut it was carrying, then turned its back deliberately. "You are a rat," muttered Sunday, looking through the window. "And another thing—" She stopped, peering out. "Hey! There's Papa Charles and Pop!"

The Twins joined her at the window. "Uh-oh," Lil said. "Something's up."

The squirrel scampered away. Bo peered over her sisters' heads to see Papa Charles stomping down the street looking like thunder and lightning, and she didn't need Sunday's giant detective binoculars to tell her that he was either rehearsing for a brand-new role as a really angry man or . . . he was a really angry man right then. Bill rolled beside him, nodding the way Bo did when she'd sit and listen to Mr. Korin get yelly about people who didn't understand that garlic was all the medicine they needed. She'd known that if she let him go on uninterrupted, they'd get to eating whatever deliciously garlicky dish he'd prepared.

"It's kind of early for them to be coming home from work," said Lee.

"Yeah, the store should still be open for at least another couple of hours," said Sunday. "I detect . . . *Something Serious.*"

As Papa Charles stomped inside, a gust of cold wind seemed to blow in from nowhere.

"You think so, Poirot?" said Lil to Sunday, who stuck her tongue out.

Bill closed the door softly behind them.

"Hello, girls," Papa Charles said, sticking his head in through the kitchen door. "Had a good day? Good. Great. Fantastic. See you in a bit." No twirling them while he shouted "HeLLOOOO, Lovelies!" in that big bear voice.

Bill gave them a very quick, very fake thumbs-up as both men headed straight to the living room.

The girls looked at each other.

"Maybe he has a fun surprise for us," said Lee, but there was a question in her voice. "A hamster?"

"Yeah, maybe, if 'fun' means something Really Bad," said Sunday.

According to Mum, acting was the perfect profession for Papa Charles because he had a lot of Personality with a capital, underlined, neon-highlighted P. "He has a lot of enthusiasm for his work," Mum had said. "That's much more important than being rich and famous." Bo was good at math, but she didn't have to be to tell that the number of auditions Papa Charles went on compared to the number of acting jobs he booked meant that not everyone valued his Personality as much as he hoped.

Lil clapped twice. "Positions, sisters," she said.

"Oh, I hate eavesdropping," said Lee. "We should just figure out where we're going tomorrow, and wait until they decide to tell us what's up. If there's anything up," she finished. "And probably there's not. Everything's fine!"

"Yeah, well, while you stare out the window and talk to bluebirds or whatever, the rest of us are going to do something," said Sunday. "Anyway, it's not eavesdropping, it's . . . *paying attention.* Think of it as our duty." She pulled a small notepad and tiny pencil from her jeans pocket. "Sometimes, the Parents need us to do it."

"Yep," Lil added. "It's for their own good. Sometimes it just takes them longer to realize it. This way, we're really helping them out."

"I think . . . ," said Bo, "I think they're right, Lee."

Lee sighed, but she stood and held the parlor door open for her sisters. They slipped quietly into the hallway.

There were so many fabulous things about their house, but one of the best things about living in a really big, really old brownstone was that there were a lot of nooks and crannies to hide—and hear—in. Each of the girls had special spots for listening to those grown-up conversations that their parents didn't want them to hear. *I mean, seriously,* thought Bo, as she squeezed into her spot behind the living room couch, *those conversations are usually about us anyway, so they're the ones who are wrong for not talking to us, right? Right.*

Sunday nodded briskly at her sisters. "Meet up in our room in oh-fifteen," she whispered.

"None of us get that 'oh' stuff," Lil whispered back. "Just say what you mean! Fifteen minutes?"

"Yes," Sunday hissed. "Which means that you do get it, so—"

"Sshhh!" whispered Bo. "I mean, please. We're wasting time."

"IT'S HAPPENED," Papa Charles was saying. It was pretty easy to eavesdrop on him, Bo thought. He projected even when he was trying to have one of these parents-only conversations. "IT'S UN-BE-LIEV-ABLE." He drew the syllables out, then paused.

"What's happened?" Bill's voice. Bo heard the wheels on his chair creak; he was probably settling in for a good, long Papa Charles monologue. Papa Bill said that Papa Charles was "always on," and Bo didn't need Sunday's supposed powers of deduction to tell that this was probably one of those times.

"The INCREDIBLE ignorance, the LACK of understanding of nuance, the UNMITIGATED gall . . . ," began Papa Charles. Bo had learned that when Papa Charles got excited, he spoke in Thesaurus.

"The new show," said Mama Hope. Then she mumbled something that Bo couldn't hear. Then they all mumbled some more. Argh! Bo hoped Lil was getting it all. Lil's hiding place was right behind the giant old wooden pantry with the glass doors, right next to the kitchen. It was full of silverware and porcelain dishes that looked like they hadn't been used since the Harlem Renaissance, and it was a risky hiding spot, not just because it was so close but because it was dusty too, which meant a serious sneeze factor. Lil loved risk factors the way Bo loved buttercream frosting.

"Asking me, *me*, to appear alongside a talking ferret—"

"A what?" asked Bill.

"I thought this was a hospital drama," said Mum. "What in the world would a talking ferret have to do with a hospital drama?"

"Are you asking me to make sense of television, Lola?" asked Papa Charles. He said *television* like it was one of the words they were not allowed to say out loud. "But I did not complain when the not-even-good-enough-for-a-coat creature was actually given a dressing room larger than mine, a wardrobe—"

Bo heard a muffled happy squeal from somewhere nearby. Lee. Probably planning little ferret sweaters for winter.

"But now they've decided that the entire hospital will be

populated by these pests! A ferret-run hospital! In Manhattan! No humans allowed!"

"Ah," began Mama Hope. "So they don't need Charles Dwyer, human actor, anymore."

"I've been written off," said Papa Charles. "We shot my entirely undignified exit scene today."

"Ferrets, huh?" said Bill. More mumbling. Bo strained to hear. Mrs. Pilkington strolled over and meowed disapprovingly.

"That's RIDICULOUS!" boomed Papa Charles, obviously shocked back into shouting. "Who can afford that?"

Bill mumbled something in reply, so Bo guessed that now they were talking about his bookstore. It didn't take much to realize that Papa Charles losing a gig wasn't a good thing, not when the bookstore was struggling, Mum's teaching artist work was drying up with every school budget cut, and while Mama Hope was kind of a big deal in the world of drawing maps for children's books, that didn't seem to be a very big world. What if, just as she was settling into this life, they had to leave it? What if her new family had to split up?

Bo strained hard to hear the Parents. *We're not spying*, she reminded herself. *We're paying attention*. Parents thought that she couldn't say it out loud, but she felt deep down in the scariest part of her heart that if she didn't stay vigilant, their patchwork-quilted family could be torn apart just like that.

"I'm going to start some bread," she heard Mum say. Uh-oh. Her mother starting a loaf in the evening meant stress, big-time.

Bo twisted her body into a more comfortable position. Parents and their whispering were so annoying! She heard scuffling nearby. Mr. Bultitude was scratching a box in the hallway. Bo tried to signal him to be quiet, and Mr. Bultitude gave her the official *I'm Just a Cat* look and kept scratching. Suddenly Papa Charles said, "Well, that's it, then. It's all over. We're in for some big changes around here."

There was a humongous crash. And then silence.

Bo ran into the kitchen.

15

LIL WAS CAREFULLY PICKING HERSELF UP from the floor and away from pieces of broken fancy dishes nearby. Bo didn't need Sunday's Sherlock Holmes-y hat (a "handmade by Lil" creation) to deduce that the broken dishes were the least of their worries.

Mama Hope was standing over Lil with her arms crossed, and Lil was looking at the floor with her lips pressed together like a panini. Bo had read in books about people turning "a shade of purple" when they were angry, and now that she was looking at Papa Charles, she could confirm that not only could that actually happen, it could happen even if a person's skin was a deep shade of brown. Bill, who she had to admit was the smiliest man she knew, was about as far from smiling as a person could get. And Mum was looking right at Bo.

"Tokunbo," said Mum in a low, scary voice. "Come here."

Uh-oh, I'm in full-name trouble. Bo slowly stepped into the kitchen. Sunday and Lee followed close behind, tiptoeing into view.

"Were you all eavesdropping?" continued Mum.

"Yes! We're sorry! We all were!" said Lee quickly.

Lil groaned. "You can't fold so fast, sis!" she said. "I had it covered—" She paused as the full heat of the Parents' glares turned toward her. ". . . Uh, I mean, yes, we are very, very sorry."

Bill went over to the broom and dustpan while Papa Charles beckoned the twins toward him with his finger.

"Yes, we were listening," said Bo. "We know it's wrong, but . . . we're paying attention to the world around us, like you tell us to. And this"—she waved her hand around—"is the world around us."

"Nice," muttered Sunday in approval.

"You know that eavesdropping is not okay. What were you thinking?" asked Mum.

"That," said Papa Charles. He clasped his hands behind his back and started pacing. "That . . . is the question." He looked around at them all, and for a second Bo thought he was going to take a bow. She stifled a giggle. Lil didn't.

After weathering another set of glares, Lil cleared her throat. "Um, so anyway," she said, taking the broom from Bill, "we're sorry." She stood straighter. "But I heard you say something about rent," she continued, and her voice only trembled a tiny bit. "And Pops losing his job to a ferret—"

"To be fair, I think the whole block heard that part," said Sunday.

"Really not the time, Sunday," Bo said. She turned to the Parents. "I think you should tell us what's going on." Because she could feel her sisters move a little closer to her, she held her head up a little higher.

None of the Parents answered for a long moment; then Mum spoke.

"Why don't you girls clean this up properly, then we'll eat and have a little Table Talk time. There's obviously a lot to talk about."

After Lil said a long grace (adding a lot of Scripture quotes on forgiveness and mercy), they'd all tucked into bowls of turkey chili with kale, black beans, and corn. Papa Charles spoke.

"So, girls, this eavesdropping is disappointing, to say the least. It's obvious that we need to have a conversation." Papa Charles's voice had its soliloquy boom to it, which could mean a lot of sound and fury signifying . . . nothing.

"Pops," Lil said, "with all due respect—"

"And there's a lot due," cut in Papa Charles. He held up the hand that wasn't holding a forkful of chili.

"Ahem," he continued. He cleared his throat long enough for Bo to be impressed. When he was done, he seemed surprised and a little disappointed to find that the girls were still looking at him. "Well, so . . . we have been having discussions . . . our situation for a while has been . . . we have to look at all of our options. . . ."

"What situation?" asked Lee.

"What options?" asked Sunday.

"Well," began Bill. Then he stopped.

"At this rate, we'll be more than old enough to handle whatever you think we can't handle now," said Lil. "Stalling doesn't help."

Bo raised an eyebrow; Lil was talking strong.

"You're on thin ice, young lady," said Mama Hope. "Don't fall through."

"Well," began Papa Charles again. Then he stopped too.

The longer the stalling went on, the more Bo wondered if she even wanted to know what the problem was. It looked like it could be Something Serious. And if it was, that meant Lee would probably cry a lot, Lil would hatch a high-risk caper that involved action-movie-level stunts, and Sunday would drive them all to distraction with her list making and deductions of the obvious. And Bo would wonder why she'd relaxed when she knew that the Happys never last forever. Mum had told her so once, and Bo had never forgotten.

"Girls. The rent has doubled at Bill's shop, and budget cuts mean that I'm not booking as many school visits as I need."

"We're all doing work that we love and believe in," said Mama Hope, "and as you may have heard, with the . . . er, ferret situation"—she glanced at Papa Charles, who scowled magnificently—"sometimes that doesn't translate into the big bucks. Or even medium ones."

Bo spoke quickly. "So do we have to split up? Move out of the city? Go . . ." Her voice lowered to a whisper. "To the *suburbs??*"

The Parents looked at each other and then back at the anxious faces of the girls.

"What? Of course not!" said Mum. "Split up? We just got

together!" Bill squeezed her hand, and Bo let out the breath she hadn't realized she was holding.

"What in the world gave you that idea?" asked Bill.

Did parents really not get that whispered conversations and worried glances did not go unnoticed? Bo had to work hard to keep her face fixed; they were in enough trouble already.

Papa Charles spoke up. "I apologize. Perhaps I was being a bit dramatic this evening. It was a shock, the weasel thing—"

"Ferret," interjected Lee. That drew sharp looks from everyone.

"But that was just me letting off steam," Papa Charles said. "All is well. Such is the life of a performer!"

"We're not splitting up, leaving the city, or anything like that," said Mum, smiling a little at Bo. "We just have to . . . rethink a few things, reorganize, be creative. There's nothing for you girls to worry about. Worrying is for adults. We do our jobs, you do yours. And your jobs are to focus on your schoolwork and respect our privacy. That reminds me, Sunday, thank you for putting the cookbook proposal on my desk. I love it. I'm so glad that you and Bo are putting your heads together on these things." She looked around the table at the sisters. "And I'm sure we'll all be interested to see a detailed presentation from the four of you on the differences between a spirit of inquiry and snooping, and the consequences of not seeing your way out of A/B conversations. Along with that should be a companion report—with citations!—on age-appropriate strategies for stress management."

"Strategies from across the diaspora would be nice," murmured Mama Hope. "Always so helpful to learn about practices in a variety of cultural contexts."

"And perhaps some backyard pottery work?" added Bill. "We'll need some replacements for what was lost in tonight's crashtastrophe."

The girls just nodded; they were probably getting off easy. And the pottery would be fun. Bo glanced at Bill, and he winked.

Mum sure had gotten the hang of the *school* part of free-schooling. *It figures*, Bo thought. Even with all of their Independent Learning and Mature and Responsible speeches, their parents were still parents. And parents seemed to think you were a baby until you were old. She exchanged looks with her sisters that said "talk later" and the family finished their meal with light conversation and slightly heavy warnings about respect and eavesdropping.

"What cookbook proposal?" Bo whispered to Sunday as they had a dessert of fresh watermelon that Mum had gotten from a man on 125th Street who drove down south every year to get what he called "*real* watermelon. Back in my day, we appreciated seeds." Bo and Sunday both had theirs with feta cheese, which Sunday took to be yet another sign of their destined-to-be-togetherness. Bo, even though she'd just been worried about being split apart, felt mulish and contrary and added less feta to her bowl than usual.

"Oh, it was this great idea I had for us. You'll love it," Sunday said confidently. Bo kept eating.

The girls cleaned the kitchen spotless without reminders; for good measure, they even mopped, which always annoyed the cats. They fed Barbara and Shirley under Rubia's watchful eye, and since it was still light, the Parents agreed to let them take a short walk.

Without a word, they headed straight to Morningside Park, which was still humming with kid activity. They passed a group of teens selling T-shirts in front of the movie theater on Frederick Douglass Boulevard, and a man selling a surprisingly large amount of fresh seafood. Riddims, the nearby Jamaican café, was full to bursting with bright colors and belly laughs; Lil pointed out a flowy green pantsuit and a very large red straw hat that would be perfect with just a few touches of ribbon and lace. A woman with impossibly long pink box braids zoomed by on holographic roller skates and two small dogs trotted at her side. At the park, they sat on a bench near the playground; Lil took out a pack of fruit snacks from the secret emergency junk food stash and passed it around as they recapped the evening.

"Look, we got off pretty easy," said Lil, tossing her floppy purple hat into the air. She'd embroidered flowers all around the brim with a special glow-in-the-dark floss, and the hat sparkled in the evening sky. "And we're lucky, even though we lost that hiding spot, they didn't see the others!" Her grin fell as her sisters gave her stone-faced stares.

Bo turned to her. "Really? That's your takeaway? *You're* going to be the lead on this group project, Lil." Sunday and Lee loudly agreed. "Do you think they're being totally honest with us?" Bo went on. "Because, you know . . . parents."

Lee nodded. "Yeah."

"Maybe we shouldn't push the wedding party anymore," said Bo slowly. "It might make them more stressed out."

"No!" cried Sunday as a toddler's ball rolled toward their bench. Bo picked it up and handed it to the tired adult walking a couple of paces behind the toddler. "When times are tough, you have to celebrate when you can. I think we have to push even harder."

Bo wanted to say that Sunday was all about pushing harder, but for once, she agreed with her sister. "Sunday's right," she said. "We just have to show that we can handle it. I mean, I was an assistant party motivator at my neighbor Dougie's first-day-of-kindergarten party. And I still have my notes."

"Of course you still have your notes!" said Sunday, wrapping Bo in a tight hug. "You really are just what this family needed."

"Can we go back to 'assistant party motivator'?" asked Lil, laughing. "Because what does that even mean?"

Bo shrugged. "Exactly how it sounds. I just kind of . . . hyped everybody up." She smiled. "To be honest, it's not that hard for kindergartners to get hyped anyway." Lil and Sunday made *oop oop* sounds, like they were on the dance floor, and while Bo laughed, she wondered: Was this family just what she needed? And if so, why did she still feel itchy sometimes?

Lee had started to hum Miss Lou's "Hill and Gully Rider"

along with Lil and Sunday's *oops*, so Bo tapped out a rhythm on the bench. The child dropped her ball again and toddled toward them; soon there was a small crowd around them, clapping, humming, adding their own beats and harmonies. A girl who was about their age tried to do a series of runs like she was Mariah Carey, but Bo noticed that Lee subtly but definitely got louder and stronger until the girl gave up. When a child started singing a song from a popular TV show, the girls joined in, and then requests started. The sisters ended with "No Mirrors in My Nana's House," and everyone clapped, and it was time to go home.

"Not too many young people like you know that one," said a woman who had been singing loudly. "Dr. Ysaye Barnwell is from right here in Harlem. Do you know who that is?"

Bo smiled. Guess these freeschool projects did come in handy. "Dr. Barnwell was one of the members of Sweet Honey in the Rock, and wrote and produced many of their songs, including this one, which was also a picture book of the same name. Dr. Barnwell has done extensive research about the healing power of choral singing, what she calls 'building a vocal community.'" The woman looked impressed, and Bo couldn't help a flex. "She also founded the Jubilee Singers."

The woman nodded hard. "Well, all right now. She still hosts Community Sings in the D.C. area. Look her up if you're ever down there. Tell her Nzingha sent you. Y'all got a Community Sing going just now without even trying! And I thank you for it." She walked away, humming.

When Lil picked up her hat from the bench, she squealed. "Hey! We got paid!"

"How much?" asked Sunday. "Maybe we can start a wedding party fund."

Lil grinned. "Some goldfish crackers and a juice box," she said.

"It's a start," said Bo. And she realized that she'd already started thinking about their Consequences project. Music was a surefire stress reliever in the Dwyer-Saunders household. And it looked like quite a few people agreed.

The next day after they'd walked Rubia and tried unsuccessfully to record the hens clucking in order to "lay down a track," as Sunday put it—after the park singalong she'd been inspired to write some "little kid songs"—they met in a corner of the Odd Room, a room that the sisters were trying to turn into an official indoor, not-so-secret clubhouse. The Parents weren't yet convinced.

"I know we had a little setback with the whole breaking the fancy dishes thing, but we still have cards to play," Lil said. "Bo, they all feel kinda bad about you missing out on your trip. So do we, by the way. We should think of something we want and ask now, while the iron's hot."

"That sounds so . . . schemey," said Sunday. "It's genius!"

Lil shrugged. "You know what I mean."

"Ooh, what about the canine adoption fair!" said Lee.

"How about *not?*" said Bo, Lil, and Sunday together.

16

"I'M THE OFFICIAL KID VOLUNTEER at Beauty of the Beast Animal Rescue," Lee said to Bo, like she was telling her a secret. Lee said it at least once a week; sometimes Bo caught her saying it to herself. Lee was also wearing a black T-shirt that said **Official Kid Volunteer**, so . . . things seemed pretty clear.

Lee had been trying to sell everyone on the idea of a canine adoption fair at the wedding Block Party. Bo had been reminding her that they were still trying to sell the Parents on the idea of the block party itself. Now, as Lee went on and on, Bo smiled politely and wondered how poopy the place was going to smell.

"Thanks for bringing me with you," she said, even though it wasn't like she had had much of a choice. Mum "strongly encouraged" her to share each of her sisters' interests, which so far had meant free puppet-making workshops in the park with Sunday, roller- and ice-skating with Lil, and now menagerie madness with

Lee. But Bo would rather be doing what they were doing now, walking a shelter dog, than getting into Lee's other big passion—the pool.

"He's so well behaved," said Lee proudly. "Remind me to tell the Parents that when I get home. 'He's so well behaved!' I'll say. 'It's like he knows exactly what to do without any training!'"

He *was* pretty good. And Bo liked the way he was walking and looking around like he hadn't seen very much yet in his little life. Still, she kept a healthy five paces behind Abiyoyo. Apparently naming was one of Lee's "official" duties, along with cleaning up many varieties of animal poop.

The girls had spent the morning cleaning, and Bo had to admit it had been pretty cool to use the concoctions they'd whipped up in a science lesson with Mama Hope. Vinegar was truly amazing. Then there was a search for Dwayne Wayne that had taken an hour. Then they'd had to find his hat.

Bo wanted time to find *herself*. It wasn't just that her sisters were always clamoring for a group baking session. Or that Mum kept "just happen"ing to need Bo to "run a snack over to Bill at the shop." Bo would go, and more often than not, Bill would be there alone, in the middle of his books, eager to tell her about the new Dhonielle Clayton fantasy that he didn't have in stock anyway, and ask her if she'd teach him to make scones.

"I have a kitchenette in the back," he'd say every time. "And I'd love to finally understand the difference between baking powder and baking soda."

But . . . baking was her special solo joy; Bo wasn't ready to give that up yet.

Lee's voice faded in and out as she told Bo about all her favorite neighborhood spots while they walked.

"Sido makes the best hummus and falafels," Lee said. "And every summer at some point we go to Rama's to get our hair braided. Lil is a really good braider, but she charges me and Sunday twice as much."

Bo was surprised to see some signs in French, and Lee explained that they were near New York's Little Senegal.

"We'll take you to Accra restaurant soon too," Lee said. "We studied Ghana back in the spring. Lucky Star No. 7 is our favorite Chinese takeout place that sells pizza too. And beef patties. Kids go there all the time, because it's like one-stop shopping. Mr. Cheng is really nice; he lets us hang out there even if we're just sharing one order of fries."

They walked past three community gardens right next to each other, and Abiyoyo barked at the fake owls. Then he barked as a street cat slipped under a parked car, and another dog somewhere barked back.

"We get our patties from Kingston Tropical in the Bronx." Bo felt like she should do more than just nod. "It's the only place Mum will go if she doesn't make them herself."

"Ooh, do they have veggie?" asked Lee. "Maybe we can go as a field trip!" Abiyoyo led them to a stoop that was lined with large potted plants. Lee tried to hold him at a respectful distance as he attempted to investigate.

"Is that your dog?" asked a serious-faced little girl who was wearing orange shorts and a white T-shirt that said **Spoiled** in bubble letters. She was making chalk drawings on her stoop. "I'm allergic to dogs. I'm telling."

"There's nothing to tell, Amy," Lee said patiently. "This is a shelter dog, and if we stay on the sidewalk and you stay on your stoop, you don't have to worry."

"I'm still telling," said Amy, going inside.

Bo laughed. "She looks about the same age as the boy I babysit—used to babysit. Dougie." She stopped laughing. She used to do a lot of things.

"I can't imagine babysitting Amy," Lee answered with a sigh. Abiyoyo looked a little too interested in the freshly planted flowers in front of Amy's building, so they moved on quickly. "Come on, let's go, we've got lots to seeee," Lee sang. Bo noticed that she was much louder than she'd been in their band rehearsal.

"AAAAH! My ears!" said a voice behind them. Bo turned to see a boy all laid out, rolling on the sidewalk, holding his ears. "I think they're bleeding!" he went on.

"Bo, that's Marcus Semple," said Lee. "Or, as Sunday would say, the neighborhood giant gnat. Where's Kareem? I'm not used to seeing the gnat without the mosquito."

"What? I can't hear you," said the boy. "Those screechy

sounds coming out of your piehole killed my ears. You *murdered* my ears, yo."

Bo laughed, but she stopped when Lee shot her a hurt look.

"I mean, it's obviously not true," Bo said. "We all know you have a beautiful voice!" Lee looked away. *How am I going to learn to be a good sister if I keep messing up like this?* "Uh, who's Kareem?"

"Kareem's my name, don't wear it out," said another boy, walking over. His red hair was cut into a fade that was almost high enough to be considered old-school, and his freckles stood out against his light brown skin. He looked like he laughed a lot.

"The Parents agree that it's too much television that makes Marcus the way he is," said Lee to Bo, as if Marcus wasn't there. "I think they give television way too much credit. Lil says some people are just born that way. Look at Kareem."

Bo laughed again, and from the satisfied look on Lee's face, this time it was okay.

Just then Abiyoyo trotted right up to Marcus and . . . licked his face!!!

"Abiyoyo!" cried Lee.

"Cute puppy," Marcus said, standing up quickly. "Why would you try to hurt him with your wretched voice?"

"You might want to take a good shower when you get home," Bo said, raising her eyebrows. "Because he just peed over there a second ago."

Lee high-fived Bo, and they both laughed as Marcus scrambled away. Kareem jogged after him, but when he turned back and waved to the girls, Bo saw that he was laughing too.

Maybe I'm getting the hang of this sisterhood thing.

"Isn't it great the shelter is so close to Pop? I've been thinking that maybe he'd want to create an Animal Annex at the shop!" said Lee as they approached the bookstore entryway.

"Pretty sure animals and books don't go together," said Bo. "Nice rhyme, though."

"Mrs. Pilkington loves read-alouds," Lee went on. "And I've been reading to the shelter animals since . . . since I learned how to read! It was a great way to practice!"

Bill was grateful for the food. "Thanks for bringing this by," he said. "It's nice not to have to close up the shop every time I forget my lunch. You never know when someone might drop by."

Bo looked around. "Um, maybe if you put a few chairs over there by the window, people will get the 'read-and-relax' vibe and you'll get more customers."

"Good idea, Bo," Bill answered. "Maybe the next time Winston and them come up, they can sit in the window and look like customers—nothing makes you busier than already looking busy." He held up a hand for a high five, and Bo hit his palm lightly.

Abiyoyo barked. "We need to get going," said Lee. "But I think some four-legged company might be just the thing this shop needs."

Bill laughed. "I'll take that under consideration, Lee. Though I do get quite a bit of that at home. Maybe if they're willing to buy a few books to sweeten the deal, I'll consider it." As he thanked them again for the food, someone behind Bo cleared their throat.

"Uh, are you open?" asked a young woman. Her hair was in a high, sleek bun, and she seemed tall because her posture was so good that it made Bo stand straighter. She was wearing the kind of red lipstick that Auntie Fola said only really dark-skinned people could carry off. She looked elegant and . . . confused.

"Yes! Come in, come in," said Bill. The girls moved over quickly.

Peering inside, the woman shook her head. "Oh, never mind, I . . . Didn't this used to be something else?"

"Now it's the best bookshop in New York City," said Lee quickly, tossing her head like she was wearing red lipstick too.

"Uh, great . . . yeah, I was just checking your hours." She turned quickly and left.

"Well, that's progress," Bill said cheerily.

As Abiyoyo pulled Bo and Lee back outside, Bo turned around and saw him behind the counter, head in his hands.

After the walk, they'd turned Abiyoyo over to the intern in the puppy playroom; Abiyoyo had spread out on the rug like he had just done the New York City Marathon.

"Right now, we have eleven cats, eight dogs, three bunnies, two turtles, one bird, three Madagascar cockroaches, and Ernest the Surly Iguana," said Lee, who was now waving her arm around Beauty of the Beast shelter like she was taking Bo on a fancy house tour.

"No joke," Lee went on, "every beast that's arrived has been welcome here! Because we mean beast in the nice, regular animal way. Not, like, the monster way."

"Uh, cool," said Bo, trying very hard not to let her nose so much as even twitch even though she could smell every single one of the twenty-nine creatures Lee had just mentioned. "Well, we've got to move fast. We promised the Parents that we'd get back in time to help with dinner." Only this many animals (why, why, why would they have cockroaches from Madagascar when there were already perfectly terrifying ones in New York?) would have her in a hurry to do household chores. "And," she added, noticing that Lee was giving a black-and-white cat an extra-long hug, "without any new animal friends," she finished firmly.

Lee sighed. "Come on, I'll introduce you to Dr. Coleman."

Bo followed Lee to the exam room, which was just like Bo's pediatrician Dr. Shepherd's office, except the exam table was smaller and Dr. Coleman didn't look like she called her patients "Chubby Cheeks." (Bo had been telling her mother that she needed a new doctor. But Mum thought it was cute and reminded Bo that she did have chubby cheeks. Which was . . . not the point.)

Dr. Coleman was friendly but businesslike, which Bo appreciated. "Nice to meet you, Bo. Would you and Lee be up for giving Armstrong a good brushing?"

"Armstrong's the tuxedo cat," explained Lee.

"Chitchat while you work," said Dr. Coleman. "And then scrub up. We've got an examination to do."

"I like her," whispered Bo as she and Lee headed back to Armstrong.

Hila, the official (adult who gets paid) assistant, set them up in another small room with Armstrong.

"He looks grumpy," said Lee, and she started to hum.

"Cats don't have facial expressions," mumbled Bo. But by the end of a fifteen-minute brushing, even Bo had to admit that Armstrong really looked like he was smiling.

The two girls sped back to the other exam room to find Dr. Coleman with another very large cat. "What should we name her?" Dr. Coleman asked.

Bo turned to Lee, but Dr. Coleman nodded at Bo. "You do the honors, Bo."

"Violet," Bo said without thinking. There was something really deep purple about this cat, like she knew what was about to happen, but she wouldn't let it ruin her dignity.

"*Violet* it is," said Dr. Coleman as she prepared a needle.

"I knew you'd get it once you saw everything," said Lee. "Now, let's figure out how to—"

"Yow!" howled Violet as the needle went in. It was a noble *Yow.* Bo surprised herself by stroking Violet's head. "Sorry," she murmured. Dr. Coleman finished the examination, and Hila whisked Violet away.

"I miss her already," said Lee.

"Don't get any ideas," said Dr. Coleman. "Your parents are still salty about that last little . . . misunderstanding."

"Bo, now you can see—we're always overflowing here!" said Lee. "The Parents don't recognize our family's full animal-care potential yet. I just don't get it. They're fine with being the only 'freeschooling' family in the neighborhood, and obviously we'd *learn more* about animals if we *had more* animals, but apparently even freeschooling has its limits, and a dog, two cats, a bearded dragon, three betta fish (RIP), a turtle, and a family of mice (who don't really count because they kind of came with the house) is that limit. But now you can help me—"

"Oh no," said Bo. "I came here today, and I brushed a cat. That's enough for me."

Dr. Coleman laughed. "You may have met your match, Lee. Something tells me Bo's not quite the animal lover you are."

"She will be," Lee said. "It's a family thing. Wait till we get some more chickens and another dog! And a bird."

"I'm going to get my bag and hit the lights," said Dr. Coleman, drying her hands. "After you wash up, why don't you meet us out front."

Bo read all of the KEEP YOUR ANIMAL HEALTHY! posters on the gray walls behind the sink. The paint was peeling in a few spots, and the sink continued to drip after they shut it off. Bo didn't have to be a genius to see that it was not exactly raining money on the shelter.

"Did I tell you I'm going to be a marine biologist? And a farmer," said Lee.

"Yeah, you did," answered Bo, but she smiled.

Violet was still meowing in clear protest as they left, so they stopped so that Lee could sing "I Wish I Knew How It Would Feel to Be Free" for a few seconds.

"She's purring!" said Bo.

"They call me the 'Beast Whisperer' around here, because I can calm and charm just about any animal that comes in, including Ernest," answered Lee. "It's not easy to tell if an iguana is smiling, but I'm telling you, I saw something like a grin! Twice!"

As they opened the front door, Bo could hear Dr. Coleman and Hila talking. She and Lee looked at each other and silently acknowledged that they didn't mean to eavesdrop, because that's not polite, but sometimes adults' voices get really low, and then of course you slow down and listen harder, and then you're in the middle of eavesdropping without even realizing it.

". . . I don't see a way to keep going. We knew this day would come," Dr. Coleman said.

"I just don't understand why," muttered Hila. "What do they expect us to do? They know we don't have any other options."

"I know what we have to do," answered Dr. Coleman. "We've been running on fumes for months now. It's time to let go. We've got a few weeks left. After that, Beauty of the Beast needs to close its doors for good." *WHAT?!!*

"Girls?" Dr. Coleman called out. "Are you coming? Don't you have to get home?"

"Coming," Lee said, and even though her voice was a little shaky, Bo thought she sounded pretty normal.

Dr. Coleman smiled and said thanks and goodbye, and then Hila smiled and said thanks and goodbye, then Bo and Lee smiled too and said goodbye just like everything was cool beans. But Bo could see from the way that Lee's face had shattered that it was everything but. They sat on the steps for a few minutes after Hila and Dr. Coleman had left.

"I heard wrong, right? I must have heard wrong," said Lee. "There's no way we could possibly close the shelter. What would happen to all of the animals? What would happen to me?"

A man walked up, holding a box. "Is this the animal shelter?" he asked.

"Yes, but—" started Bo, but he didn't let her finish.

"Good," he said. He dropped the box on Bo's lap and then left really fast like he knew he was wrong.

Bo heard whimpering. She looked at Lee; Lee looked back at her.

Lee opened the box.

A scrawny, scruffy, shivering little puppy stared up at them.

Bo opened the box more and let him smell her hand, whispering, "It's okay, little guy, it's okay" over and over. Before Bo could say anything else, Lee lifted him out, leaving the box on Bo's lap. There was a note inside.

"My puppers!" said Lee. "It's a sign!"

"Lee . . . ," Bo started. "We should call Dr. Coleman. Or your parents. Or somebody." But even as she spoke, she knew it was too late. Lee's eyes were shining.

The puppy stopped whimpering and barked at Bo.

"What's your problem, Barkerson?" Bo said. She read the note aloud: "'Please look after this dog. I promise he's been checked out. I can't keep him. Sorry.'" She shook her head.

"Barkerson!" said Lee. "That's perfect! You're a namer too! I knew you'd come around. He's perfect for us."

"Wait," said Bo. "I mean, it—he—barked, I called him 'Barkerson.' Not a big leap. And he's not yours, or ours. . . ." Just then the puppy leaned over, licked Bo's hand, and barked again. Lee pet him quiet.

"We can't call Dr. Coleman. You heard them; we're too full already!" Lee said. "And look, he's been neutered, so he's definitely been under a doctor's care. . . ."

"I don't need to look," said Bo, side-eyeing the dog. He made a sound that could only be described as an *Awooooo* back at her.

"Oh my goodness, Barkerson loves you. I mean, he's practically your dog! Also, I think he just sang a B-flat. He's musical! He's gifted! Let's just take him home and figure it out from there. Lil and Sunday will know what to do. I knew I'd—I mean we'd—get a new dog somehow! You are the best sister!" She started singing a sped-up "Redemption Song" softly, and Barkerson settled into her lap.

Bo opened her mouth, then closed it again. Lee and Barkerson looked at her, waiting.

"I can come up with some nice fills for that," Bo said, bobbing her head. "I don't know if I can get my snare tight enough for a good reggae sound, but . . ." Then she sighed. "We're going to have to come up with something better than hiding him in a closet." Lee squealed, and Barkerson barked again.

"You be quiet," Bo said to him, but she didn't mean it.

Because of course Lee had a spare leash in her backpack, they dropped the cardboard box in a recycling bin and walked Barkerson down Adam Clayton Powell Jr. Boulevard. Or rather, Bo noticed, he walked them. At 125th Street, he looked around at the street vendors, tourists snapping pictures of the Apollo Theater, and the line outside the sneaker shop, and Bo could have sworn he smiled.

"He sure seems like he knows the neighborhood," she whispered to Lee. "Do you think he lived around here?" Bo frowned. "Why do I care? And why am I whispering?"

"I thought I knew every dog in Harlem," said Lee thoughtfully. "But maybe I was wrong."

Bo had learned that Lee was serious when she said things like that, so she didn't laugh.

"Bad dog!" said Bo as Barkerson jumped on her for the tenth time.

"That doesn't work," said Lee. "Watch. No. No jumping, Barkerson," she said in a firm but kind voice. "No jumping. Sit, Barkerson. Sit." Barkerson stopped and, eyeing Bo, sat.

Lee clapped. "He's so smart! Sit! Good dog. Good sit, yes!" She took a treat out of her backpack and gave it to him.

"You just happened to have dog treats?" asked Bo, shaking her head. "Seriously, what exactly are we doing with this dog right now?"

"Oh, it's you guys again," said Marcus behind them. "But with a scabies rabies sidekick. What's that smell? I can't tell which one of y'all it is."

Bo couldn't believe she thought he was funny just a little while ago. She turned and glared hard enough that both he and Kareem stopped in their tracks.

"Dang, I was just kidding," Marcus muttered. He cleared his throat. "So you're walking that dog? For the shelter?"

Kareem groaned. "No, they're running a cat, for the church. Bruh."

Bo turned her laugh into a cough.

Lee gave Barkerson another treat. "Something like that. Hey, have you seen this dog around the neighborhood?"

Both boys said no. "Is it lost?" asked Kareem.

"I mean, you see it right here," said Bo. "Do we look lost?"

"You really giving me that opening?" asked Marcus. Bo gave him another glare, and his smile died. "Okay, I see you with the Evil Eye. Um, where are the other ones, anyway?"

"Bruh," said Kareem again. "These ones don't want you to say the other ones."

Lee rolled her eyes. "If you mean our sisters, they're minding their business. I recommend it." She looked very pleased with herself; Bo wanted to tell her that ruined the effect of a good burn, but instead she just backed Lee up with an extra hard stare the boys' way.

Marcus and Kareem kept walking in the same direction, a few

steps behind, talking loudly about what sounded like a basketball game in which they'd scored seven hundred points apiece. As they rounded the corner on their block, Ms. Tyler peered out at them from her open first-floor window.

"Speaking of evil eyes . . . Block Auntie alert," loud-whispered Kareem. "See y'all later." The boys slipped away quickly.

"Scaredy . . . boys!" Lee whispered. "I don't use 'scaredy-cat' as a pejorative," she explained to Bo.

Bo patted Lee's arm, because what else could she do? *Scaredy boys? Pejorative?*

Ms. Tyler sucked her teeth in Bo's direction. "You live over in that house too now, huh?" she said, pushing the words *that house* out of her mouth like curse words.

It was only the fourth or fifth time she'd asked Bo the same question, but Bo just replied, "Yes, Ms. Tyler," because she'd recognized Ms. Tyler as soon as she'd moved into the brownstone. There was a Ms. Tyler on Sedgwick Avenue. There was one who worked in the office at her old school. They were everywhere.

"How many of y'all living up in there now?" Ms. Tyler narrowed her eyes.

"We're two co-housing families, Ms. Tyler!" said Lee brightly. Bo thought that using words like *co-housing* didn't help the situation. No other Black people Bo knew talked the way her new family did. "How are you today, Ms. Tyler?" continued Lee. "My mom would like to welcome you over for tea anytime you're free. She thinks you might like her coconut biscuits."

"I'm busy," said Ms. Tyler. "And it's summer. What y'all doing having tea? Running the streets with those boys, that's what I see."

Sunday had explained to Bo that while the rest of the block hadn't exactly welcomed the Dwyer-Saunders crew with wide-open arms, Ms. Tyler had been an especially hard nut to crack. Bo wondered if Ms. Tyler had already sampled Mama Hope's coconut biscuits; that might explain things. Of course, Bo and Mum's arrival probably hadn't helped things. And then, of course, there were the animals.

Right on cue, Ms. Tyler narrowed her eyes even more. "You people running a pet store in that house? You got a permit for that? I know you're not trying to violate codes, because—"

"Oh no, ma'am," Lee said quickly, smile still pasted on her face so it didn't seem like she was really interrupting an elder. "We do have quite a few pets, but they're all ours, and you might notice that they're all very well cared for and trained." She pointed to Bo. "Bo just got this adorable guy, Barkerson."

What?! Bo gave her sister a *Who, me?* look. "Would you like to meet him?" Lee continued.

"That mangy thing?" Ms. Tyler sniffed. "Looks like you just picked him up off the street five minutes ago. Probably full of fleas."

Ugh, fleas. Bo hadn't thought of that. But elder or no, she was tired of this lady, who Auntie Fola would probably call an "old biddy." "He's not wild or mangy, he's just . . . a special breed," she said, lifting her chin. "He's actually quite rare and can do all kinds of tricks." She said a silent prayer. "Sit, Barkerson," she said loudly.

And he did!

"Um, very good, good doggie," said Bo, glancing at Lee. "Roll over?" she went on, not quite keeping the question out of her voice.

Barkerson gave her a look that Bo recognized as *You're pushing it*, because she'd perfected that look when she was four. But then, he rolled over! After he did it again, he stood and stared at Ms. Tyler as if to say, *How you like me now?*

Lee squealed and clapped.

"Back home, we didn't treat dogs like people." Ms. Tyler sniffed. Bo knew that even though Ms. Tyler had lived on the block "since Langston Hughes lived in Harlem," as Bill liked to say, "back home" was still Jamaica. Bo knew what it was like to miss home.

"The Twins' family is from Jamaica," Bo said, nudging Lee.

"That's right," Lee said brightly. "And Bo's mum makes the best bulla cakes!"

Barkerson calmly stared and raised a hind leg, and Bo knew it was time to quit while she was ahead. "Uh, it was good to see you, Ms. Tyler," she said, grabbing the leash and Lee's hand. "Maybe I'll bring you some of my mom's treats one day!"

"Bo's a great baker too!" Lee called out as they hurried away. "In fact, you should come over and—" Bo yanked her away.

Sunday and Lil were waiting outside when they got home.

"Mama's in her studio working on her New Wakanda map, so she'll be busy for at least an hour," said Lil. "Papa's auditioning people for his *Bodega Dreams* web series, so he could be busy for hours."

"And Pop is still at the bookshop," said Sunday. "I'm pretty sure he was expecting Mr. McKnight and Uncle Winston to stop by, so he'll be there forever." Bo had overheard enough snippets of conversation to know that even though Bill's Bookshop didn't sell too many books, he had a few regulars who traveled from Brooklyn to listen to *Democracy Now!* and *Roland Martin* on somebody's phone while they argued about politics.

"Mum is teaching," said Bo. "Then she's meeting . . . um, Pop at a community board meeting or something." *More like bored meeting,* Bo thought, but the Parents loved that sort of thing.

They sat on the stoop to think. Lee hummed softly to the dog, and he wailed back. Bo took her drumsticks out and tapped a rhythm on the stone ledge.

"Yo, that sounds pretty good," said Lil. "Maybe we can train him and then bring him on the subway platform. He can make us a fortune!"

"Can we just figure out what to do with him right now?" asked Bo as Sunday gave Lil a light flick. "In case you all forgot, the first time I was here, it didn't go so well with an unexpected, uninvited guest dog."

Barkerson looked straight at Bo and barked.

"If you guys can create a distraction for about twenty minutes, I'm pretty sure I can rig a pulley system up along the side of the house that can carry him directly to the practice room," mused Lil.

"Then we can have an extra-long practice session to disguise the sound of any barking until we figure out next steps."

Her sisters looked at her.

Just then three girls walked up. Well, they didn't exactly walk. If someone told Bo to show them what *saunter* meant, she'd show them a video of these three smirking, shiny girls coming toward them. Suddenly Bo felt very grubby.

"What's up?" said the one who was obviously the leader. She even stood a little in front of the other two, Bo noticed, in case they forgot who was the boss.

"Hi," Bo said back, before she noticed that her sisters were decidedly silent.

"Who are you?" said the girl to Bo. "And why are you hanging out with these weirdos?"

Bo opened her mouth, then closed it.

"What do you want, Reese?" said Lil in a bored voice.

"And the answer is no, by the way," said Sunday, standing up like she was going to do something. Since Bo was pretty sure that the most Sunday could do was recite a poem or speech these girls away, she was impressed that Sunday had put that much bass in her voice. Bo prepared for battle. From the looks of her sisters, this wasn't a time for playing nice.

"Oh, good, because the question was 'Are you ever not weird?'" Reese turned to one of the other girls. "Right, Maya?"

Bo tried to hold back a laugh, but she didn't quite succeed, and Reese's attention returned to her.

"What are you laughing at?" she asked Bo, looking her up and down. "Nice drumsticks," she added, in a way that made it clear she thought they were anything but. Unfortunately Bo would have to agree with Reese's obvious disgust at her appearance; she'd worn her most grubby and worn-out clothes for a morning at the animal shelter, and from the way Reese's friends were sniffing, she smelled as bad as she looked. But none of that mattered. She took a deep breath.

"I laughed because you said 'weird' and 'weirdos' in the space of two minutes, and it's been a long time since I've been around someone so unoriginal," she said. "I'm used to a more creative crowd, I guess." She tapped her sticks again, just to let them know. Lee hummed a little louder, and Lil and Sunday quickly followed suit.

"'I'm used to a more creative crowd, I guess,'" mimicked Reese as Maya put her hands over her ears. Reese laughed loudly at her own "joke."

"Yep," said Bo slowly, standing up and moving closer to Sunday. "Definitely used to a more creative crowd. And I mean that in . . . in a *pejorative* way."

Reese rolled her eyes. "Are you going to nerd me away or something?" She put a hand on her hip and smiled a nasty smile. "If you're friends with these *weirdos,* then clearly you're *just as weird.* I feel sorry for you because of your *weirdness,* how about that?"

"These," said Bo, "are my *sisters.*"

Reese's other friend gasped.

Reese went on. "How is that even possible? This family is so weird. My mom doesn't even want me hanging around here, to be honest."

Reese turned to the other two. "Lita, Maya, come on, the air stinks over here. It's gross." Barkerson began to growl, and Reese and her friends backed away with a little less attitude.

"He's a trained attack dog," said Lee in a high, thin voice. "So watch your backs!"

Barkerson, of course, chose that moment to flop down and present his belly for rubbing, and Lee couldn't resist. "Aww, puppers," she cooed.

"We're supposed to look intimidating, sis," whispered Lil through tightened lips. "Can you at least fold your arms?" But Reese and her friends had turned the corner anyway.

"What was that about?" asked Bo. "They were like the mean girls in a bad movie!"

"Reese's actually done some 'professional' modeling and acting," said Sunday, making big air quotes. "Papa Charles even saw her at an audition once. We met her when we moved here last year. Unfortunately. She lives at the end of the block and is always complaining about bodega cats."

Lil muttered a few words they weren't actually allowed to say out loud. "She started in on us as soon as we moved here and hasn't stopped. I think it's, like, her extracurricular activity. We don't let it get to us, though."

"Speak for yourself," muttered Sunday glumly.

"Yeah," said Lee. "Speak for yourself. But do it after we figure out what to do with Barkerson."

"*I* know what we can do with him." Mama Hope's voice rang out from the brownstone doorway. "We can drop him off at the place where he belongs, which is not here, on our way to the pool. Summer session's starting."

"Woot!" said Lil as Lee wailed in canine protest speak. "Now that we're all Sharks, I can officially beat you on the swim team."

There was that "Shark" thing again. At this point, Bo was pretty sure that her swim level, Trout, was not an equivalent.

"I just want to perfect my backstroke," said Sunday, "so I look like I'm in an old-timey movie. I may decide to be a synchronized swimmer one day."

Backstroke!

"Sounds just as lucrative as children's book cartographer," said Mama Hope lightly. "Go inside and get your stuff, girls. Bo, your mum said your suit is in the box marked 'Summer Five.'"

"Suit?" said Bo. "As in swimsuit?" She was not about to embarrass herself in front of her sisters. "I'm . . . not signed up here. I took lessons at Riverdale Road pool last year. Now I'm done."

"Yep, your mum's meeting us there. And she said"—Mama Hope smiled—"that you'd probably say that swimming was in your past, but to tell you that in your bright, new now, you're going to be swimming like a fish!"

I already do, thought Bo. *A trout!*

"Don't worry. The Sharks do more than compete; we have

fun!" said Sunday. "And it means we don't have to wait for a parent to go into the water with us at the beach. That reminds me, Mama Hope, when are we going to Robert Moses? I'm working on a mystery that takes place at the lighthouse."

"*Can* you swim?" asked Lil. "I mean, because you will be a Trout if you're in the beginner group. Not that there's anything wrong with that."

"Uh . . . ," started Bo. "I think *Trout* meant something different at my pool."

"Of course there's nothing wrong with that," said Mama Hope, taking her phone out of her purse. "And while we're on our way to a new beginning for Bo, you girls can explain to me how this dog came to be at your side." Barkerson looked up at her and lifted his leg. "Because, unless you all want to eat my Tuna Surprise every night for the next month, he's going back to the shelter immediately."

"He didn't exactly come from the shelter," started Lee. "At least, not from inside. See, what happened was . . ."

"Here we go," said Sunday. Mama Hope was already calling Dr. Coleman as Lee explained.

There's a whole lot wrong with this, thought Bo, silently fuming as they started walking down Frederick Douglass Boulevard. She had a whole lot to say to Mum when they got to this pool. Trying new things was one thing, but this—this was going too far!

17

THE BRIGHT COMMUNITY CENTER BUILDING didn't look large enough to hold a pool inside, but here it was, deep and wide and smelling very chloriney. Mama Hope handed them off to Mum, who seemed to be carefully avoiding Bo's eyes. A small group of little kids was practicing their kicks with foam boards, and the Twins immediately went over to a cluster of teenagers who were nonchalantly diving into the bright green water at the deep end. Bo heard a lot of giggling and "You can do it"s as she and Sunday followed Mum to the bleachers. That *Hooray Summer!* joy was everywhere, except in Bo's heart at the moment. Was there such a thing as a summer grinch, she wondered? Because if there wasn't, she was going to invent it right this second.

As the Twins rejoined them, Coach Miguel grabbed Bo's hand and smiled a wide smile that showed a lot of teeth.

Please don't say it, please don't say it.

"Welcome!" he said. "Splash Fit is glad to have you."

Of course he said "Welcome." Bo glared at Mum, who looked away. She could see her sisters' lips twitching out of the corner of her eye.

"You two go ahead," said Sunday to the Twins. "I'll see you after my test."

After they left, Bo and Sunday followed Mum as she walked with Coach Miguel to the office. He picked up a clipboard.

"So, Sunday," he said. "Ready for your Shark test?" Sunday grinned and nodded, and he sent her over to a light-skinned woman with short locs who was wearing what looked like a scuba diving suit. Before she left, Sunday gave Bo an extra hand squeeze.

"So, Bo, I understand from your mom here that you've been taking lessons at Riverdale Road pool, but she thought you might want to . . . refine your technique. What level did you last test on?"

"Swimming's not really my *main* thing," said Bo, trying to sound casual. "I mean, I'm at just the right level for me. I'm more of a landlubbing type. Salt of the earth, you know?" Coach Miguel just looked at her. "Yeah, I'm a real city girl, keeping it concrete." Mum rolled her eyes and exchanged a glance with Coach Miguel.

"I got you," he said. "And you're in luck, because we special-ize in . . . salt of the earth city kids here." He gave her the same look Mrs. Dougie gave Dougie when he said he didn't know how melted chocolate had gotten all over his face. "I'm just going to do a little assessment to make sure we match you up with the right instructor."

"Could you excuse us for a moment, please, sir?" she said

politely. When Coach Miguel smiled bigger and nodded, she pulled Mum aside. "Come on, Mum! This is hopeless! And also not fun! And also something I really, really don't want to do!"

Mum patted her shoulder. "You know how some things are nonnegotiable? This is one of those. You are swimming. Here. I was so glad when I found out this place was within walking distance. And your sisters already train here—it's serendipity!"

Bo scowled as she watched the Twins join the teenagers diving off of the high board. "Yeah, they *train*. Like for *competitions*. I have a feeling this place is a little different from our old pool. Look at the color. Definitely more chlorine than we're used to! Who knows what that could do to a delicate kid like me?" Just then a group that looked like it was made up of preschoolers dove into the pool and raced across. Bo gave Mum a pointed look. "I thought we were easing into our new life, Mum. And you always say that I should be proud of who I am—shouldn't I claim my identity as a Trout?"

Mum laughed. "Paddle proudly, my delicate sweetie pie! And you don't have to compete. I just want to make sure you're safe, and you're doing this with your sisters—it's a fun thing. We have some beach trips planned for the summer. You can show your sisters your favorite spot on Orchard Beach! Do you really want to be stuck having to swim with an adult all the time? Your sisters are all Sharks; you should be too. And anyway, we got a family discount."

Bo didn't have time to ask why Mum could find money for

swimming lessons and not their trip, but that was probably a good thing. Mum had that *don't try me* tightness underneath her smile.

"Here comes Coach Miguel. Have fun," sang Mum like she wasn't throwing her first- and only-born to the (sea) lions. "I'll be in the bleachers with my knitting." Mum strolled off like she had just dropped Bo off at a birthday party. And Coach Miguel was coming over like he had a really good present that she was going to love whether she liked it or not. Ugh! There were limits to how much change she was going to take.

One thing about the shallow end—it was always warm. Bo practiced her kicks and tried not to think too hard about the reasons why that might be. She looked up at Mum, who was knitting and chatting with another parent in the bleachers like she hadn't just thrown Bo to the water wolves. Somehow a short assessment by Coach Miguel ("You're right! You *are* a Trout!") had morphed into an actual lesson, and Bo now lined up in the pool with three other children who looked like they hadn't learned to tie their own laces yet. Her coach, Crystal, had a friendly smile and didn't hover. And at least no one knew her here, except her sisters, who were obviously pretending they didn't see her standing in about three inches of water while they were practically deep-sea diving.

"It be your own people, right?" said an old lady slowly coming down the ladder into the water.

"Huh—I mean, excuse me, ma'am?" asked Bo.

The old lady adjusted her bathing cap and pointed to Mum. "I saw what went down. I can tell you don't want to do this. You feel betrayed. But trust, it's a good thing. Our people have a complicated relationship with the water. You'll thank your mother for this one day."

Okay, thanks for the tip, old lady who I don't know, Bo thought. But this was a genuine elder, so she just nodded and smiled politely. Bo was about to ask her if she needed any help, but suddenly the lady pushed off from the wall and swam a series of strong, swift laps while Bo watched with her mouth dropped open.

"That lady is a good swimmer," said a little girl in Bo's class. "I like your bathing suit."

"Thanks," said Bo. She sighed. "How old are you?"

"Eight," answered the girl. "I'm Tiffany and I have a wedgie." She poked her lip out into a pout. "I don't like swimming," she said.

You and me both, Bo wanted to say, but her Responsible Self kicked in. "Let's be buddies. We can help each other, okay?"

The little girl nodded. "You look really big in this pool. Are you ten?"

Bo was the only one in her class who was standing easily in the shallow water. She sighed again. "Eleven, since we're in each other's business. Here, I'll stand in front of you while you pull out your wedgie, okay? No one will see." Coach Crystal offered some smiley advice that worked, and Bo found that her arms didn't get as tired as they usually did. As she turned to practice kicking again, Bo realized that her first Splash Fit swimming lesson was almost over and . . . it hadn't been that bad, even though she'd never admit that to Mum. Everyone else had been busy doing their own thing, and no one was paying attention to the big kid in little water. As she waited her turn to climb up the ladder and out of the pool, she smiled a tiny smile all to herself.

A loud, ugly laugh made her turn toward the door, and her smile fell fast. One of Reese's henchgirls, Lita, had just walked in and was staring straight at Bo like Bo was a circus act, even though Lita was the one wearing a gold bikini and sunglasses at the indoor community pool. Slowly pulling her floaties off of her arms, Bo stared back, holding her head high even as she got splashed by her classmates' kicks. When the girl smiled a small, mean smile, Bo wasn't surprised. She was exposed.

18

AFTER THE POOL, everyone was subdued on the walk home; even a stop at Lee Lee's didn't bring on the usual cheers, and another stop at FairMarket "to pick up a few things" didn't prompt the usual grumbles. Her sisters had seen Lita too and tried to cheer Bo up by commenting on Lita's "waaay stupid attire."

"Like what was that fabric even," scoffed Lil. "Fast fashion garbage! Totally unsustainable!"

They ate their warm and fresh rugelach in the little plaza where the giant Harriet Tubman sculpture stood. Mama Hope was working on a map for a book about Harriet Tubman and took photos of every little detail.

"I just realized that she's facing south," said Sunday. "I thought it was all about going north in those days."

Mama Hope looked up from her sketchbook. "The artist, Alison Saar, has said she was showing Ms. Tubman like she was going back down south to help more enslaved people."

Bo wondered what it had been like, to get free over and over but then risk it all to help other people do the same. Did Harriet Tubman ever want to just enjoy her free life and let somebody else take over? Or have a different job on the Underground Railroad, one that didn't involve going back to the place she hated most?

When they got home, Bo turned to Mum, hoping she'd suggest a little kitchen together time for the two of them. But Mum squeezed her shoulders and whispered, "I know that wasn't easy; I'm glad you have your sisters to cheer you up!" and told them that she was off to the bookstore to see Bill, and reminded them to moisturize well so they wouldn't be ashy. Bo tried to make sure that her "Have fun!" was the loudest.

A little while later, smelling of chocolatey shea and cocoa butters, the girls drifted off to different areas of the house to practice. Sunday was improvising something soft and classical on the keyboard, maybe Florence Price, while Lil, who was preparing a presentation on the history of rock and roll, was rocking out along with Sister Rosetta Tharpe. Lee was singing warm-ups for the cats, who Bo could swear were actually singing along.

Bo was glad for some rare solitude but struggled to play, so she put down her sticks and studied Sheila E. and Cindy Blackman videos instead. She made a mental note to ask Lil if she could design them something like Sheila E.'s vintage "Holly Rock" look. Or maybe teach Bo to do it—Lil had already taught her to make a slim tote bag for her drumsticks.

She closed her laptop and opened her dresser drawer to look

at her collections. The stamps, the rocks she and Mum used to call "diamonds" . . . She hadn't gone through them all in a while. Bo wondered if Dougie had kept his promise to leave Dinobotland untouched until her next visit. It was usually hard for him to wait until he counted all the way to ten in a game of hide-and-seek. But she'd promised him a whole tray of cupcakes if he kept his promise.

Even though she was alone, she looked around before she pulled out her recipe folder. Maybe she'd just fess up and make the Smilecake a science project; then she could talk to Mum about some flavor ideas to finish the recipe, and it could be just the way she liked it. But if it became a project, like everything else they did, it would have to involve her sisters. She sighed and slid the folder back into the drawer.

Rubia barked outside, and Bo went over to the window. The Parents were in the wild tangle of trees and flowers behind their backyard, the old community garden that had been locked up for years, according to Papa Charles.

"Whoa!" said Sunday, coming into the room behind Bo. "How did they get in there?"

"Something good's going down, I know it!" called out Lil. "I detect news!"

More "new"; Bo quieted the rumble in her anxious stomach by thinking of the beats in the opening to Stevie Wonder's "Superstition," and followed her sisters outside.

"Whoa!" said Bo, stepping into the garden through the creaky wooden door. She ducked to avoid some low branches. "It's, like, magical and creepy at the same time!"

"Exactly! It's perfect!" said Sunday, and the others looked at her. She shrugged.

Pop Bill nodded, guiding his chair along the crooked path that sliced through a wild wall of greens, yellows, reds, pinks, and oranges. A rusty barbecue grill was perched upside down in a corner. Pebbles crunched under Bo's purple Chuck Taylors, and she could feel her heart lift a little as she breathed in the scents of the lush foliage. She took comfort in the fact that the garden was as new to her sisters as it was to her; they told her it had been locked and mostly obscured by a wooden fence since they'd moved in.

"We've been calling it the Wacky Botanica Gardens," said Lee, pointing to a red-and-white wooden house with the words CAT CLUBHOUSE over a tiny entryway. "But we've only seen it from the Odd Room window. In person, it's . . . it's . . ."

"Magnificent," breathed Bo.

"We call it a gift, a blessing," said Mama Hope. "The best welcome to the neighborhood we could imagine!"

"I thought it was an old community garden," said Bo. *Emphasis on old. And it didn't look like there had been much community going on in a long time.*

"It is," answered Pop Bill. "But it's been locked up for a while. Corey Industries has been buying up property in the neighborhood at a frightening rate—they're trying to get my shop right now, but that's another story—anyway, they've been real aggressive. They own the building next to the garden and claimed that meant they bought the garden too."

"But Corey underestimated this community," Papa Charles said. "Don't mess with Black folks and their gardens."

"Black women and their gardens especially," said Mum. "A group of women formed a coalition—you know I love a good coalition, Bo—and highlighted the history of this garden. It had provided nutritious food, science education, a play space, it was utilized and appreciated in so many ways. . . . Corey tried to say that the people didn't care about their neighborhood, but it had fallen into disrepair precisely because it was taken away from the community."

"The people fought back," said Bill. "And they won. After nine long months, Corey was ordered to unlock the garden and turn it back over to the community. Today."

Bo looked around. There were remnants of the garden's glory days—a rusty watering can lay against the shed, yellow dandelion plants stood defiant, and an abandoned plastic toy truck was sticking up out of the soil. A sign on the shed door read MONTHLY FRUIT AND VEG BOXES—SIGN-UPS NEXT WEEK!

"So where is the community?" asked Lil. "And why do you have the keys?"

"Remember that community board meeting we went to the other night?" said Mum. "After we heard the whole story, we, uh, volunteered to be the garden caretakers."

"We thought it might help, well . . . endear us to the neighborhood," said Pop Bill. "You might have noticed that we . . . don't ex-actly blend in." He looked tired, Bo realized. Very tired. She knew the Parents spent long hours talking about budgets and "frugal but fun" living when they thought the girls were asleep. Bo was usually the last to close her eyes; there was so much to take in, so much to remember, so much to lose.

"Perish the thought!" said a voice behind them. "Who wants to blend in? Boring!"

"AUNTIE SUNFLOWER!" Sunday and the Twins ran over and hugged a short, smiling, dark brown–skinned woman dressed in baggy hand-painted jeans and a bright pink T-shirt that said **Black Lives Still Matter** in gold lettering. Her locs were piled into a high bun on her head, and she was carrying a toolbox. Bo approved of her purple Doc Martens, huge gold hoop earrings, and wide smile. So this was the famous Auntie Sunflower who Bo had been hearing about for weeks. "The definition of Black Girl Magic!" "A legend!" "Even Ms. Tyler loves her!"

As Sunflower pulled all of the girls, including Bo, into a hug, she looked directly at Bo and winked. It was a wink that said, *I know, this is a lot, we're a lot, but it just might be fun too.*

When the hugs finally ended, Sunflower surveyed the gar-den. "I've always thought there were possibilities here. And I had a tiny idea that you all would be a part of that." She lowered her voice. "How are things with Ms. Tyler?" she asked. "I heard you're a drummer," she said to Bo. "Cool, cool. Has she, uh, mellowed out about the practicing?"

Four heads shook back at her. Bo grimaced. She tried to schedule her practices at the most inoffensive time possible, when most people would be at work, or not asleep, but Ms. Tyler was always sitting at that window of hers, dozing off. ("Until her neighborhood gossip switch gets triggered," Lil always said. "Then she pops awake like a cobra!")

"She says we go on all day long, and she can't hear herself think," said Lee.

"Which is probably a good thing, old, evil crone," muttered Lil. Mama Hope frowned at that, but not too hard. "Bo made us a new practice schedule, though, so it's better."

Bo knew there was room for improvement. There were still times when both she and Sunday were practicing very different exercises at the same time, for example, and even though they were in different parts of the house, it got a little . . . loud and "percussive," as Sunday would say.

"We can't help it if we're enthusiastic about music," said Sunday. "And if some people don't appreciate the arts."

"Maybe not yet," said Auntie Sunflower. "But the reason why I wanted you all as neighbors was for some positive change, and I'm sensing that this could be a breakthrough." Mum had explained the full story to Bo—that Sunflower inherited a legendary Harlem spice mix business empire and had owned the brownstone that the Dwyers and Bill had bought. She also lived next door when she wasn't traveling, and it had been her idea to turn their adjacent backyards into one giant one for Rubia and the hens to use.

"It would be nice to really feel a part of the community," said Mama Hope. "When we got here, I thought we'd really know our neighbors, look out for each other. . . . We've been on the outside since we moved in."

"They definitely look out and *at* us," muttered Lil.

Sunday shook her head. "I don't get why people think we're weird."

"I mean . . ." Bo stopped. Maybe things were different in Brooklyn, but yes, this home of many colors and the literal zoo *were* strange, even for New York City—didn't they get that? And there was something . . . loud about her new family that made Bo nervous and a little excited at the same time. Yes, they were weird, but they were wonderful too. It didn't take long to see that. Sunday was using her magnifying glass to closely examine and make up names for the foliage, and Lee was singing an old Afrobeat song called "Jerusalema" while Lil made up a dance. Mama Hope and Mum were talking to the flowers, because Mama Hope said she'd heard that helped them grow, and now that Papa Charles had a little more free time on his hands, he was trying to convince Bill to stage (and costar in) a two-man production of his original play, *Two Men in Harlem*.

Right now they looked the way she used to feel when she got to the cafeteria late and had to find a lunch seat when the tables were already full of laughing friends. She watched her family and saw something familiar in their eyes that made her feel more like a sister than ever. If there was one place she knew well, it was "on the outside." "You know what?" Bo said. "*They're* the weird ones."

"Nobody's weird," said Mum gently. "But we do want to be a part of the community that we live in." She knelt down over a patch of earth. "This could make a wonderful herb garden! I could do outdoor cooking classes!"

Bees buzzed nearby as the family walked through the surprisingly large garden. "A flower garden would be lovely," said Mama Hope. "And beekeeping—I've always wanted to try that! We could even call it 'Bee Lovely'!"

There was a large shed in the back of the garden along a high fence, and Sunday grabbed Bo's hand and pulled her over to it. "Now, that's what I'm talking about! Headquarters! Spy school!"

"You mean a design studio," said Lil.

"It could be a community classroom," said Bo, picking up a yellowed flyer that had been underneath a flowerpot. "Mum, look, Harlem Grown. You know those people."

Mum clasped her hands together. "Yes! They're a wonderful organization. I bet they'd help us get a hydroponic garden going, some workshops. This could be a perfect location for a youth farmers market. . . ."

Bo jumped in fast. "And a perfect location for the community wedding Block Party." She tilted her head toward Sunday.

"Is that really a thing?" asked Pop Bill.

"We can make it a thing," said Sunday quickly. "We're creators, not mere consumers, remember? We can make anything!"

Lee jumped in. "What better way to reopen the garden and get to know our neighbors?" she said quickly.

"A community celebration is the kind of thing you're always talking about," Sunday added. "We'll ask everyone to bring a dish to share, like a potluck, so it won't be expensive."

"And I bet places like Lee Lee's and Mikey Likes It and Sugar Hill will donate delicious samples," added Lil. "This is the perfect way to get around those pesky block party regulations!"

"They did say at the community board meeting that it's been a couple of years since there have been the parades and street fairs the neighborhood used to have all summer long, remember," mused Bill.

Mum raised her eyebrows. "But—"

"Bill . . . um, Pop, maybe you can advertise the store, and, Mum, your business would definitely be popular if we used your recipes for some of the food," said Bo.

Mum was still walking around the garden. "Look! There's an apple tree, a pear tree . . . and we can grow peppers, tomatoes."

"Strawberries?" asked Lee. "Strawberries would be great!"

"I'm thinking a rainwater collection system," said Lil. "And look at the wildflowers. Lee, you'll love this—some companies are using flowers as a goose down alternative for puffy coats and stuff. We should do a presentation together. You do the report part; I'll make myself a coat."

Bo walked around, taking in the earthy smells and bright green weeds and wild berries that had held their ground despite neglect. "There are a lot of community gardens around here," she said. "How come this one got left out?"

"Ooh, maybe it's haunted," said Sunday, running over. "There's probably a tragic story behind it all!" She rubbed her hands together, sounding way too happy about the prospect.

The Parents explained that the developer's tactics had included skunk spray and WARNING: POISON signs all over, and it had become a habit for residents to just stay away.

"It's been a hard few years in this city," said Bill. "People probably just got tired too, struggling to mind their own business."

"And that brings us back to community," said Lil. "The way I see it, the way we all see it, is that this could be a wonderful learning opportunity—the perfect summer project. It will allow us to contribute to the family . . . coffers in a creative way, since we can't really go out and get jobs, and it's community oriented, which are words that you guys love. We kind of *have* to do the Block Party here."

"We don't call her 'The Closer' for nothing," whispered Sunday to Bo, who nodded, impressed.

They had a glorious dinner picnic in the garden, with a surprisingly good fruit salad made by Mama Hope ("All I had to do was cut up some fruit, and Lola showed me how to make a simple ginger syrup"), all kinds of sandwiches on thick slices of fresh-baked brown bread, and then a caramel cake that Auntie Sunflower had brought along as a surprise. She'd also brought deviled eggs, but the cake made up for that in Bo's mind.

As they munched and explored all of the nooks and crannies of the garden, the girls did a lot of nudging and whispering. Auntie Sunflower joined the huddle.

"So, seriously, folks," said Auntie Sunflower, "I leave for a few months and come back and the family's all new!"

"And improved!" said Sunday. Bo wanted to hug her for that. Auntie Sunflower looked at Bo and winked again. As they all began cleaning and weeding the garden, they sang, and a few people walking by glanced over. The girls had a final quick huddle, and then Sunday and Bo called everyone to attention.

"Ahem!" said Sunday. She began to sing. "We'd just like to remind the happy couple that there's this great opportunity to spread the cheer. . . ."

"We can create, not consume, and have a wedding party right here," continued Bo with an impromptu rhyme to back Sunday up.

"We can share the joy with our neighbors and friends," sang Lee.

"So . . . just say yes before the picnic ends!" finished Lil, taking a bow.

The Parents laughed.

"I half expected to see you all wearing matching outfits by now," said Auntie Sunflower. "What's your band name?"

"Band name?" asked Bo.

"Well, yeah! You're a drummer, and you've got guitars, keyboard, and a lead singer—yes, Lee, you *are* a lead singer—so I mean, you absolutely have a band!"

The girls looked at Auntie Sunflower, looked at each other, then looked back again.

Auntie Sunflower held up her hands. "I'm just saying. Think about it." Then she added, "This really is an incredible design opportunity. I could start working now and have things ready in about three weeks. I can soundproof the shed in our yard and build a door from our yard into this garden, so it'll be easier for you to go in and out. And then what better way to unveil the renewed community garden than with a—"

"WEDDING BLOCK PARTY!" yelled the girls.

"Organized by us," said Bo. "Remember, we'll handle everything."

"Mama, there's a party!" cried a little girl, trailing her mother and siblings down the sidewalk. "An outside party with big girls! Can I go?" Her mother shushed her and rushed her along.

The sisters gave their parents a significant look, as if to say, *See?*

Papa Bill grabbed Mum's hand. "It could be fun," he said.

"It could be a lot of things," murmured Mum. Then she smiled. "But definitely a lot of fun. Okay, girls, it's a—"

"YAY!" Bo, Sunday, Lil, and Lee joined hands and immediately started a singing victory celebration.

"See what I mean?" said Auntie Sunflower to no one in particular. "A band!"

The Parents decided that the girls would have three weeks to prepare, and they would have to submit a plan and a final research paper at the end (ugh). The sisters decided that if they worked quickly, there would be time for an ice cream run to top off a wonderful day. They made a unanimous decision to get Harlem Sweeties cones, and Bo and her sisters kept working and singing. The more they sang, louder and freer, the more families passed and peered curiously into the garden. And Bo held her head high and sang louder.

19

EVERYTHING ABOUT BO'S LIFE felt like one big field trip these days, so she had been a little surprised when their first actual field trip day arrived. It was hot, but there was a breeze; the trip was going to involve music and tortillas from scratch; and no one had mentioned anything about a reflection essay, so Bo thought the day was promising.

"This is like waiting for the G train," said Lil, tapping her feet. "We're going to Times Square and then Queens, not Kaffeklubben Island."

Bo agreed (and thanked Mama Hope's geography games for being the reason that she knew where Kaffeklubben Island was). They were so close to being out the door, but the Parents were droning on and on, repeating the long list of instructions they'd gone over the night before, and that morning at breakfast.

"If there's a car with only one person inside, do not get on," repeated Lee.

"Don't stand in the doorway," said Sunday.

"You mean 'Stand clear of the closing doors,'" said Lil, in a pretty good announcer imitation.

"And no earphones, AirPods, earbuds, whatever while we're in transit," added Bo. She'd been relieved to discover that she wasn't alone in having to follow annoying subway rules. This was also her sisters' first summer of riding the subway without adults, and last night they'd agreed that they were thrilled, and more than a little nervous. From now on, if all went well, they'd be allowed to take public transportation on their own. No solo trips allowed, though; at least two sisters had to travel together at all times.

"We got it, we promise, goodbye," said Lil, grabbing her backpack and slipping it carefully over her shoulders. Since they were all wearing the **Say Her Name** shirts that Auntie Sunflower had gifted them with a few days earlier, Lil had embellished hers with sequins at the collar and seams.

"Do you know your stop?" asked Mum as she helped Bo slip her messenger bag over her shoulder.

"We got it, 103rd and Corona Plaza," said Bo, hugging her mother quickly and giving the other parents a fast wave and smile. Bill reached out and patted her shoulder.

"Have fun!" Bill said. "And hand sanitizer! Make sure you each have hand sanitizer!"

Bo smiled back. Bill was trying, but not too hard, which she appreciated.

Sunday grabbed Bo's hand and led her outside. "C'mon, sis,"

she said. "I've got sanitizer and wipes for both of us." Sunday, on the other hand, was the living definition of *go hard or go home.*

"So whose idea was this again?" asked Lil. Though it was ten-thirty in the morning, officially after rush hour, the Times Square subway platform was bustling and pretty crowded. It was different without her mum, but since the others looked all casual, Bo kept her face expressionless, bored even.

"You okay?" asked Sunday. "You look sick."

Bo sighed. The train was pulling in, thank goodness. The girls glued themselves together, Lil leading the way and Sunday bringing up the rear; they pushed their way onto the 7 train and crowded around a pole.

At Court Square they were all able to get a seat. Elevated trains were Bo's favorite, and the 7 was something special. From Manhattan to Queens, the Flushing line ran through a United Nations of communities. Bo's part—the trip plan and outline—was done; she turned slightly to watch the city go by below. Lil was scribbling in the margins of a packet about Queens that they were supposed to have already read, and Lee was reading a book about manatees and probably trying to figure out how to build a pool for them in the backyard.

"We're going close to the end of the line," said Sunday, as though Bo hadn't studied the subway map for a week as part of the route plan. Bo nodded. "The thing I love about the 7 is that it's like riding through a mini world on one train trip!" Sunday went on. "All these different neighborhoods, getting on and off, hearing all the languages. It's so cool."

Bo looked at Sunday. "I'm from here, remember," she said gently.

"Oh! Yeah! I know . . . sorry. I just get excited."

"Yeah," said Bo after a pause. She smiled. "I actually haven't ridden the 7 that much. Mum and I go to Flushing sometimes for soup dumplings from Shanghai You Garden and turnip cakes from Joe's Shanghai. We're going to take a dumpling lesson from my neighbor Mrs.—" Bo paused, wondering if that plan had changed too, along with everything else. "My *old* neighbor, I guess."

"What's she like?" asked Sunday.

"Well, she's been working on a book called *101 Uses of Ginger*, and—" Bo stopped. She wasn't supposed to talk about her old life anymore. "I mean, she's interesting. No big deal, though. I hear there's a noodle shop that makes good dumplings in the neighborhood."

"Oh yeah!" said Sunday. "The Noodle! Like, that's literally what it's called. If I had a noodle shop, I'd call it . . ." Bo sat back with one ear open as Sunday buzzed on and on.

"Done!" shouted Lil, closing her packet and ignoring the looks from other people in the subway car. "Yo, did you guys know Louis Armstrong did collage?"

"Um, yeah," said Sunday. "It was in the research packet that the rest of us read before today."

"Oh. Well. Anyway, we should do a collage project."

"Bo suggested that last week," said Sunday patiently. "Did you read the outline she made at all?"

"We're almost there," said Lil, ignoring Sunday. "90th and Elmhurst."

Lee looked up. "Already?"

The busy shopping area at 103rd and Corona Plaza was junk food tempting to the extreme. Sunday glanced longingly at the doughnut shop until Bo promised fresh churros that evening. That cheered up everyone, including Bo. She loved feeling *essential*. Mrs. Dougie had been called an "essential worker" many times over the last few years; she even had a sweatshirt to prove it. Bo hoped that making the churros would give her an opportunity to sit and process this day.

Lil turned to Bo. "Yo, I guess you didn't really get a summer break, huh?" she said. They passed a construction site; a Corey Industries truck was parked nearby. "What would you normally do in the summer?"

"Last year I went to cooking camp for a week," said Bo. "Then we took a trip to Mystic, Connecticut, with my auntie Fola." She smiled, and looked over at Lee.

"Oh yeah, we love that place!" said Sunday quickly. Sunday seemed to like letting Bo know that they'd already done everything.

It wasn't long before they were in front of a sturdy brick house.

"We're here," said Bo, pointing to her map. "I thought it would be fancier."

"Maybe it is on the inside, like me," said Lil, giggling. "Oh, wait, I'm fancy all the way through." The others shushed her as they walked inside.

Bo had to admit, she hadn't been so sure about this field trip; she didn't know much about jazz, and what she did know was Esperanza Spalding, mostly because of her beautiful hair, and once Mum had taken her to see Cindy Blackman, who was doing a free show in Central Park. That had been fun, and Cindy Blackman's four-way coordination had been amazing. Trumpets just seemed . . . spitty and loud.

"Respect," she whispered when the tour guide told them about Armstrong's skill at scatting and improvising. "He was like an OG freestyler!" And his band the All-Stars! Danny Barcelona had that snare drum *singing* on his solo in "Stompin' at the Savoy." Bo tried hard to memorize it; she was definitely going to give it a try during her next practice slot. The house seemed alive. The shaggy carpets were temptingly plush. Armstrong's warm, gravelly voice was playing on speakers throughout, and Bo felt like he might come out at any moment and invite them to jam with him. She'd need to bring Mum back to see the kitchen, Bo thought, impressed with the bright blue cabinets and side-by-side ovens. She had a feeling that Louis Armstrong appreciated food with soul.

She wrote in her trip journal that Armstrong was a world-famous foodie and signed letters "Red Beans and Ricely Yours," in honor of his favorite food. Bo became a big fan after she heard that.

Lil was especially in love with Armstrong's practice of collage, while Sunday almost fell on the floor laughing at stories of his sense of humor. They had to drag Lee away from a photo of Mr. Armstrong and General, his Boston terrier, who even Bo had to admit was pretty cute. As they walked around with two other families, Bo resisted the urge to sit on a couch or even turn on the old-school TV. It felt more like a home than a museum, and by the end of the tour, Bo felt like she'd been visiting a family member for the afternoon.

Outside, the sun seemed to be shining hotter.

"Icees," said a little voice behind them. The girls turned to see a child who'd been in the tour with them, often skipping ahead of her family. "I want Icees!"

Bo could hear that tears were not too far away. She did what she always did and looked around for the adults. She squatted down to eye level with the little girl. "Are you okay?"

"Um, I think we shouldn't make her talk to strangers," said Sunday. "And she looks like she's about to . . . um, blow."

Bo smiled gently. "Why don't we wait for your adult together," she said in a soft voice, being sure to stay low and close but not touching the little girl; she didn't want to scare her and send her running down the street—or worse, into the street. She motioned to Lil. "Can you go inside and let the museum people know what's going on?"

"Should we get her an Icee?" asked Sunday. "I mean, maybe we could all use one."

"Nice try," said Bo. The little girl sniffled. "Now look what you did."

"Sorry," said Sunday.

"We can't do something like that without her adult's permission," Bo said.

Lee was humming a familiar song, and that gave Bo an idea. "*I could be a warrior!*" she sang along with Lee, gesturing to Sunday to join in. Slowly they started singing the Chloe x Halle classic, and the little girl stopped crying, joining in at the end for a long, drawn out "*Meeeeeeeeeeeeeeeee!*"

Lil returned with an anxious-looking mother and father.

"Mindasia!" cried the mom, gathering the girl up in her arms. "We were worried sick! Why did you do that?!" She looked over at Lil. "Thank you so much," she said.

Lil pointed to Bo. "Oh, that was all my sister's doing. She's got all the little-kid knowledge."

"Well, then, thank you," the mom said to Bo. "Thank all of you!"

"Those were some good harmonies," said the father. "Louis Armstrong would have been proud of the music you were making."

"What do you say, Mindasia?" said the mom.

"Thank you for singing and taking care of me," said Mindasia dutifully, adding some sniffs that Bo suspected were entirely artificial.

As they walked away, Mindasia cried out, "That one said she would get me an Icee!"

Sunday grimaced. "Oops."

At Nixtamal, they ate as many tortillas as they made during their cooking class with Mum's friend Fernando and then topped it off with his gift of huge containers of superfresh chips and salsa that they devoured at a nearby bus stop.

Lee leaned back. "Oh my goodness, who knew learning to cook could be so delicious!"

"Um, everyone knew that," said Lil. "It's just better when you get someone else to learn to cook and you still get to eat."

"Wait till Bo teaches me all of her baking secrets," said Sunday. "We will be living permanently on treat street."

"Bo can keep us there on her own, muffin girl," said Lil. Actual bus passengers approached their bench, and the girls began to pack up their things. "Come on, let's head to dessert. By the time we get there, we'll be ready for LEMON ICE! WOOO!" The other three groaned.

"Maybe we can do the lemon ice thing on our next trip," said Bo. "We have to go back to Louis Armstrong House to use the archives for our research papers anyway."

"Trust me—once we walk all the way to the Lemon Ice King," said Lil, "we'll be ready to have some. It's like eighty-seven blocks from here."

"I'm ready to get off my rear," said Lee, standing with the others.

"And fresh lemon ice will bring good cheer. Ahh, I rhymed!" She and Lil high-fived. Bo looked at Sunday, who mouthed, "Twins."

As they walked down the wide sidewalks, they passed a playground where little children were playing a serious game of tag.

"Someone's gonna cry in about ten seconds," said Bo. "Aaand . . . there it is." Right on cue, a thin, high wail rose.

"You really know kids," said Sunday.

Bo shrugged. "I mean, I *am* a kid, so . . ."

"Yeah, but you have expertise," said Sunday. "All that babysitting—you could teach us that too."

"I did the Red Cross course," said Bo. "It's not that hard."

"You're really organized too," said Lee. "Like, *really* organized." She glanced at Sunday. "It must be pretty hard to share a room."

"HEY!" cried Sunday.

"Dibs on the big practice room when we get home," said Lil.

"Is that on the schedule I made?" asked Bo.

"Yeah, I'm pretty sure it's my turn today," said Sunday.

"But we switched last week, remember?" asked Lee. "Isn't it my turn?"

"I can practice scales while you do vocal warm-ups, Lee, but not bass," said Sunday. "And I can't hear myself think when you're going wild on the guitar, Lil."

"Oh, so your ragtime interludes aren't disruptive when I'm learning Prince?" retorted Lil. The bickering continued until they got to a red light at 42nd Avenue.

"I have an idea," said Bo slowly. A few old ladies carrying

shopping bags nudged each other and pointed to the Twins, smiling.

"Every time," muttered Sunday. "It's like twins are magic or something. They're just regular girls!" she yelled in the ladies' direction.

"Shhhhh, Bo has an idea!" Sunday continued.

"You were literally the one yelling," whispered Lee.

This really is like a TV show, thought Bo. "Okay, so even though right now it seems like a really not-so-great idea because there's anything but harmony in the air . . . what if we practiced together?"

Lil rolled her eyes. "We tried that, remember? That's why you made the schedule."

"Which we very much appreciate," interjected Sunday.

"You're so good at that stuff," added Lil.

"Welcome!" said Lee, giggling. After a beat, they all joined in.

"Okay, first of all, you guys are going to have to start treating me like you treat each other," said Bo. "I can't take you walking on eggshells all the time!"

"We should be taking pics of the neighborhood," said Lil. "For our presentation." Bo nodded. Bo's sisters had told her they did presentations all the time—they hadn't been joking. She'd done six already—three in a group and three solo—and it was not her favorite thing. They stopped; one of the many rules was no walking with phones out. As Bo looked around, her sunny mood dimmed a little. She knew what so many FOR RENT signs meant on storefronts.

"Isn't it kind of weird this neighborhood is called Corona?" asked Sunday. "I wonder if they ever wanted to change it."

"Did you see the article in our research packet? This neighborhood was hit really hard by the virus," said Lil. They walked on in silence for a while. A light and welcome breeze lifted the leaves of the trees dotting this stretch of sidewalk.

"Pop jokes about it," started Lee, "but he asked me what I thought about bringing Mr. Bultitude to the bookstore for company because he hardly has any customers."

"He at least had his friends from the block come in all the time when we lived in Brooklyn," said Sunday, nodding as she snapped a photo of party dresses in the window of a shop called Oh So Dressy. "But people still don't know us in Harlem."

"People still don't *like* us in Harlem," said Lil. "You know I'm right."

Bo thought of Ms. Tyler. "I think Sunday's right," she said, and tried not to laugh when Sunday grinned, pumped her fist, and said, "Yes!"

"We could invite them over to play with the animals," said Lee. "Animal therapy is such a mood booster. I did a report on it. And then maybe they'd want to adopt from the shelter, and—"

"I don't know about all that," said Bo quickly. "I just meant, remember what the Parents said about their plan for the community garden? Now that we're having the Block Party there, I think they're going to need to do more than just open the gates. We need to think bigger and better."

"And badder," said Lil. "We should always think badder."

Bo took a deep breath. "Let's make a list. What do we need for a good block party?"

"People," said Lil.

"Activities," said Sunday.

"Dog adoption fair," said Lee. Everyone ignored her. Soon they arrived at the Lemon Ice King, and Lil had been right: everyone's appetite was back. As they strolled to the train station, Block Party conversation resumed.

"What flavor cupcakes are you making, Bo?" asked Lee.

"If you need a baker's assistant . . . ," said Sunday.

Bo kept her eyes on her notebook. "I, uh, haven't decided yet." She hadn't even begun to work on the Block Party cupcake recipe. And when she did, she was going to work on it alone. "So anyway, what I'm thinking is that we need . . . entertainment."

There were only two other people in their car on the train back to Manhattan: two men in a very animated discussion about the greatest tennis player of all time.

"Duh, Serena," said Lil as the girls settled onto a bench.

"I like the entertainment idea," said Sunday.

"But what if Papa wants to do a monologue?" said Lee. They all got quiet after that.

"What about music?" asked Sunday.

Funny you should mention music. "Well, I was thinking . . . ," Bo started shyly. "Well, what Auntie Sunflower was saying. We should be a band. Weddings have bands, right? Why don't we practice together, like, all the time? Louis Armstrong House made me think—we have all the ingredients to officially be a band. We could debut at the Block Party!"

"Like, a band for real?" asked Lil. She pulled a sketchbook out from her heavily embroidered backpack. "Oooh, I can design the sickest costumes!"

"I can write songs!" said Sunday.

"I bet I could train Rubia to play the tambourine," said Lee.

"Oh, that won't look weird," said Lil. And after a pause, they all laughed, even Lee.

20

THAT NIGHT, THEY ALL PILED INTO the Twins' room to discuss the developments of the day as soon as the lights went out. Sunday and Bo brought in couch pillows and spread their sleeping bags on top.

"We're the guests," said Sunday, "so you guys should let us take the beds."

"The only reason why we're not in your room is because it's overrun with your mess," said Lil. "I don't know how Bo stands it."

"I'm going to get it organized," said Sunday. "I'm just . . . waiting for the right time." She looked at Bo. "I'm sorry. Is it really that bad?"

Bo shook her head. *YES!* She didn't know how Sunday could live in such a mess. Then she remembered that she was living in it too and pretended to cough so she wouldn't have to say anything. Auntie Fola always said, "If you can't say anything nice, at least you tried in your head." Maybe she should tell Sunday how she felt.

"So, first of all, props to me in advance for the gorgeous outfits I'm going to make us. You're welcome, by the way."

Sunday threw a small pillow at Lil. "I'm not sure we're all going to fit in here tonight with all your exponential ego growth going on."

Lil pulled on an eye mask over her satin cap and lay back in her bed. "I did the hard part. I'll leave the rest to you all." Lee tossed another pillow at Lil's head. "Ow!"

"A band is about the music. Shouldn't we discuss that first?" asked Lee.

"I was thinking you'd be lead singer, Lee," started Bo.

"What if I trained Rubia to be lead singer?" Lee replied. "Stop laughing, you guys, I really think I could do it!"

Sunday rolled her eyes. "You literally have the best voice of all of us, silly." Lil tossed Sunday the pillows, and Sunday threw one at Lee's head. After a shy glance Bo's way, she threw one at Bo too. A pillow fight broke out as the cats stared disapprovingly from the doorway. Finally Bo called a truce. "Shhh! We're gonna get busted!" They settled back into their sleeping areas, pulling their satin bonnets back on. "Hey, we really do have to come up with a plan," said Bo. She looked at Lil. "Together."

"Yeah, yeah, you all know I was kidding," said Lil.

Sunday looked at Bo expectantly. "So, what's the band plan?" They all laughed and shushed each other.

"Go to bed, girls!" called Mum from downstairs. "In your own rooms."

"You know why you need a full night's sleep, right?" Bill chimed in. "To give your phones a rest!"

The girls groaned. After a few silent minutes of pretending to go to sleep, Sunday whispered, "I have one of my little ideas. It's sort of related. From something Bo did." Bo looked up, surprised. "Remember how we helped that little girl, Mindasia, by singing?"

"Mostly because Bo knew what to do," said Lee.

"Exactly. So why don't we put her babysitting experience to use? I mean, if you agree, of course." Sunday turned to Bo with a pleading eye.

Bo raised an eyebrow. "What do you mean? You want me to babysit at the Block Party?"

"I mean—and this may be my greatest little idea yet—that we could be a babysitting band! Like, we offer to babysit kids in the neighborhood and play music for them, maybe even teach a little of the basics!"

"*I* have a lot of experience," said Bo. "I took the class, remember?"

"Awww, like music teachers who come to your house," said Lee. "That would be so cute! We still have a lot of little-kid instruments—the claves, the bells . . ."

"Sunday, you got that idea because you binge-watched *Baby-Sitters Club* when you were supposed to be doing your math project," said Lil. "But I like it. . . . It has business potential."

"I got the idea because of, well, everything! We can all take the class, right? We're going to be a band, there are lots of kids in the hood, we can make some money—"

"I really like the sound of that," said Lil. "I'm in. The outfits will have to be fire! Everyone's going to have to give me ten percent of their allowance. Costume-designer budget."

"Doesn't Reese babysit? She'll be mad," said Lee.

"Ooh, then I like it even more," said Lil. "I'll make our outfits for free . . . ish. A deep discount."

"There's no rule that there can only be one babysitter in the neighborhood," said Bo. "And if we're doing it as a group, as a band . . . and if you all take the class, then . . . I like it. It's a great idea."

"Yes!" yelled Sunday, and they got an immediate "Go to bed!" from all four parents.

"We need a band name," whispered Lee. "How about Adopt Don't Shop?"

"You definitely win the one-track mind award," said Bo.

As Sunday slipped a notebook out from under her pillow to record whispered band name suggestions, song ideas, and more, Bo smiled to herself in the dark. She was pulling her weight. As long as the ideas and organizational skills kept flowing, her sisters would want her around. And Bo was realizing just how much she wanted to be around.

The next morning, after a rushed breakfast, the girls were ready to set up in their newly designated Band Rehearsal Room, formerly known as the Odd Room. The Parents had loved the band idea and officially handed over the "keys" (a broom and dustpan), and Mama Hope said she'd make a sign to put over the door. Bo thought she saw tears in Mum's eyes when she'd heard the news.

"Bo, I so wanted this for you," Mum said as she wiped the table down.

Maybe this was a good time. "Mum, I can help you clean up the kitchen," Bo started as her sisters thanked Mum for the "lightest, fluffiest pancakes EVER!" according to Sunday. "I wanted to tell you—"

"First band practice, Bo!" said Sunday. "This was your idea, so you have to be the first to walk into the room."

Mum shooed Bo away. "Go, go, practice and enjoy! I'm going to make the band something special for dessert tonight. Have you seen the recipe folder—oop, never mind, go, GO!" Mum laughed and pushed Bo out behind her sisters.

Bo had suggested that each of them bring something of their own to the rehearsal room for decoration and inspiration, and though they were four very different band members, she thought it looked pretty good already. She'd filled a large vase with some of her favorite drumsticks, and Sunday had a glittery purple keyboard cover that looked like something from a movie set. (It was; Papa Charles had snagged it when he was an extra in *Fame II: The Getdown*. It was even signed by the actress who played Coco Fernandez, the main character.) Lee had a bunch of clickers and bells and instruments made from dog collars and other pet toys, and Bo had to admit that Lil's neon polka-dotted shorts, yellow tights, and retro off-the shoulder T-shirt made her look already famous.

"I have shades for all of us," Lil said, handing out pairs of sunglasses.

"I can't put these over my glasses," said Lee. "And I won't be able to read the music without my glasses. Neither will you, Lil, even though you fake it all the time."

"Speaking of reading music," said Bo. "We need songs."

"And it just so happens that I've got them!" said Sunday. "Well, sort of. I have lyrics. A whole notebook full."

"Hmmm," said Bo. "What if we start with some songs we already know, like melodies—remember when we did 'Mary Had a Little Lamb'? My band teacher at school used to say that was a foolproof formula for a hit song—putting great lyrics to familiar melodies."

"But we only have Sunday's lyrics," said Lil with a straight face.

"Har, har," said Sunday. "Bo, that's a fantastic idea."

"Lee, you're obviously our lead singer," said Bo.

"Um," said Lee. "I don't know. . . . That's kind of . . . scary."

"You have the best voice of all of us," said Sunday.

"And you sing all those songs to the animals!" added Lil.

"It's different when it's animals," said Lee. "And don't tell me people are technically animals," she said as Sunday started to speak. "You know what I mean."

Bo walked over to Lee. "How about if our first performance is for animals? At the shelter?" She looked at Sunday and Lil. "Sort of a pre-debut before our wedding party debut?"

"Really?" asked Lee, brightening.

"Really," said Bo, giving the others another meaningful look.

"Yeah, really," said Sunday, sighing. "Forget Carnegie Hall. I've always wanted to sing for a bunch of pit bulls."

"They are so misunderstood," murmured Lee.

"Really," added Lil. "As long as there are no complaints about the look I create for us. Capisce?"

"We get it, nous comprenons," answered Bo. "And because I got a perfect score on my Yoruba app yesterday, ó yé mi too. Sunday, any demands?"

"Just that we stop talking and start playing!" said Sunday. "Let's goooooo!"

21

"STOP!" YELLED SUNDAY.

Rehearsal was . . . not going well. Even though they had settled on the shelter for their band debut—"At least the animals won't care that we don't have a name yet," Sunday had pointed out—Bo noticed that they couldn't agree on much else.

"Was that the doorbell?" Bo really just wanted to escape to the kitchen and bake something. She would never admit it, but sometimes the bright red paint on the rehearsal room walls made her head pound louder than her drums. In fact, the shouty walls, the four ginormous trunks always open and overflowing with Lil's band uniform ideas, Sunday's notebooks, dress forms, half-built robots, and jumble of broken instruments didn't exactly scream harmony. Neither did the band, at the moment. They'd spent the first fifteen minutes shooting down each other's band name ideas, and then every attempt to get "Loud/Free/Me," Sunday's latest composition, exactly right was coming out all wrong.

"This song is kind of . . . silly," said Lil, as they launched into it for the tenth time.

"What's silly is the way you keep trying to add . . . rock riffs or licks or whatever to a House song," said Sunday. "It doesn't make sense, it just makes noise."

"We're supposed to be soothing the residents," said Lee. "Why don't we practice Shelter Dog Blues? This could be a regular gig for us if we do a good job. You could come to the shelter with me every day!"

"Oh joy," said Sunday. "Back me up, Bo. It doesn't sound good, right? Can we get on the same page for once, please?"

"We're never going to be known for more than making noise anyway, with songs like 'Loud/Free/Me,'" snapped Lil. "And with you always writing the songs, we're always on *your* page, all the time."

"Maybe we should take five," Bo said, trying to push the attitude back down her throat. "I'll make us a snack. And, uh, I'm pretty sure I heard the doorbell. Maybe Ms. Tyler—"

"I didn't hear anything," said Sunday. "But I did hear Lee sing 'if you will' instead of 'if you would,' and that brings a completely different meaning to the story I was trying to tell with these lyrics. . . . We're running out of time, and I'm afraid we have to run that again." She hit middle C on her keyboard for emphasis, accidentally also hitting the bossa-nova button. A bouncy beat tried to lift the spirit of the room.

It didn't work.

"If you didn't keep taking five to do a 4/4 beat," muttered Lee, "we'd be done with rehearsal by now."

"Again," said Lil, thumping her guitar lightly. "One, two—"

"Wait, wait. I want to start from this chord progression—"

Bo, breaking the sisters' unofficial Hands On Your Own Instrument Unless I Said You Could Touch It rule, walked over to Sunday's keyboards and pushed the "Off" button.

"Oooh," said Lil, glancing at Lee and raising her eyebrows. "It's on." She strummed a few warning chords.

Bo took a deep breath. *Solidarity,* she thought. *Sisters and Community. Everything Mum wants, and I can't mess it up.* She'd try again and play nice this time. "Sorry. I was just frustrated . . . with myself. I was a little off on that last one."

"I was off too," said Sunday after a pause. "I know it. I'm sorry, sis. And maybe . . . maybe I was being a lot."

"You think?" said Lil. They looked at her. "Oh, all right, I messed up too. But it was on purpose. I can play this perfectly if I want to." She lifted her guitar to play. "Wait, where were we?" That warmed the room up a little, and they all laughed.

Lee looked at Bo and smiled. "Sooo . . . about that snack . . ."

"Can I help you make it, Bo?" asked Sunday quickly. Too quickly. Bo's heart sank.

"We should all help," said Lee.

"It's really okay. I got it," said Bo, trying to keep the bass out of her voice. "I want to. I offered, remember?" She saw the Twins exchange a look out of the corner of her eye, but they just shrugged.

Sunday followed her downstairs anyway, because of course she did.

"*I'll* help," Sunday said. "And I really like what you're doing in the drum solo," she added. "Oh, by the way, I told Pop you might want a shekere. I used to have one, but I can't find it."

"No way," said Bo. She didn't say anything about the shekere; she'd love one, but she also didn't want to say she wanted one. She felt contrary and Eeyore-ish and weird about the arguing... if she could just have a *moment*—

The doorbell rang.

"I'll get it," said Sunday.

Yes! Bo hurried to the kitchen. What if she was the reason for the bickering? What if they realized they were trying to add a square peg to a set of round holes and it was just throwing everything off? They probably never argued before she came. *I'm supposed to be the one who keeps order, and I don't know what to do.* She dug up a pretty good assortment of snacks and brought a tray, piled high, to the elevator just as Sunday was coming back from the front door.

"Oh, I was going to help you," Sunday said softly. When Bo just shrugged, she tilted her head. "Are you mad?" she asked, sounding surprised.

Yes, I'm mad, and anxious, and confused! Bo wanted to say. But she just leaned against the elevator wall and said, "I'm sorry about rehearsal."

"Why are *you* sorry? We're all messing up!" said Sunday.

"Well," said Bo, "the fighting and stuff . . ."

"Your name was Bennett, you weren't even in it," answered Sunday, waving her hand. "Anyway, that was ages ago."

The sisters had little trouble convincing their tired parents that they'd handle all garden cleanup duty, since it was now the site of the Block Party. When Ms. Tyler had come to their door to let them know that she'd heard Barbara and Shirley clucking all night, Sunday blurted out the news.

"Maybe it's the fact that you live five buildings down that the sound carries in a funny way. You'll be able to hear us officially up close and personal—our band is throwing a big Block Party in the community garden! To celebrate Pop and Mum's wedding!"

Ms. Tyler sucked her teeth. "What, you talking about a party on that patch of dead leaves behind your house? It's been sitting like that for years. And what band? All I hear is noise, all the time." She peered inside, sniffing. "You all running a bakery or something?"

Bo thought fast. "I'll be right back, Ms. Tyler!" She ran to the kitchen and came back with a thick slice of bun topped with bright yellow cheese. "Mum just made bun this morning," she said. "We'd be honored if you'd taste it."

Ms. Tyler sucked her teeth again, saying "Just cause I have manners" as she took the offering. "Where'd you get real Jamaican cheese from? I know your mama didn't make that too." She took a bite.

"Bo and her mum know all the best food places in the city," volunteered Sunday. "So now we go to Kingston Tropical in the Bronx for patties, and we get cheese from Champion sometimes. And now when we go to the Brooklyn Museum or back to our old neighborhood—did you know I was on the Friends of Clinton Hill Library committee there? Probably not, because we never talked like this before, but anyway, when we go there we get Islands' oxtail and Ali's curry goat roti and doubles, well, Lee just gets doubles, but Bo's mum can make it all if she wants to, also Bo's an amazing chef too, and . . ." Bo sighed hard, and Sunday finally trailed off. Bo wondered if Sunday was trying to convince herself that she liked having Bo around.

"Isn't the bun delicious, though?" Sunday said, leaning toward Ms. Tyler. "I mean, soooo good!"

Bo rolled her eyes. Sunday was definitely working hard to convince herself of Bo's worthiness.

Ms. Tyler chewed thoughtfully. "Hmph. Well, it's good." Two minutes later, she almost smiled when Mr. Bultitude rubbed against her stockinged-in-the-summer leg, and she left with a sizable hunk of bun wrapped in aluminum foil.

"Don't forget to tell the other old—elders—about the Block Party!" yelled Sunday as Ms. Tyler marched away. "Do you think she heard me?"

"My auntie Fola heard you, and she lives in Queens," said Bo.

*   *   *

"Remember that even if the party is just us," Mum said gently, as they finished giant bowls of fruit salad for lunch, "it will still be a beautiful celebration."

"I mean, yeah, sure, in the Parents Always Say That Kind of Thing sense, I guess," said Lil, "but we're trying to go big."

Sunday nodded as Mama Hope walked in. "We've got it all worked out. This will be the beginning of a lot more. I can picture us on SummerStage! Prospect Park Bandshell!" Sunday and the Twins immediately started planning a summer tour, and a new wall chart got started. Occasionally one of them would yell out a random place like "UN Plaza!" "Harlem Meer!" "Washington Square!" and add it to the list. Even though they didn't have outfits yet, Lil suggested a video shoot by the pond in Morningside Park. Sunday kept trying to insist on band meetings at Caffe Reggio in the Village, but only Papa Charles took that seriously, because he said that place always reminded him to rewatch "Richard Roundtree's groundbreaking performance in *Shaft*."

Bo tried to smile and act nice even though sometimes she felt like the ground was going to break under *her*—so much wasn't steady or routine these days. Her sisters didn't always stick to the practice schedule and seemed to think everything about the Block Party would come together like the dump cake she'd watched people bake on one of those "cooking" programs that seemed designed to show just how much food people could waste.

Being in this family made her think about doing fun new

things sometimes, like doing her own cooking videos. But she knew that if she mentioned it to Mum, Mum would just tell her to talk to her sisters about it and make it a Table Talk topic or something and then it wouldn't be hers anymore. Anyway, it was hard enough staying focused on being good at sisterhood; belonging in a family that didn't quite seem to fit in anywhere was not easy. She wondered if she was just too *regular*, and if that was a disappointment in her new wacky and sometimes wonderful world.

The babysitting business plan took a little more persuading than the garden plan. Sunday found an online babysitting course for them to take, and Lil worked out that if they each took a 15-percent cut from their allowances for three weeks to go toward paying the Parents back for it, they could take the course that Saturday morning, in just a couple of days. "We'll make it back in two gigs," Lil told her sisters. After that, the Parents agreed, on the condition that they started with people they or Auntie Sunflower knew, which didn't leave them with a lot of people, but it was a start. And then there was the big thing: they had to babysit at the bookstore.

"No way!!" Bo blurted out without thinking. Mum gave her a sharp look.

"Think of it this way," Bill said gently. "You'll be helping me out. It'll make the store look busy. And you can use any books you like for read-alouds!"

The Parents also reminded them about annoying practical

details, like having to bring their instruments to other people's apartments, and that having "light supervision just in case of emergencies but of course there won't be any" could also be a selling point.

Sunday wrapped Bill in a big hug, and the others cheered.

Bill looked at Bo. "And, I was waiting for the right moment to share this, but, um . . . my guy Dwight has a drum set that he's been trying to offload; he said he could drop it off at the shop anytime. So you could have a set in both places."

"It's not easy to get used to two different sets," said Bo. "Each one has its own personality."

"Bo," said Mum under her breath.

"I mean, thank you," said Bo, and her sisters cheered. Clearly it was decided. Obviously everyone thought it was a great idea. To Bo, it sounded like a lot of Bill time that she wasn't sure she was ready for. Somehow, every day brought her closer to everyone except Mum.

"This is what I'm talking about," Sunday said a few days later as she pulled up weeds (along with a few flowers) in the garden. "They're desperate. Papa Charles hasn't won an audition in forever, and I heard Pop say he sold one book all of last week. They need this boost just as much as the rest of the grown-ups around here."

Bo had to agree. She'd gone to the bodega the day before, and a few people had been standing around talking about how they couldn't afford to stay in the city but had nowhere to go.

"I feel stuck," a guy had said as he'd ordered two bacon, egg, and cheese sandwiches. He had told Bo the week before that this bodega had won New York's number-one chopped cheese in 2017, even though she hadn't asked.

"Yeah, I guess," Bo said to Sunday. "Mum was really excited about her cookie-delivery business, and she put up lots of flyers, but people are funny about food if they don't know you, and I don't blame them." In this household, Bo was funny about food because she *did* know them, so . . . "Anyway, if they tried her cooking . . ."

"That's why we've got to work on getting people to the party. And getting babysitting gigs will help," said Lil. "And . . . exciting news! We have our first TWO. I got the message this morning."

"Good thing we finished the course yesterday," said Lee.

"Even though *some people* were watching fashion videos the whole time," said Sunday.

"Excuse you. Farai Simoyi is an inspiration—I was studying," said Lil. "And multitasking, for the band's benefit, remember. Plus, the thing with all of us doing this together is that you guys will re-member the details. Now, back to my announcement." She looked at Bo. "Drumroll, please . . ." Bo tapped the stone bench she was sitting on. "Amy Johnson was the first, and the Bullocks are the second! Yay!"

The sisters looked at her. "Amy Johnson?" said Lee. "Um . . ."

Bo thought that summed it up pretty well. Every time they saw Amy on the block, Amy warned them that she was "telling."

And then she proceeded to do something way worse than the nonexistent thing she was accusing them of doing!

"Who are the Bullocks?" Bo asked.

"As in Kareem Bullock," said Sunday. "As in Marcus Semple's shady sidekick."

Oh yeah. Bo nodded. "Got it, red hair, right? He didn't seem that—"

Sunday put up a hand. "Remember when we watched that old cartoon *Bébé's Kids* at Auntie Sunflower's house? Kareem's little brother and sister are like that, but with more energy."

"Look, this babysitting thing was your idea," said Lil.

"And it was a good one," said Bo. Sunday shot her a grateful look. "We got this."

"You're right, you're right, we should be celebrating," said Sunday. "Our first gigs! And at least we'll be together for them. Hey— what about Dougie?" she asked Bo. "We could babysit him. I'd love to finally meet him."

"Hmmmm," Bo said.

Lee wiped sweat from her brow with a bandana she'd pulled from her khaki overalls pockets. She was cleaning the Cat Clubhouse and, Bo suspected, looking for ways to expand it into a Cat Hotel or something. She sang as she cleaned, an oldie that they always sang when they were cleaning, "Ain't No Mountain High Enough."

"We should do that one at the party," said Lil. "I can design us some gold shorts and halter tops." She turned to Bo. "What's your position on tiny hats?"

Bo shrugged. "If it helps you get back to helping me plant this lavender, I love tiny hats."

Sunday started to harmonize with Lee, and soon Bo and Lil joined in. They got so into it that no one noticed that they'd attracted a little audience—though it wasn't exactly a friendly one. Bo turned; Marcus Semple and Kareem Bullock were leaning against the garden gate.

"You guys think you're What's Up, don't you?" said Marcus. Bo was offended; everyone knew What's Up didn't play their own instruments. After the last awards show performance they'd watched, she wasn't even sure they sang their own songs.

"Speak of evil," said Sunday, "and evil appears."

"Yeah, we were just talking about you, and no, it wasn't good," said Lil.

Sunday was just getting started. "We're *actual* musicians, thank you very much." Lil played a little air guitar for emphasis.

"You'll see it at the block—I mean, private garden—party," said Sunday. "Oh, wait, you're not invited, though."

Bo got why Sunday had done the quick name change to make it all sound more exclusive, but she leaned in close to Sunday and whispered, "Remember, Kareem's mom is one of our first baby-sitting jobs!"

"Um, I meant, hi! Great to see you guys!" said Sunday in the least-convincing happy voice ever. Rubia barked.

"Oh, look, it's the cheaty one and the grumpy one," said Marcus, pointing to Bo and Lil. "What private garden party? And what kind of party will it be if nobody comes? Because nobody will."

"You still mad just 'cause I dunked on you three times?" asked Lil, leaning forward. "I'm heading downtown to The Cage next." Bo was no basketball player, but even she knew The Cage was for serious ballers. Her sister could win a trash-talking tournament, but from the way he kept dropping the ball he was trying to dribble, she guessed that beating Marcus wasn't exactly difficult.

"Let's bounce, Kareem," Marcus said, tripping over a flowerpot. Bo bit back a giggle.

"I kinda want to stay," said Kareem, hopping onto a large rock near Lee. "My mom says I have a green thumb."

"Traitor," Marcus mumbled. Then he strolled over to Bo.

She smiled sweetly at him and handed him a rake. "Sure I'm not too grumpy for you?"

He pointed to the stack of flyers she'd placed in the corner under her messenger bag. "What are those?"

"Like we said, we're having a garden party to celebrate my mum and Bill—Pop's wedding." Why was it suddenly awkward to say "wedding" to this boy she'd only met once? He wasn't really nice, or even cute! Except when he laughed.

"Cool. For people on your block, huh?"

"Well, the general neighborhood," Bo said. "So you and Kareem can come too. If you want."

"And," said Lil from the other side of the garden, "you'll see some real musicians throw down!"

"Who'd you get?" asked Kareem. "The Nubians? I heard they were doing a summer tour."

"Even better," said Lil. "The . . . um . . . It's us!"

"What language is that?" asked Kareem, looking confused.

"We're a band now," Bo explained. "We don't have a name yet, but we're playing the garden party, so . . ."

Marcus laughed. "You guys are a band?!" He really wasn't cute at all.

"Yeah," answered Bo. "We *girls* are a band, and we're good."

"As good as Gloss?"

"Who's—" Bo started, just as Lee mouthed, "Reese!"

"And how did you get in here anyway?" asked Marcus. "Scared the gates open with your screeching?" Rubia barked again from the other side of the fence, and the boys looked her way warily.

"We're better than Gloss," said Bo calmly. "And we're glad you'll be there to see."

"Me and Marcus got bars," said Kareem. "You should have us perform. We could really move the crowd. If you can even get a crowd."

Lil rolled her eyes. "You mean those pitiful little nursery rhymes I heard y'all stuttering last week?" She gestured to the stone path. "Help me arrange the stones, and maybe we'll consider letting you audition." Marcus and Kareem looked at each other and shrugged, then they started picking up rocks.

"So you don't have a band name?" Marcus asked Bo after they'd worked for a while.

"Working on it," she answered. "Any suggestions?"

"Wacky and the Wackettes—Lee could be the lead singer of that," he said, as though he'd been waiting to deliver that one.

"I heard that!" said Lee.

"So, anyway, the garden party," said Bo, changing the subject. "Y'all should come out. The garden is going to have an all-new setup. It's going to be amazing."

"Free food?" said Marcus. "I'm there, even if I have to endure the caterwauling you're calling music. Ha, get it—CATerwauling. All those animals in your band too?"

"I play the trombone," said Kareem out of nowhere. "I'm auditioning for the Middle School Jazz Academy at Lincoln Center. And I'm in Jazz Power Initiative up in Washington Heights. We sing and stuff."

"Yo, I'm trying out for *Showtime at the Apollo*," said Marcus. "Watch me."

"Watch you what?" asked Lil. "What can you do? Walk by the Apollo every day?"

"Don't worry about it," said Marcus.

The boys stayed and worked for a surprisingly long time under the summer sun, and they seemed sincere in their thanks for the orangeade and chocolate cake that Bo brought out to share. But when she mentioned that to her sisters later, Sunday scoffed.

"Who's not going to be thankful for chocolate cake like that? Even those boys have a tiny bit of sense."

Bo looked at Lil. "What did you mean, let them audition?"

"Oh, I was just talking," said Lil airily, waving her hand. She took off her gardening gloves to wipe the sweat from her forehead. "Who's starting the group reflection entry for today?"

Sunday raised two hands. "Ooh, I will. I've got a lot to say."

"Quelle surprise," said Lil dryly. "I'll be in charge of refreshments. I want to talk to my people at Mikey Likes It; I have a new flavor idea: Big Ups To Butterscotch."

"Just get one of the old flavors for all of us," said Sunday. "See if there's any Truffle Shuffle left."

"We will so get in trouble if we get ice cream before dinner," said Lee.

"We're interviewing the owners for the new neighborhood guide that we're going to share at the garden party. It's *research*," said Lil.

"In that case," said Sunday, "Go to Sugar Hill too, we can have *all* the ice cream!" She held up a hand, and Lil tapped it with a smile.

"I got you," Lil said.

"What neighborhood guide project?" asked Bo.

"The one I just came up with now! You can be in charge of the outline. I'll buy everyone's ice cream. Thank me later." She headed toward Frederick Douglass Boulevard.

"It is a good idea—that's what makes it so annoying every

time," said Lee, shaking her head. "Listen, Auntie Sunflower said she'd stop by one day soon; she found an Urban Family Farm School class that we can take so we can really set this garden up right—food, medicinal herbs . . . This is so exciting!"

"I don't know why I ever thought freeschooling would mean less school," Bo muttered to herself.

Sunday heard, and laughed. "Mum said you'd say that. She's really excited about this one, though. She said that once we take the class, we'll be able to help with her community garden cooking demos."

Mum knew about this? And talked to Sunday before she'd told Bo? Bo sighed. There was new, and then there was just . . . too much. But there was also Truffle Shuffle ice cream. Bo couldn't be mad at that.

22

THE SISTERS HAD BEEN DOING their history projects all morning, and it was time for a break. Even though the humidity made them feel like they were wearing wool coats in a hot shower, they'd planned to use this time to hand out their flyers/Block Party invitations. But first, tea. Lee had made iced lemon ginger tea, and after they sat on the ledge next to the Harriet Tubman statue, she poured it carefully into her sisters' brightly colored travel cups. They silently lifted their cups to the bronze statue that seemed to be in perpetual, determined motion forward, then they began their meeting. Sunday pointed to Bo. "What's on the agenda for the rest of the week?"

Bo nodded. Once Sunday had seen her color-coded notebook and accordion-folder system, she'd nominated Bo to be in charge of the daily group planner, and the Twins had agreed wholeheartedly. They didn't agree on much, so Bo was honored and tried to decorate the planner with her best stickers and do a good job.

"It's Thursday," she said, opening the spiral-bound planner. "So that means, Sunday, you're going to your engineering workshop at NYU and the Museum of Math with your dad—"

"Whomp whomp," said Sunday gloomily just as Lil yelled "Lucky!" and Bo laughed.

"Lil, I'm . . . with you," she said slowly. Mum was allowing her to ease into the whole freeschooling thing, shadowing each of her sisters for a day for these first few weeks while she waited to "discover" what she wanted to "uncover." A Lil day usually meant . . . a strong possibility of roller-skating stunt jumps on the playground or getting fitted for a dress made out of FedEx envelopes. Or, somehow, both.

"Marcus Garvey Park, here we come!" said Lil. "Let me get my sewing tote."

Bo had to laugh. Yep, it was going to be both. "Yay," she said feebly. She patted her hair, reminding herself of the pretty flat twists Lil had stayed up late to do for her the night before, even incorporating shiny beads in an intricate pattern in the front.

Sunday raised her eyebrows. "You could have been teaching me to make a cake or something, but . . ." She shrugged. "I'm not saying I'm offended, but . . ."

Bo stopped laughing and mumbled something close to words, but she really didn't have an answer. It was getting harder and harder to avoid Sunday's requests for more baking lessons. There were some things that were still hers. Baking was her thing. If she baked with her sisters . . . first they'd be all interested, then they'd want to learn more, and it all might even be fun, but it wouldn't be hers anymore.

"I should get going," said Lee. "Gigi is probably starving, she hates her new diet, and Bluto really needs a morning song, and—"

"Please go now," said Lil. "You're torturing us!" As the girls double-checked for snacks, keys, and emergency phone chargers in their backpacks, Bo looked around. *We must look pretty weird,* she thought. But Mum was always saying that was the beauty of NYC: you could be as weird as you wanted, and no one cared. Sometimes Bo thought people should care just a little, though. Notice each other's weirdness and celebrate it. That would make life a lot easier. And, she suspected, a whole lot more fun.

Even though Bo and Mum had visited Marcus Garvey Park often, usually during a break from shopping on 125th Street, when they'd sip drinks from Serengeti Teas and munch on sweet potato fries from Harlem Shake, Bo had never paid much attention to how, well, historic it felt. The Harlem Fire Watchtower was definitely a part of that, and thanks to the freeschooling life, Bo now knew it was the only cast-iron one left in all of New York City, since they'd been built in the 1850s. But there was also something, even about where it was, where East and West Harlem came together, and the Black and Brown people of every age lounging, running, laughing, kissing (ewwww!!!), and just being happy that made Bo feel like something special could happen to her, like getting a master class in drumming *and* cooking from Questlove.

"Let's hit up the playground first," said Lil. "I haven't been on a swing in ages; we can hang for a while before we give out flyers. Then I want to practice tricks on the bleachers in the amphitheater. The first show doesn't open until next week, so I'm pretty sure no one will catch us."

"Us?" asked Bo as they walked toward the playground gate. The sprinklers were on, and a crowd of children shrieked and giggled as they ran through. "Remember how you just sprained your wrist on a . . . kickflip?" Bo had to admit that Lil's stunts were pretty impressive. Marcus seemed impressed too, and whenever they ran into him, which was often, he kept trying to compete with some basketball maneuvers that he called "old-school Harlem Globetrotter style," which seemed to mean that he laughed off every mistake and said "I meant to do that."

"Yeah, kickflip," said Lil, taking her skateboard out of her backpack and pushing off toward the swings. "And I still shredded my guitar solo, though, so . . ." She shrugged and looked back at Bo while a white man and his toddler scrambled to get out of her way. "I can't wait until we debut! Name or no name, we are going to bring down the house!"

"Greenhouse," said Bo. But Lil was right. They had already graduated from simple nursery rhyme riffs to full-blown original songs. Bo would usually start things off with a rhythm, Lee would hum, and then they'd be off and running. The whole row of swings was free; they jumped on and swayed.

"Excuse me," said an annoyed adult voice. "My son wants to use the swings. I don't want any trouble here."

Bo hopped out of her swing and turned around, confused. "Oh! Sorry! I didn't know anyone was . . ." She looked past the tight-lipped white woman who'd spoken and saw that there was still a free swing at the end of the row. "There's one over there. . . ." The little boy with the woman started to walk toward the empty swing, but his mother held him close.

"I'm just saying, aren't all of you a little too old to be over here? It's not fair to the children?" She ended her sentences as questions, but Bo thought this woman was pretty sure of herself all the time.

"*We're* children," said Lil. "We're not going anywhere."

With a lot of huffing and puffing, the mom slowly followed her little boy to the empty swing. They were the only two white people in this part of the playground, but somehow they seemed to take up a lot of space.

"I really wanted to go over to the slide," whispered Lil, "but we're staying another few minutes just to make the Big Bad Wolf-mom mad."

They lingered on the swings a little longer, but the playful mood had evaporated. Then Lil suggested they hand out flyers, so they did, offering one to everyone except the increasingly sour-faced mom, who walked by them multiple times muttering something about "solicitation laws."

"Come on, I want to do some ollies before we go home," said Lil. They left, walking slowly past the pool to the amphitheater, where the Classical Theatre of Harlem performed. Bo had been making enough progress in swimming class that she could imagine herself swimming there. In fact, the last time they'd gone to Jackie Robinson Park, she'd been afraid to even picture herself in that pool, but these days she was peeking through a door into a whole new world.

"Hey! Strange sisters!" Bo turned around.

Marcus and Kareem caught up to them, panting.

"Just for that, you guys have to hand out flyers," said Lil.

"We were just coming to tell you that Reese can help with your party," said Marcus. "Her dad is friends with a guy who knows Trey Jones's cousin's wife. They were on *Neighborhood Idol* before it ended."

Bo groaned. Reese again. "What's *Neighborhood Idol*?"

"And why are you even talking to that girl about our party?" demanded Lil.

Marcus and Kareem explained that there had been a long-running community talent show in the neighborhood. "People came from all over. Even my Jersey cousins came out to see it," said Marcus. But when the community center had shut down, the talent show had ended. "I heard they were trying to get a deal to do it in the Apollo," said Marcus, "but it was too expensive."

Hmmmm.

On their way out of the park, a few of the people they'd given flyers to came up and asked more questions, like "Is the food really free?" "Who all gon' be there?" and "Who's the DJ? Y'all know Stormin' Norman?" Bo didn't see the huffy Big Bad Wolf-mom anymore. But she couldn't stop thinking about her. Maybe Lil was doing the same, because at the edge of the park, Lil suddenly stopped and started dancing. Lil could really dance, and Bo wanted to join in, but as a few people came over and supplied some impromptu beatboxing, she just hung back and clapped for her sister while people yelled "Ayyyyyyye!"

After a few minutes, Lil took a bow. "Let's swing!" she said to Bo and the boys. And even though they knew they'd be late getting home, the four of them marched back to the swings, then went on the slide, and then played tag, and finally walked home, sweaty and triumphant, having taken up space and hoping they'd meet an Icee lady along the way.

23

AFTER HER THIRD SWIM CLASS, Bo began to really enjoy it. The breathing practice was very calming, and even in a pool full of people, she felt a peaceful aloneness in the water. While her sisters practiced diving and time trials, she'd float on her back and let herself be slowly carried from end to end. And her "buddy" Tiffany hugged her at the beginning and end of every class.

This sister thing, sometimes it was still new and fun like an Easter outfit or being first on the ice after the Zamboni's done. Everything about the band was fun, even fighting over a band name. Sunday wanted Story of Our Lives, while Lil was pushing for something short and exclamation pointy, like Killing It! or Blastoff! No one was seriously considering Lee's suggestion, The Ark. Bo was keeping her list to herself for now. She wanted it to be spectacular, showstopping, "superfresh," as Papa Charles would say (unfortunately). He'd just gotten a part as the English teacher in an eighties throwback movie and was always doing embarrassing things like pop locks and inviting random people into the garden for a rap battle.

"Papa Charles, they didn't even have real hip-hop back in those days," said Lil once, after he'd scared some people away by shouting, "Ah one two, ah one two!" as they'd been pulling weeds.

The sisters were in the bookstore for their last rehearsal before their first gig, which Sunday had billed as their "Soothe the Savage Beast" performance at the shelter. That is, if you didn't count all the practicing they'd done in front of the home animals. Once, Lee had even snuck Barbara and Shirley into the practice room. Bo couldn't do anything other than laugh the first time she saw the chickens, Rubia, Mrs. Pilkington, Mr. Bultitude, Dwayne Wayne (in a tiny bucket hat that Lil had made), and even Urkel all lined up as the "audience" for a show. But once Lee had started singing, they'd actually seemed to be . . . listening? Bo was thinking she might do her next research paper on music and animals.

Humming along to "Backyard Blues," Bill tapped the edge of the counter, and Bo almost missed her cue. She tossed her sticks up in the air and caught one on the way down. She looked up quickly as she picked up the other and got back on the beat right away. None of the other girls had noticed. She kept playing; this band was all about flow, and Bo knew that stopping in the middle of a song was very anti-flow.

"STOP!" sang Lil. It took a moment for the rest of them to realize that she meant it. Sometimes Lil and Sunday added "flair" at unexpected moments in the song.

"Wow," said Sunday. "That kind of fit right into the song. Let's keep it."

"But maybe make it an actual note and not a screech meant to explode our heads open," said Bo. She stole a quick glance at Bill, but he was working very hard to organize a book display. He usually didn't get involved when they were rehearsing, unlike Mum and Papa Charles, who tended to have a lot of "suggestions."

Lil glared at Bo and her other sisters.

"What?" asked Sunday.

Lil sighed meaningfully. Dramatically. Completely over-the-top-ishly, thought Bo, but that was Lil.

"What?" Lee asked again.

"This," said Lil, "is a song about dreams, am I right, Sunday?"

"And reaching for the sky," added Sunday. Bo admired Sunday's songwriting talent, even though sometimes Sunday went way overboard making sure they all understood the emotion behind her words.

"Being totally, whole-bodily, enormously, fantastically excited about life," continued Lil, "and you're singing like you're waiting for the bus, Lee!"

Lee ducked her head. "Oh. . . . Sorry."

Bo wondered what the deal was. If she knew anything, it was that Lee loved to sing at the top of her lungs while she did things.

"You're sucking the soul out of the song," continued Lil. "It's like letting the air out of a balloon. It's like negative ease in a sewing pattern."

"I mean . . . ," started Bo. Lil was going a little far.

"It's not *that* bad," continued Sunday.

"Let's take five," suggested Bo.

"Who wants a snack?" asked Bill. "Bo, why don't you come in back and help me grab a few things."

Bo put down her sticks and slowly followed Bill out of the main store to the small kitchen area in back. She bit back a sigh; probably time for some special "talk" or forced, awkward bonding moment.

But Bill just smiled and helped her fill a tray, piling it high with pretzels, carrots, cucumbers, and the freshly baked chocolate toffee chip cookies that Mum had made that morning; the silence in the room was heavy.

"Uh, the drum set is really good," Bo said. "Thanks again for getting one for me to keep here."

"Oh, thank Dwight!" said Bill. "You'll get to meet him at the party. I don't know if I thanked you enough. It's such a nice idea."

"Well, it's all of us, not just me," Bo said quickly, feeling a little fake. "I hope people come to the party."

"You know, since you girls have been practicing here and stopping by with the animals and stuff, I've actually had a few people come into the store. I tell everyone to take a flyer and tell their friends." He winked. "And if they make a purchase, I offer them whatever delectability your mum has baked up that day."

"Is that a word, *delectability*?" asked Bo. She smiled so Bill could tell she wasn't being rude.

"Trying for some points on the Word Wall?" Bill laughed. "Not sure, but I'll back you up if we need to battle."

She smiled again and stepped around his chair carefully as she balanced the tray. "Thanks for the snacks, Bill . . . Pop."

Bill waved her out. "Like I said, thank *you*. You girls are bringing a little light and life into this store."

"Thanks, Bo!" said Lee brightly when Bo returned with the food.

"Yeah, well, Pop is the one who hooked us up," Bo mumbled.

"So I was just saying that if the shelter show—" started Lee.

"Soothe the Savage Beast," interrupted Sunday. "I mean, it's the perfect name!"

"If the shelter show goes well today, maybe we can ask Dr. Coleman if she wants to have a very small, teeny, tiny, you-won't-even-notice-it animal adoption info table at the Block Party," finished Lee. "Don't you think that's a great idea?"

"And I was saying that Pop could sell books and encourage people to come to the store," said Sunday.

Bo held up her sticks. "That all sounds great," she said. "Even the adoption table, as long as they don't bring a whole ark of animals with them. We can use ours as stand-ins."

"You said 'ours'!" Lee cheered, and Bo rolled her eyes, but she smiled.

"We got, like, two more minutes to snack," said Bo. "Then we should get back to work. We've got to nail our timing on 'Happy Paws.'"

Lil and Sunday exchanged glances. Bo knew that look. They'd been *talking*.

"So . . . are you still planning on making the cupcakes for the party?" asked Sunday.

Bo raised an eyebrow. "Why, do *you* want to?"

"No, it's just that we were wondering how the recipe was coming along. You haven't talked about it much . . . and we were thinking . . ."

"We were thinking we might have a lot of people," finished Lil. "Should you organize us into some kind of baking assembly line?"

"I got this," said Bo quickly. *She* was the organized one. She looked at Sunday. "And organization isn't exactly *everyone's* forte." She felt a little twinge when Sunday looked down.

"Um, you guys . . . ," said Lee softly. She was holding their big planner.

"Are you sure?" asked Lil. "I mean, I hate cooking, but maybe I can build a contraption that gets the batter into the cupcake tins faster, or something. Ooooh, a project!" She picked up her mini sketchbook and began to write.

"Hey, we might have a problem . . ." Lee spoke again.

"You've been doing all this planning and organizing for all of us," said Sunday to Bo. "We just—"

"I said I got this," said Bo. "Let's keep practicing."

Sunday shrugged. "Okay, let's gooooooo, then. I need to finish my Mary Lou Williams versus Hazel Scott project, because ever since we went to Louis Armstrong House—"

"GUYS!" yelled Lee.

"See? You can be loud when you want to be," muttered Lil. They all looked at Lee.

"You know how our first two gigs are Kareem's little brother and sister, and Amy?"

"Yeah, one of them's on Monday. That's why we're practicing," said Sunday. "Amy, right?"

"No, the Bullock kids are Monday," said Lil.

"They're both Monday," said Lee. "At the same time. That's what I've been trying to tell you. We're going to be babysitting all three of them at the shop, together. Monday."

THE SHELTER SHOW WAS A HIT; Abiyoyo barked up a storm to their original composition "Ruff Riding on the A Train," and a group of kittens had stopped falling over each other to listen as Lee did some runs on their cover of Ella Jenkins's "Baa Baa Black Sheep." Afterward, the sisters helped Hila and Dr. Coleman feed the animals.

"That was amazing!" Dr. Coleman said as she filled water dishes. She hummed a little. "What was that last song? 'Beats and Bear Cubs'? Loved it!"

"An original composition," said Sunday.

"I've got a perfect band name for you," said Dr. Coleman. "Dolittle! Look around—the animals are so happy!"

Outside, the girls high-fived each other enthusiastically.

"I really didn't mind singing to the animals at all," marveled Lee. "And I really think Violet and Abiyoyo were harmonizing."

As they were approaching Ms. Tyler's building, Sunday turned to her sisters and smiled. "I have an idea," she said.

"Sunday . . . ," started Bo, but she was too late.

"Hey hey, Ms. Tyler," sang Sunday.

"Who raised you to say 'hey' to your elders?" grumbled Ms. Tyler from her window.

"Uh, I meant, hello, Ms. Tyler, how are you today?" said Sunday, curtsying. She almost fell over but caught Bo's arm before she hit the ground.

"You about to drop that toy piano you got there," said Ms. Tyler. "Be careful. I don't want your parents coming here to sue me or something if you hurt yourself."

"Oh! This is my portable keyboard, and it's what I wanted to ask you about!" said Sunday, winking at her sisters. "You know that garden party we're having? To celebrate Pop's wedding to Bo's mum?"

"Your mum made any bun lately?" Ms. Tyler asked Bo. "My friend Bertice up the block told me she has some kind of cookie business. Is that true?"

Bo nodded. "Yes, she does, ma'am."

"Humph," said Ms. Tyler. "Would have been neighborly to offer free samples, but that's none of my business."

"Well, I—" started Bo.

"That's what I was talking about!" interrupted Sunday. "So at the garden party, there's going to be food and music from our band and . . . a community talent show!"

"Community talent show?" repeated Ms. Tyler, Bo, Lil, and Lee.

"What are—" started Bo.

"Come on, Ms. Tyler," said Sunday, winking at her sisters again. "I'm sure you have a talent. . . . Do you sing? Dance? Oooh, I know—are you a puppeteer?"

There was a pause. "Magic," said Ms. Tyler. "I used to do a little magic."

"Whoa, like you're a witch? I knew it!" crowed Sunday.

Ms. Tyler's eyes narrowed. "You trying to be a comedian? I *mean* I was a magician. Did shows on the playground every Saturday." She tossed her head. "My name was Madam Mystery." She chuckled. "I was eleven years old. . . ."

Sunday looked at her sisters. "Just like us!" She inclined her head toward her sisters. "We'd love to have you be in our community talent show!"

"Uhhh, yeah, just like us," said Lil. "You should do a magic show at our garden party!"

"It'll be like a reunion with your younger self!" said Lee. "And Rubia can be your assistant!"

"Who?" asked Ms. Tyler.

"Never mind my sister, she's talking nonsense; you know these kids," said Sunday. "But what do you say? We'd be honored, right?" She looked at Bo. "Right?"

"Um, yes, Ms. Tyler," said Bo. "Honored."

"They used to have *Neighborhood Idol* back in the day," said

Ms. Tyler. "But that was for the young folks. Half-nekkid half the time . . ."

"Our show is for the whole community," said Sunday. "You can be old and fully dressed the whole time!"

Ms. Tyler squinted again.

"Uh, that's not quite what I meant, but, um, you get the gist, right?" said Sunday. "Anyway, yay, magic!"

"Humph," said Ms. Tyler again. "If you're going to be out in that garden, well . . ." She trailed off. "You all thought about putting an herb garden back there? I might talk to your parents about that. We'll see about the talent show."

"Yay!" said Sunday, and after a beat, her sisters joined in.

"What was that about?" asked Bo after they left Ms. Tyler.

"It's a way to get people to come," said Sunday. "I bet Auntie Sunflower will agree with me. People will definitely come if they're a part of it, and that's the whole point, right? I've been thinking about it ever since Marcus and Kareem brought it up."

"Ugh, now we have to let them be in it too?" asked Lil. A few children were trying to jump double Dutch on the sidewalk, without much success, and the sisters gave them a wide berth. "And I thought the whole point was to celebrate the wedding. Somehow this got . . . big."

Tell me about it, thought Bo.

"It is a good idea," said Lee. "It could be fun. And . . . I think I'll feel less self-conscious if other people are performing."

"What do you think, Bo?" asked Sunday.

Did it matter what she thought? And did she even know what she thought? Bo shrugged. "Yeah, I guess. Whatever," she said. They were home. "I'll be in the kitchen," she said.

"Are you going to work on the cupcakes?" asked Sunday.

Bo didn't answer.

"We'll be out back," called Sunday.

"I'll bring out some snacks," Bo said. "Be there soon." Mrs. Pilkington and Mr. Bultitude appeared at her feet. "Hey, guys," she said. "I actually missed you." She sat on the living room couch with the cats for a few minutes, looking out the window and listening to them purr. From the looks of it, the double Dutch kids had been joined by some bossy ladies who "came out here to show y'all how it's done." Once the ladies got hold of the ropes, Bo had to admit that they did just that.

The familiar ring of the ice cream truck's bell made Bo smile as she remembered Dougie yelling, "ICE SCREAM!" She grabbed a couple of bags of chips and went out to the backyard.

Lee was sitting with the hens and still talking about the shelter performance. "It could be a whole part of our new business!" she said. "We can do musical pet-sitting too!"

"We should charge double for that," said Lil. Rubia barked. "Oh, what do you know?" said Lil, rubbing Rubia's head. Rubia barked again, and Lil grabbed a few pretzels and stood. "It's my turn to walk Rubia, right? Anyone want to join me?"

Lee said that she was going to feed Barbara and Shirley and

tell them about the shelter show, and Sunday had some reading to do. When Lil looked her way, Bo shook her head.

"I'm going to just hang out," she said. She didn't say anything about cooking or baking, but she had some ideas about caramel extract that might finally finish off the party cupcake recipe. And then maybe one day, she and Mum could sit down and read *Cherry Bombe* and laugh about "baker's block" together.

25

AFTER THE SUCCESS OF THE SHELTER SHOW, Dr.

Coleman had posted a photo of the girls on the shelter's Photoview page, and a City College student had reposted. Word got around, and the babysitting email account got its first inquiries. The sisters were even recognized at JJ bodega down the block, which then agreed to let them post a flyer about the party.

Rehearsals were smooth, even though Sunday had a lot of suggestions. "What if I start with a root position C chord and go into a G, then A-minor—"

"No minor chords," said Lil. "They make me cranky. And when do I get to go off?"

"Here's something I've been wanting to do ever since we went to Louis Armstrong House," said Bo. "I saw a video of these Afro-Cuban drummers, Obini Bata, that gave me some ideas." Her sisters were impressed.

Lee sang lead loud and proud, often under the approving

stares of Dwayne Wayne and Urkel. Rubia was usually an enthusiastic harmonizer, and now that Ms. Tyler's regular visits had more to do with seeing what recipes Mum was working on than complaining about the noise, it was okay. She had even told some of her friends on the block about the garden party, and a couple of them stopped by a few times to help with cleanup. Even though they did more talking than cleaning, the girls enjoyed their tall tales.

"You know I planted an ackee tree here ten years ago," said Mr. Lloyd for the hundredth time.

Ms. Tyler sucked her teeth. "You know you're just making up stories. You can't grow ackee in New York—these girls know that. They have their own school, you know. Real smart."

The sisters stole surprised looks at each other but kept their mouths shut.

Well, well, well, thought Bo. She turned to Lee and whispered, "Next she'll be feeding the hens for us!" Lee giggled and Ms. Tyler gave her a suspicious look.

"Ms. Tyler, I think Barbara and Shirley have some fresh eggs waiting just for you!" Lee said quickly. "Let's go check!" She led Ms. Tyler through the door into their own backyard.

"Can we grill at this party?" asked Mama Yemisi. "I can make some good suya." Bo smiled. When Mama Yemisi had found out that Bo was short for Tokunbo, she'd practically adopted Bo and Mum, promising them a hotel hookup from her cousin in Ikoyi when they rescheduled their trip to Lagos. She hadn't laughed when Bo's eyes had watered the first time she'd brought them pepper soup, and she had helped Bo start a Nigerian recipe notebook, detailing her methods for cutting chin chin into perfect squares. Today, she and Mrs. Valentine were having a kind of food *Verzuz* competition between black-eyed pea dishes, Texas caviar and moi moi. Bo had never tasted either one, but the debate made her laugh so much she volunteered to judge the battle anyway.

Lil walked over. "We need to get going to Pop's so we can set up for . . . *The Nightmare.*"

"When you say it like that, you don't exactly sound like someone who got into babysitting because you like it," Bo answered, laughing.

"I'm sorry, I'm kidding, really, I'm kidding." Lil smiled. "But just in case, I'm going to get Mama's old portable DVD player and *Emmet Otter's Jug-Band Christmas* to watch as a last resort. Remember? That was the name of the evil puppet band."

"Mmm-hmmm. Only in this family would it feel totally normal to watch a Christmas movie about an animal puppet band in the middle of the summer," said Bo.

"Classics don't have a season," said Lil. "It's like classic clothes. Ooh, don't forget the knits on those otters! The costume design on those puppets is epic. I might do a whole Muppet knits episode on my vlog this week. You in to help out?"

"Sure, why not," said Bo. "The way you all talk about these kids, if I make it through our first babysitting gig, I'm ready for anything."

"Two hours later, Bo was on the floor of Bill's shop, buried underneath a pile of board books.

"Oof!" she called out as another copy of *Bright Eyes, Brown Skin* was added to the pile. "How many of these do you have in stock?"

"It's my number one recommendation for baby gifts," said Bill. He wasn't doing a great job of hiding his smile. "I tend to keep a healthy number. There are two more cases in the back."

"Yay!" yelled Stevie Bullock. He started chanting, and his sister, Zora, ran over from Sunday's side and joined in. "More books! More books!"

Bo sat up. "No more books!"

Sunday ran over. "Read-aloud! Let's do a read-aloud!" She pulled Bo out of the books. "But first we need to stack this up. Neatly." As the Bullocks opened their mouths to protest, she added, "And loudly. You can yell 'YES!' every time you put one back. NEATLY."

"YAY!" yelled the Bullock twins. Sunday looked at Bill and mouthed "Sorry!" as the Bullocks let out their first robust "YES!"

"Thanks," whispered Bo. "What's that in your hair?"

"Remember when I thought it would be a good idea to show them the science of slime?" Sunday said sadly. "I'm not sure if they really got the point of my lesson." She put her hand to her hair and laughed. Then her eyes widened. "Zora! Cats do NOT eat books!" She ran over to Zora, who had abandoned the book tower for the cage holding sleeping Violet from the shelter.

"Why is this cat here again?" asked Lil.

"Because we thought that maybe Amy's parents or Kareem's mom might adopt her," said Lee. "Remember? It's like an adoption fair preview before the garden party."

"What do you mean, remember?" asked Bo. "Did we actually put that in the babysitting plan?"

"Do you even know how to babysit?" asked Amy, tapping Bo on the shoulder. "I'm telling."

"What? Yes, of course we do," said Bo. "And there's nothing to tell, Amy."

"I'm telling my mom I'm bored," said Amy, folding her arms. "This is boringsitting!"

"Boringsitting! Boringsitting!" yelled the Bullocks.

Bill came over to Bo. "If you want adult intervention, just say the word," he said in a low voice. He looked around. "At least while the store's still standing."

Bo's eyes followed his. She was not giving up yet. "We got this," she said. "But, uh . . . stay close."

Bill smiled, gave her a salute, and went back behind the register, only wincing a little when Stevie opened a random paperback and left it, facedown and splayed out, on a chair.

Bo stuck her fingers in her mouth and let out a loud whistle. Everyone looked at her. "That's my special freeze signal," she said.

"Sitters can unfreeze after five seconds. Sitt . . . uh, sittees, um, Stevie, Zora, and Amy, you have to wait thirty seconds for a special surprise."

"How will we know thirty seconds?" asked Stevie.

"Count one—one thousand, two—one thousand, three—one thousand," explained Bo. "Say 'one thousand' in between each number as you count to thirty. Ready, go!" She ushered her sisters into a corner as the kids counted.

"We can do this. We'll do a dance party to tire them out, and then there are some games I used to play with Dougie. . . ." She thought for a moment. "And for Amy, we can let her be in the band, play the tambourine or shekere or something. And be a helper. I think she just wants to belong. That's what makes her so annoying." *I know how that feels.*

Her sisters nodded. "THIRTY!" yelled the kids.

"Lee!" Bo pointed to the Bullocks. "Can you sing the scavenger hunt song Sunday wrote? Find a book that starts with each letter of the alphabet."

"But—" started Lee. Just then Stevie Bullock, who had found the watercolors that Lil had packed, yelled, "If the cat's name is Violet, we should make her Violet!"

"'*Scaaaaaaavenger hunt!*'" sang Lee. "'*Da-dunt-da-dunt-da-dunt, we're going on a scaaaaaaavenger hunt!*'" The Bullocks ran over to her.

"Was that a high E?" said Sunday. "I'm impressed!"

"Now," said Bo to Amy. "We're not babysitting you anymore."

"I know," said Amy. "You're *boringsitting*. And I don't think you should get paid to play with us. You're not even playing good."

Bo forced a bright smile. "No, I mean you're going to be our special assistant," she said, nudging Sunday.

"Oh!" said Sunday, "Yes, you'll be our amanuensis!"

Amy's eyes narrowed. *Now she looks like Ms. Tyler*, Bo thought. "What does that mean?"

"Not what she thinks it means," said Bo. "I mean that you are going to be our helper. Like a friend helper. We know how smart you are, and we want you to be able to show it!"

"Teacher Maria always puts my work on the bulletin board in the hall, not the one under the class sink," said Amy proudly. "Adam's are always under the sink."

"See?" said Bo, looking at her sisters and urging them to applaud. "You were born to shine!"

"Hey, Born to Shine, that's a good band name," said Sunday.

Lee darted over, still singing, "*I'm at Rrrrrr!*"

"Speaking of band," continued Bo quickly. "How would you like to be a guest star in our band today? We're going to do a special store concert, and we want you to join us onstage!"

"We do?" asked Lil.

"What stage?" asked Amy.

"We do," answered Bo. "And did you know Lil is an engineer? Yep, she is, and she's going to create a stage area for us in—"

"*Da-dunt-da-dunt-da-dunnnnnnnt!*" sang Lee frantically.

"In two minutes!" said Bo. "Now!"

Lil pulled some beanbags around their instruments and grabbed a couple of flashlights from Bill. "Uh . . . ta-da!" she said.

Bo handed Amy a shekere. "Okay, you and me, we're percussion. We're the heart of the band." She ignored Sunday's cough and took out some claves. "Now, we might let the Bullocks play these. You can decide if it's appropriate." She waved Lee and the Bullocks over. "Stevie and Zora, I have some very special instruments here. I hope you can handle them. Do you want to try?"

"YAY!" yelled the Bullocks.

"I don't know," said Bo, looking at Amy. "What do you think, special assistant?"

"I'm a manensis," said Amy, standing tall. "I want a shirt like hers." She pointed to Lil. "Who's that? She looks cool."

Lil looked down at her shirt. "That's Sade, and she *is* cool, like me. You're right—you're effortlessly chic. Hmmmm, let's see. . . ." She ran to the kitchenette and came back with some red dish towels, then tied them around Amy's waist like a sash. "Effortlessly chic, just like Sade . . . and me."

Amy put her hands on her hips and sashayed in a little circle, then she held up the claves and looked down her nose at the Bullocks. "This is a bookstore. Books are for reading. Did you finish putting everything away?" The Bullocks nodded solemnly. "Then . . . okay. This bookstore is also for music. You can play these." She nodded at Bo to hand them the claves, and Bo slowly and ceremoniously dropped them into the Bullocks' hands.

"Thank you, Special Assis—Amanuensis Amy! Okay! This band is ready to go! Lee's on bass and vocals. Sunday's on the . . . keys." Sunday grinned and gave her a thumbs-up. "And Lil—"

"Has a five-minute guitar solo," Lil finished.

"You don't even know what song we're doing," said Lee.

"It doesn't matter," said Lil. "I'm still getting a solo."

Sunday ran over to her keyboard and went into a dramatic chord progression. "Let's goooooooooo!"

By the time Ms. Bullock and Kareem arrived to pick up Stevie and Zora, the band had played four encores for Bill and Violet and had danced their socks off (literally) in a dance party.

"Mommy! Mommy!" The Bullock twins hugged their mother, all sweetness and smiles. "We learned about synco . . . synco something," said Zora. "And Son music in Cuba!"

"And next time, we're going to sing songs like Ella Jenkins!" added Stevie. "Sitter Lil said I can use her ukulele."

Ms. Bullock smiled. "Wow, I'm impressed! You two look very happy—and so do your sitters?!" She looked at the sisters as Stevie and Zora made a couple of last laps around the store. "And you all have survived? I know my kids can be . . . challenging." Kareem coughed, and she looked over at him with a raised eyebrow. "I think this one was very grateful that he had soccer today at Riverbank. He usually has a pretty hard time managing his siblings."

Sunday smiled. "We specialize in challenging cases," she said. Ms. Bullock's eyebrow went higher.

"What my sister means," said Bo, "is that Stevie and Zora are a joy—curious and energetic."

"Noice!" muttered Lil. She handed Ms. Bullock a very small tangle of yarn. "I taught them the knit stitch. They made you . . . a scarf?"

"Put it on, Mommy!" said Zora.

"Hmmm," said Ms. Bullock. "It's so beautiful that I might just . . . hold it in my hand for a while." She looked around. "What a lovely shop this is! I can't believe we haven't come in."

"Ma, you should see if Mr. Saunders has that book you wanted," said Kareem, finally looking up.

In twenty minutes, Ms. Bullock bought a thick volume called *New Daughters of Africa* and the entire set of Jada Jones books for Stevie and Zora. And then three copies of *Bright Eyes, Brown Skin* for gifts. After she'd paid the girls and left, the sisters hugged each other and cheered.

"We. Did. That!" yelled Sunday.

"I had fun," said Lee. "And did you see Ms. Bullock petting Violet? I think she wants to adopt her."

"Then she'd be too late," said Bill, coming forward, "because she's now the official Bill's Bookshop cat!" Lee squealed and hugged him.

Sunday shrugged. "There's something kind of literary about

a bookshop cat. Maybe even . . . mysterious, like a bookshop cat detective!"

Amy tapped Bo on the shoulder. "Am I done being a manensis?"

"Uh, yes," said Bo. "Your parents should be here soon. And thank you—you did a great job."

"So where's my percent?" Amy asked, unsmiling.

"Percent?"

"Sitter Lil told me that a smart businesswoman always gets paid for her labor."

Bo turned and looked at Lil, who shrugged.

"Uh, yeah . . . I guess I did say that."

The celebration was slightly subdued when the Johnsons arrived. But they also bought books, and Amy blurted out the garden party and talent show news before the sisters could.

"Oh, honey, we should . . ." started Mrs. Johnson, looking at her husband.

"Maybe we should, but I don't know if we can," Mr. Johnson finished. He smiled at the girls. "We met as members of Dance Theatre of Harlem."

"Ooooh, that's so cool," breathed Lee. "We're going to take lessons there this summer."

"We are?" asked Bo. The Johnsons voiced hearty approval and waited patiently as Amy proudly told the sisters her story of meeting Misty Copeland. "She's . . . not in Dance Theatre of Harlem," Bo whispered to her sisters.

"It's Amy; we're just going with it," Lee whispered back, smiling and nodding.

The Johnsons paid for their books and paid the girls, who in turn paid Amy, to a hearty round of laughter from the adults. They left with garden party invitations, promising to spread the word and to return to talk to Bill about a community dance class in the store.

"I'm feeling pretty unstoppable," said Lil as they walked home. "Exhausted, yes. But also unstoppable."

"I'm so glad it worked out," said Lee. "I was really nervous."

"Thanks to Bo!" cried Sunday. "My sister is the BEST!"

"Woot!" They group hugged Bo, and she hugged them back, feeling pretty unstoppable herself.

"We really killed it as a band," said Sunday. "I can't wait till people hear us at the garden party."

"I'm going to need some help finishing up these outfits," said Lil. "Y'all's hand-sewing skills better be sharp."

"Can we bask in our musicianship for a minute, before you get all Ann Lowe on us?" said Bo.

"Aw, I'm touched that you watched my last vlog," said Lil. "She was an amazing designer, right? I'm going to make a tennis skirt inspired by her, for lessons this summer."

"Nobody wears tennis skirts for free tennis in the park," scoffed Sunday. "And you have to fix my racket, air guitar queen."

"Tennis?" asked Bo. "We're taking tennis lessons?" Her sisters told her not to worry; it was laid-back and low-key. Free tennis lessons in the park meant a lot of waiting on line to practice hitting.

Bo just smiled a weak smile. *Nothing to see here, folks. Just another new thing!*

As they got closer to 125th Street and St. Nicholas, they heard the sounds of music coming from the subway station.

"Wow, now that's musicianship," said Sunday. "Let's go check it out. We might be inspired!"

The tired-but-triumphant babysitting band descended the stairs into the station, where a crowd surrounded the buskers. With the acoustics of the station, the lead singer's voice rang clear and true, surrounding them.

"That drummer is pretty sick," Bo said. "I really need to get on those paradiddles. Let's get closer. We can put something in their box."

"We already gave money to Amy," grumbled Lil. "Let's not go wild."

"Whose fault was that?" Bo answered as they got closer. "But it was a good call, Lil. And if it makes you feel any better, I think it will bring us more business."

"Wow, whoever that is really has pipes," said Lee. With some difficulty, they pushed their way to the front of the crowd. A glittery gold sign was propped up, with one word on it: GLOSS. A set of glossy red lips was positioned inside the O, and in front of them, looking and sounding like superstars, were Reese, Lita, and Maya.

They were AMAZING.

The sisters went back upstairs and stood in front of a CVS in silence.

"Hair braiding?" asked a woman sitting on a folding chair near the corner.

"No, thank you," Lee said.

"But did you see Maya's blowout, though?" demanded Lil. "We need to up our hair game if we're trying to be a band. Obviously our outfits are on point."

"What outfits?" asked Sunday. "You keep talking about them, but we haven't seen anything, and the garden party is less than a week away!"

"Now do you see what I mean about not singing lead?" asked Lee. "I'm nothing like Reese."

"Let's walk," said Bo. "We're in the way." As they started toward home, a voice rang out from behind.

"Hey!" yelled Reese. "Y'all are rude, not even buying a CD."

"Sorry!" said Lee. "You have CDs?"

"Be quiet," muttered Lil, nudging her twin.

"Who has CDs anyway?" asked Sunday. "I only know what they are because of my dad."

"We heard you were scaring kids and figured we'd show Harlem what a real girl band sounds like," said Lita. "I guess we did that."

"I heard you were engaging in animal torture at the shelter too," added Maya. "It was a noise nightmare."

"Hold up, wait a minute," started Lee, moving forward.

"Now, that's what I'm talking about," said Lil, pushing her twin forward. "Let them know, Lee!"

Bo turned to face Reese and her friends, who were standing with their hands on their hips. "Nice set," Bo said coolly. "Can we help you with something?"

"Maybe you can make it make sense," said Reese. "Why would you think anyone, or anything, would want to listen to you?"

"We're a band," said Sunday. "We had an official gig."

The girls laughed, and Lita, the one who had seen Bo at the pool, laughed the hardest and then whispered in Reese's ear.

"Marcus Semple said y'all are hosting a talent show in that nasty garden," said Reese. "Is that true?"

"It's a garden party, to celebrate a family wedding," said Bo.

"Well, if you need a real band . . ." Reese trailed off and shrugged. "We might be able to help you out. At least if we play, people in the neighborhood won't hate you more than they already do."

"Ooooh, you know what?!" Sunday looked ready to explode.

"Come on," said Bo. "Let's just go." She led the way home; the triumphant mood was gone, and they walked in silence. That mean laughter was still ringing in Bo's ear. Some things weren't new.

"They're still standing there laughing at us," said Sunday, looking back. "We should challenge them."

"Seriously, Sunday, you know you can't fight," said Lil, hopping off of her skateboard. "Can you hold my skateboard, though?"

"I don't mean fighting. I mean, like, a battle of the bands," said Sunday. She turned around. "Us versus . . . what's their name again?"

"Gloss," said Bo. "And that's a bad idea."

"Why?" asked Sunday. "We were just talking about how awesome we are!"

"That was for a bunch of abandoned animals and captive kids," said Bo. "Not a *real* audience!"

"Hey, the shelter animals have good taste," protested Lee.

"As much as I love competition," said Lil, "maybe Bo's right. We're just getting started. We all saw it. Gloss is, like, almost professional. Super-ugly outfits, though."

Lee gave her a look.

"Okay, okay," grumbled Lil. "The outfits were good."

"I can't believe you, all ye of little faith," grumbled Sunday. "We are just as good—no, better! We just gonna let them do us like that? Why are we even playing at the garden party, then, if we're so bad?"

"You're right," said Bo suddenly. "Why are we? Maybe we should just focus on hosting. That's enough." If they didn't have to practice, she could get those cupcakes finalized, and her sisters would never have to know how close she'd come to failing.

"Bo! I can totally help you with the cupcakes, or whatever you need," Sunday said. "We're all going to work together. We got this, remember? And the band was your idea!"

"We have less than a week, Sunday. This isn't one of your long stories with an unrealistic happy ending," said Bo. "We've got less than a week, and a year's worth of things to do, as usual! Projects, classes—I don't even have time to think!" She didn't know how loud she'd gotten until she realized that everyone else had gone real quiet.

Lil cleared her throat. "Lee, you want me to braid your hair?"

Lee nodded. "I'll get Rubia so I can brush her while you braid. Can you help me practice for the geography bee? I've been slacking off."

"Yeah, if you help me finish my museum model. I want to show Auntie Sunflower after the party. She's friends with Mike Jung, and she might show it to him."

Bo gave Sunday a look that said, *See?*

Sunday joined the Twins in the elevator. "Can we talk more about this?" she asked Bo.

Bo shook her head. "I wouldn't get a word in edgewise. Talking to you is pretty one-sided." That came out meaner than she'd meant, but the elevator doors closed before she could apologize.

After color coding the pantry, Bo felt better. Who cared if Gloss was good? They sure were good, though. But Gloss wasn't a musical babysitting band, offering education and childcare—that genius stroke of Sunday's set them apart. Bo decided to go upstairs and tell Sunday exactly that. As she went up in the elevator, she smiled. As for the garden party talent show, well, if Mr. Jimenez from down the street was actually going to recite his spoken-word poetry about the wonders of rice, and Mary from the bodega was going to demonstrate 101 ways to recycle phone cards . . . then their band could perform and have fun with it. Even if they still didn't have a name.

She heard scrambling as she approached the bedroom she shared with Sunday; the door was closed, and she opened it carefully. Bo was used to tripping over one of Sunday's stray books or slipping on a piece of paper. The room was—

Cleaned up? Bo looked around. Whoa! Sunday's mess was gone; her bed was even made. Mr. Bultitude and Mrs. Pilkington sat under Bo's desk, looking as wide-eyed and surprised as Bo felt. Had Sunday even . . . vacuumed?

"Ta-da!" yelled Sunday, coming out of their walk-in closet with a wide smile. "I thought this would cheer you up."

"Wow, I mean . . . I don't know what to say. . . . I was worried that you'd be discouraged. . . . I didn't mean to go so negative," Bo said. "I—you—whoa, this room is so much bigger than I realized!"

Sunday laughed. "And now, the pièce de résistance . . . open your dresser drawers!"

"Huh?"

"Check it out—I organized all of my stuff in my dresser, and I know you like systems, so I arranged your stuff in the same way. I even put some stuff together. Turns out I had a bunch of stamps, and quartz rocks too, so I added them to your collections. I never knew how many cool collections you had! You don't talk about it much. We should make a display! I had a great idea—a family museum project. I—Bo? Are you okay?"

Bo ran over to her dresser and pulled open the drawers. Her stuff, her precious stuff. The stuff that only *she* touched. "But . . ."

"You're shocked, right? I know we're supposed to keep our stuff separate, but I know that was only because I was so disorganized. Now I'll do better, because we'll manage this together."

"I can't believe this," whispered Bo.

"I know, it didn't seem like I could do this, but I told you, I can get organized if I focus. I just needed a little inspiration, and I got it from you, of course! You're always—" Bo ran out of the room. She didn't even bother with the elevator; she just ran down the stairs.

"Bo!" called out Sunday.

She passed Lil and Lee, who were in the parlor. Lee was being fitted for what looked like a space suit. Rubia sat next to them, and barked when she saw Bo. Bo kept running, out the door, all the way to the B train.

26

BY THE TIME BO GOT to her old building, she was *hangry*. The elevator was working, and when she got to her old floor, the garlicky smell of Mr. Korin's cooking was like a big hug. At Dougie's door, she paused. What was she going to say?

The door opened. "Bo!" said a surprised Mrs. Dougie. "What a lovely surprise!"

"Um, hi," said Bo. "Were you going out?"

"No, no, I was just taking some trash downstairs. What perfect timing—would you mind staying up here with Dougie while I run down?"

"Of course!" said Bo. She breathed in. Just like old times. "That's what I'm here for!"

Mrs. Dougie hugged her. "Such a treat to see you. You know, I thought—"

"BO!!!!!" Dougie ran and jumped at her.

"Heyyy, Dougie," Bo answered, laughing.

"He missed you," Mrs. Dougie said dryly. "I'll be right back."

Dougie talked a mile a minute as he led Bo into the apartment.

"Did you bring snacks?" he asked.

"You're supposed to offer me some, Dougie," she said. "And I'm actually really hungry."

"Like, hangry hungry?"

Bo nodded solemnly, then she let out a pretend angry growl. Dougie laughed.

"We have Samoas," said Dougie. "Mommy doesn't know I know where they are."

"Well, we have to wait until she comes back, then," Bo said. "But there are certain anytime snacks, right?" She started tapping out a beat on the counter, and Dougie immediately did a reasonable imitation of a beatboxer, then he said, *Fruit and veggies, we can eat anytime! I'll give you yours, then I can get mines!*" He grabbed two bananas from a big wooden bowl on the countertop.

"You remember!" said Bo, high-fiving him.

"I got bars," said Dougie. "My new friend Bella likes to freestyle."

"Who's Bella?" Bo asked.

"She lives in your old apartment! Do you want to go there?"

Bo shook her head slowly. "That's okay. So actually, I came to see how Dinobotland was holding up. I was thinking we could finish it now!"

"Oh, okay!" said Dougie, shrugging. "I think it's in the coat closet. I forgot about that."

Mrs. Dougie returned and immediately began assembling a substantial tray of snacks, including some Samoas. Dougie winked a large wink at Bo.

"It's funny, I just talked to your mum this morning," said Mrs. Dougie. "She didn't tell me you were coming by."

"Oh, she's swamped," Bo said vaguely. "She, uh, probably had a lot on her mind. I came to tell you about the wedding party we're having. Uh, I wanted to invite you in person!"

"Yes, the garden party! Lola told me—we can't wait!" said Mrs. Dougie. "And I'm so looking forward to meeting Sunflower Rogers. So young and yet pretty legendary already."

"*Don't sleep on me, cuz I am legendary,*" rapped Dougie, returning to the room with a large box. "*My style and rhymes make me a visionary.*"

Mrs. Dougie smiled and rolled her eyes. "Has Dougie told you about Bella? They spend a lot of time dropping lyrics—"

"*Bars*, Mommy, *bars!*" cried Dougie.

"Sorry—bars. Anyway, it was good luck that a family with children moved into your old place, and—"

Bo accidentally on purpose bumped the large box. "Ooops!" she said loudly. She didn't want to hear about new people in her old apartment. "What is this anyway, Dougie?"

"Dinobotland!" said Dougie. "I put it away. We have to start over."

"Oh!" Bo tried to sound casual. "I thought you were going to keep it just where we were so we could finish together."

Dougie shrugged. "That was a long time ago. And I play with GearIts more now. I made a spaceship for my Simone Biles doll."

"Less than a month, but okay," said Bo. "My sister Lil has GearIts. They're actually pretty cool." She laughed. "Actually, last week she built a cake-o-lator out of them, to shoot squares of cake directly into her mouth while she's studying."

"It must be so wonderful for you now, having sisters," said Mrs. Dougie. "I can't wait to meet them. Oh! We've had two Gatherings since you left, and they've been fantastic! We're going to host an eighties hip-hop symposium next month, and Kool Herc has definitely confirmed that he'll consider thinking about attending."

"Can we play now?" asked Dougie. "And you're still gonna make me a whole tray of cupcakes like you promised, right? Since I didn't finish Dinobotland? I did the opposite!"

"Sure, yeah." Bo nodded, grateful to change the subject. Next Mrs. Dougie would mention Mum.

"You go into the living room," said Mrs. Dougie. "I'll just ring Lola and see if it's okay for you to stay for dinner."

"Uh . . . ," started Bo. "I, um, I . . ." The doorbell rang.

"We're popular today!" said Mrs. Dougie, walking to the door.

"*Popular, I'm popular, I got so many friendssss,*" sang Dougie. "*Popular, I'm popular, my buddy list never endsssss.*"

"Dougie, we're going to have to talk," said Bo. "You live in the heart of hip-hop. Your rhymes have to be on point. Where did Bella move here from?"

"Queens," said Dougie.

That explained it.

Mrs. Dougie returned . . . with Sunday! Bo's mouth dropped open.

"Hey, sis," Sunday said. "This has been such a fun project!" She walked over to Bo and put an arm around her shoulder. "Just follow my lead," she whispered.

After Mrs. Dougie had settled them all in the living room with bananas, crackers and cheese, and a healthy stack of Samoas, Dougie, Bo, and Sunday focused on building Dinobotland with the GearIts. Every few seconds Bo would sneak a look at her sister, only to find Sunday sneaking a look at *her*. Sunday and her gift of gab had come just at the right moment; she'd "explained" that Bo had invited her to explore the neighborhood as part of a project they were doing. Sunday had added that she'd told Bo to go on ahead while she took a few playground photographs downstairs.

"Uh, yeah . . . ," mumbled Bo. "I was about to mention that my . . . that my sister was with me."

Mrs. Dougie fussed around them for a little while, looking through Sunday's detective notebook, admiring Sunday's hair, which was in a pretty spectacular twist out, thanks to Lil. Then she got on the phone, and Bo pulled Sunday aside.

"How did you get here?" she whispered.

"The same way you did, except I knew you were there, so I

wasn't riding the train alone and against the rules, which is more than I can say for you," Sunday hissed back.

"Were you spying on me?"

"I like to think of it as protecting and detecting," Sunday said. "For real, I was worried!"

"You're whispering. Telling secrets is rude," Dougie called out. "I'm telling."

"Do you by any chance know a girl named Amy?" Sunday asked, and Bo elbowed her.

The children spent a quiet hour laughing and building with GearIts and dominoes; Dougie and Sunday enjoyed each other, and to Bo's surprise, she didn't mind. This was different, but it was mixed in something warm and familiar.

"Did Bo tell you about our band?" Sunday asked Dougie. Dougie shook his head.

"Yes, we have . . . a band," said Bo. "An all-sister girl band." She smiled at Sunday. "And we're good."

"That's crimination," said Dougie. "What about other kids who aren't girls?"

"We welcome allies," Sunday said cheerfully. "And special guest stars." She looked down. "We also babysit."

"You know, since I'm allowed to come back here as long as I'm with my sisters," said Bo slowly, "our babysitting band can come hang with you whenever your mommy needs us." Sunday looked up and smiled.

"What's your band name?" asked Dougie. The sisters looked at each other.

"We're working on it," said Sunday.

"We better have one in time for our garden party debut," said Bo.

"WOOOOOT!" yelled Sunday, and Dougie joined her.

"You can come back with Bo," said Dougie. "You might be my second-best friend."

"What about Bella?" asked Bo.

"First and a half," said Dougie.

"WOOOOOOT!" said Bo, just because.

On the way home, Bo showed Sunday where Kool Herc's house was and introduced her to the aunties in the West African grocery. The subway wasn't too crowded, and they found seats near the back of the car.

They turned to each other.

"I'm sorry," they said at the same time. Then they laughed together.

"Like twins," Sunday said with a sad smile.

"I've never heard them do that," said Bo.

Sunday shrugged. "Yeah, I guess that really only happens on TV, not in real life. But it was how I always wanted it to be for me and my . . . twin."

Bo nodded. "Oh, yeah . . . but I . . ." She stopped.

"I know," said Sunday. "You're not my twin. I went too hard, like I always do. And I didn't respect your privacy. I'm so, so sorry. I should have known better. I was just so focused on trying to make you see that things weren't so bad. . . . The Parents will be furious if they find out."

After a pause, Bo said, "I'm sorry I stormed out like that. And thank you for covering for me. Breaking a rule like that . . . ugh, I can't imagine what Mum will say. And I've been trying so hard, because she's so happy."

"I mean . . . ," started Sunday. "I know I don't have a great track record, but . . . I can keep my mouth shut."

Bo looked at her. "And I don't have to say anything about . . . boundaries," Bo said. "And I know you were trying to do something nice. It's just . . . I was trying to keep a small part of myself for myself, you know?"

Sunday nodded sadly, and Bo took a deep breath. "I love living with you all, and freeschooling, and everything . . . and Bill—I mean Pop—he's great, and you are such a great sister. It's just . . . a lot of *new* for me. I've been feeling a little . . . overwhelmed."

"You always seem so cool, calm, and collected!" said Sunday. "Like way older than the rest of us."

"I really wanted to seem that way," said Bo. "But it's a lot of work. I think sometimes I need to just take a breath."

"Pop is always telling me to do that," Sunday said. "What's it like?" After they both giggled, she went on. "I get it. We're a lot.

I'm a lot." She got serious. "The truth is, I don't always have an easy time making friends."

Bo thought of Celia and Amber. "Maybe we have more in common than I thought."

"I had all these plans for when you moved in, for how we'd be like twins, but I think I was just thinking of two of . . . me."

Bo wanted to give something too. "Even if we're not twins, I'm still learning to be a sister," she said. "And you're a great teacher."

"By the way, I know Dougie was just talking," said Sunday. "Don't worry—you don't have to bring me back there."

Maybe sharing more of me doesn't mean I'm less of me, thought Bo. "Well, now you're Mrs. Dougie–approved; I have to bring you back." She smiled at Sunday.

"Um, did I just hear you say 'Mrs. Dougie'?" asked Sunday.

Bo laughed. "Long story," she said.

They changed trains at 149th Street–Grand Concourse and were back on 125th and Lenox in a few minutes. They walked toward the sound of drums; there was a community health fair going on, and a drum line was performing in front of the statue of Adam Clayton Powell Jr. at the State Office Building. More than a few of their neighbors were clapping and dancing on the plaza. Dr. Ohadike, whose office motto was "Eye care is my passion, eyeglasses are great fashion," told them that he and Mr. Cheng, who owned Lucky Star No. 7 Chinese takeout, were coming to the garden party with dueling fried rice dishes.

"We have a jollof battle in the works too," Bo muttered to Sunday after Dr. Ohadike left. "Not to mention the rice and peas clash that's been brewing among the 227 Crew. It's gonna be a real rice war." They texted Lil and Lee as they watched the drummers. "Whoa, that kid in the back is a double stroke roll master," said Bo.

"I have no idea what that means," said Sunday. "But it sounds like she's good?"

"You sure you don't know?" Bo shot Sunday a little side-eye, but with a smile. "I thought the keyboard was 'percussive.'"

"Okay, yeah, I told you . . . I'm a lot!" Sunday blushed. "But this beat—what if you do something like this, and I start with a root position C major chord and go into a—"

"A-minor, right?" Bo said. "Here's something I've been wanting to do. I've been practicing triplets, watching Bernard 'Pretty' Purdie videos. Maybe we don't just do a remixed nursery rhyme at the party . . ."

"Maybe we do one of our own songs!" Sunday cried. "YESS!"

"Aw, they probably think they'll get better if they keep watching real musicians." A voice came from behind Bo.

"Reese, you are, like, the definition of lurk," said Sunday, sighing. "You can't stay away from us, can you?"

"We were invited here. We're actually *on* the program," said Lita. "We go on after the DJs. Because we're a real band."

"That sounds like battle language if you ask me," said Bo.

"It does?" answered Sunday, raising her eyebrows. When Bo

nudged her, she cleared her throat. "Yeah, it does! It's on! Battle of the bands!"

"What are you even talking about?" asked Reese, looking around.

"You sure you want to do this, Gloss?" asked Bo. "Because you don't even know what we can do."

"You know that's right!" Sunday was warming up.

"Do what?" asked Maya.

"Battle of the bands at the garden party," said Bo and Sunday together, then they laughed.

"Oh, now we're invited?" drawled Reese. "You might have to check with our manager, Libba. We might be booked that day."

Bo nodded. "Well, we'd love to have you. And we'd love to battle you in the community talent show."

"It's on!" called out a boy who was standing behind them and clearly had no business of his own to mind. Bo glared at him.

"Fine with me," said Reese, raising her eyebrows and flipping her hair at the same time. "We'll ask Libba if we can squeeze your little 'battle' thing in. Your choice to embarrass yourself. Again."

"Yeah," added Maya and Lita in unison. And in harmony, Bo noticed.

Lil and Lee appeared. When they got close to Bo and Sunday, they looked from their sisters to Gloss, then back again.

"Uh, what did we miss?" asked Lee.

"Whatever it is, it looks like it's not over," said Lil. "Not by a long shot!"

27

THE DRUM LINE FINISHED, and some people drifted away to continue their 125th Street shopping. A DJ with a salt-and-pepper beard and a British accent took center stage, slipping smoothly into seventies funk and Afrobeat music that got some older spectators moving in ways that made the kids in the crowd give them a lot of space.

Lil and Lee had questions.

"Where did you guys go?"

"What was that about?"

"Did you see what they were wearing?"

Without having to say anything to each other, Bo and Sunday decided to keep the story short.

"Uh . . . I wanted to personally invite Dougie to the garden party," said Bo.

"All of a sudden?" asked Lil, looking skeptical. "And this DJ is fire—I wonder if I can get lessons. . . ."

"And I went along for research," continued Sunday loudly, "for our history of hip-hop project. DJ-ing—that would be great for our research, Lil! Scratching, remixing . . ."

"What project?" asked Lee.

"The one we're doing this fall," said Sunday. "I'm going to propose it tonight at dinner. You'll love it. Beatboxing, leg warmers, Kangol hats, Adidas."

"Doesn't sound that different from now," Lil said. "But what does seem different is—"

"Don't forget the neon," sounded a voice from behind them. "And off-the-shoulder sweatshirt dresses. I've seen many pictures of those!"

"Auntie Sunflower!" They managed a group hug in the crowd, and this time Bo felt comfortable joining in.

Auntie Sunflower smiled. "I'm so proud of you all. This garden party has the whole block talking! I was just over at the George Bruce Library. They said they're going to have a library card sign-up table outside the gates."

"Not to toot my own horn," said Sunday. "But—"

"Yeah, we know, toot toot," said Bo, smiling, and Sunday nudged her.

"I *did* work on that!" said Sunday. "And they'll bring used books for sale too." Auntie Sunflower high-fived her. "One day I'll have a used book for sale at the library," Sunday added dreamily. "Hey! We should put a Little Free Library in the garden!" Now the DJ was providing a house music soundtrack for some teens who had started an impromptu open mic on the plaza, and a couple was doing what Sunday called "fancy dancing" a few feet away.

"The Apollo is right there. They better come out and see this Black excellence!" said an older man, leaning over his walker to the man next to him. "Brother Albert, you remember how we used to do?" Brother Albert nodded and smiled.

"Isn't that the man who's always in Flamekeepers Hat Club?" whispered Lee. "I see him when I take Rubia out." By the look of the man's crisp straw hat, Bo guessed Lee was right.

Sunday skipped over to the man and his friend. "Hi! I'm Sunday! We're your neighbors, and we would love to have you, um, do how you used to do at our community talent show and garden wedding party!" She stopped to take a breath. "There will be food—well, everybody who comes has to bring some—"

"You don't have to worry about that," said Brother Albert suddenly. "My mac and cheese used to win awards! The secret is chili."

The first man almost laughed himself out of his walker. "He's just talking," he said.

"I'm listening," said Sunday. "And so will my pop. He's all about chili."

"I'll tell you," said Brother Albert. "If that lady who makes those cookies I had a couple of days ago at the bookstore is going to be there, I will too!"

Sunday clasped her hands together. "Yes! She will!" She

waved Bo over. "That's her mum!" She took a breath. "*Our* mum, right?" Bo smiled, but she couldn't say anything yet. "And that's our pop's bookstore!" They gave the men some flyers, promised to make sure that dominoes would be on hand, and went back to their sisters.

"Did you hear that Theo the therapy dog is coming to the garden party?" asked Lee. "Kids can read to him. It's going to be so cute!"

Auntie Sunflower nodded. "You are on a roll, ladies! But what I want to know is—"

"Maybe Pop and Dr. Coleman can start a therapy animal reading program at the bookstore," said Bo. "We can set up that back storage room and designate it a full-fur zone so people with allergies know what's up."

"Yes!" said Lee.

"How's it going with—" Auntie Sunflower started again.

"And that can be a part of our musical babysitting business," said Lil. "For an additional fee, of course." She rubbed her hands together. "So what was that about a battle of the bands?"

"Yes, the music!" said Auntie Sunflower. "How are things on the music front?"

Bo spoke first. "We're going to battle Gloss at the garden party, like Sunday said . . . and I, uh, agree."

Auntie Sunflower's eyebrows went up.

"Whaaaat?" cried Lee. "What happened to a nice little

community talent show, not a competition? What happened to not being ready? What happened to Gloss being semiprofessional and us being . . . not?"

"Our outfits are better, though," said Lil. "Not that it's a competition."

"Listen, we got this," said Bo. "We just got caught off guard, but they're not better than us." She glanced at Auntie Sunflower, who smiled.

"I get the feeling I missed something," said Auntie Sunflower. "But . . . it sounds like you're working it out."

"We are. We played the best gig for Amy and the Bullocks—which is not a bad band name, even though it has nothing to do with us . . . ," said Sunday. Bo nudged her. "Anyway, just a couple of hours ago, we knew we were all that! We've got the skills."

A line dance had started, and a DJ named Tara had taken over. A familiar song rang out.

"This is my jam!" Auntie Sunflower said, joining the dancers.

Lil and Lee looked at each other, then back at their sisters.

"You seem . . . different," said Lil. "Like a team of two."

"More like all *four* one . . . ," started Sunday, holding up four fingers, then grabbing Bo's hand. This time Bo squeezed back.

"And one *four* all!" finished Bo. They started to cheer themselves but were quickly shushed by a woman in the crowd whose heels were so high, Lil had to take a photo.

"I'm scared," said Lee. "But I'm in."

"Yes! *That's* what I'm talking about!" said Sunday. "And I

know, I know, everything is always what I'm talking about. Can I help it if I'm just enthusiastic about life?"

"Yes," said Bo, but she was laughing.

"So anyway," said Lil, "I've been watching episodes of *Sister, Sister, Moesha,* and *A Different World* for inspiration, and our look is going to be tough but chic, lots of color."

"Basically, you," said Sunday. "You're just giving us what you would wear."

"And do the Parents know you been watching all those shows?" asked Lee. "I just gave them a persuasive essay to get permission for *Cat Hospital* and *For the Love of Dogs,* and I'm still waiting for an answer."

"I had the nostalgia factor in my favor," said Lil. "And I said *for the culture* a lot."

"Okay"—Bo held up a hand—"so how are we going to make sure we beat Gloss, convince our neighbors to come to the party even though there will be funky animals that aren't even ours, save the funky animals that aren't even ours, make sure there's no funky potato salad with raisins or something in the potluck mix, decorate the garden, and finish our freeschool work in less than a week?"

"That's what I'd like to know," sounded Mum's voice. "But first, perhaps you can tell me about your little excursion, Bo, because I'd really like to hear about that."

Lil and Lee slipped away so quickly that Bo made a mental note to ask them if they'd ever thought of trying out for track.

"So, seriously, you're going to *love* this story," started Sunday in a brave attempt to "storify" and deflect.

Bo smiled. "It's okay, Sunday. You don't have to cover for me."

Sunday looked from Bo to Mum, then nodded. "Okay, but . . . I just want to say that I was with Bo the whole time, Mum Lola, or at least within eyesight! And Bo did a great job of showing me her favorite landmarks, and I was thinking that we could all go back, and . . ." She trailed off. "I'll just . . . stop talking." She gave Bo a quick hug and lifted a fist of solidarity, then Mum asked her to pick up some tea from Serengeti.

"Ginger turmeric and one of your choice. Bo and I are going to bake," said Mum. "And we'll meet you at home for a nice afternoon iced tea."

Sunday gave them a thumbs-up. "You had me at 'bake'! And going to Serengeti means free samples, so thank you!"

Bake, huh? This sounded like it might go way better than she would have thought. Was there a catch? With a start, Bo realized that she had been waiting for this for so long that she didn't know what to feel. Still, she was pretty sure that it wasn't exactly going to be a reward for running off to Dougie's. More like an opportunity for a Very Serious Conversation.

But Mum just hugged Bo's shoulder and was silent on the walk home. She even stopped to check out the vendors who lined 125th Street, picking up a few bars of black soap on the way. In the kitchen, she already had some butter, flour, eggs, and brown sugar out. "Let's go check Barbara and Shirley for a couple more eggs. This recipe has five," she said. "I love that we can do that."

Bo nodded. "I thought that the chickens were going to be the kookiest thing about living here," she said slowly, "but it's pretty cool." Outside, Rubia barked a happy hello when she saw Bo.

"You two seem like buddies," said Mum.

Bo shrugged. "Rubia's not so bad, I guess." She rubbed Rubia's head.

"What kind of cake are we making?" Bo asked when they got back inside.

"I have a new base cake recipe," said Mum. "I'm calling it 'Sistersweet.' I can customize it for each of you girls. I've been playing around with this one for a while, Sunshine Surprise Smilecake." Mum pointed to an already finished cake on the counter as she put the electric kettle on. "I couldn't get the flavor quite right until today."

"It was the anise, wasn't it?" said Bo. Oops.

Mum turned around. "How did—did I already tell you about this?" She stretched. "I've been so overloaded lately, I don't remember what I've said from one day to the next."

"Well, it's perfect timing," said Bo, and she meant it. Mum always knew when she needed something special. Maybe after they had their first slices of Sunshine Surprise Smilecake, she'd tell Mum that she'd known all along.

"Anyway, I switched it out for cardamom. Do you think she'll like it? Bill said she'd love it no matter what, but I really want to get it right."

Bo looked up. "She who?"

"Sunday, of course!" said Mum.

Bo looked at the cake, then looked at Mum. "That cake is . . . for Sunday?"

Mum laughed. "Well, naturally, we'll all eat some, of course. . . . Honey, don't screw up your face that way!"

Bo swallowed. "Oh . . . yeah . . . of course! Wait, um, tell me again?"

"*Did* I mention it? I've been trying to come up with one for your sister since forever. She's been so open to having me in her life, and I know it's hard. Bill calls her Sunshine sometimes, which I think is so cute. He told me some of her favorite flavors, and I've been tinkering. . . ."

Mum hadn't been working on a surprise gift for her at all. "I'm sorry, Mum. I know I'm in trouble."

After a pause, Mum spoke. "So, what did it feel like, going back to the old place?"

Bo thought for a moment. "It was kind of familiar, and new at the same time. It was good to play with Dougie . . . and also good to introduce Sunday to him. Not how I expected it to be."

Mum nodded and handed her a bowl. "Here, whisk this." As Bo started whisking the dry ingredients, Mum went on. "You must have really been feeling some type of way to do something like that. So what's going on? I thought this summer was going so well. It's been so good to see how well you and your sisters get along. You haven't mentioned any problems." She started creaming the butter and brown sugar in the mixer.

Bo took a deep breath. "I never have a chance to mention anything! I like Bill and his jokes and his chili, and Sisters and Community, but it's just . . . I used to make you happy, and now you seem the happiest because you don't have time for me. You don't have cakes for me." And she didn't deserve one anyway.

Mum turned off the mixer, and the cats took that as a cue to move forward, into the doorway. "Out," Mum said without even turning around, and they both stepped back. "Oh, honey, you can't believe that! I'm happy because we have this life now, together! It's what we always dreamed of."

"I know you dreamed of it, Mum, and I mean, this is so cool, but . . ." She couldn't hold back her tears, and Mum wrapped her in a big hug. "But I don't want you to think I'm not happy, it's just hard sometimes, I don't want you to worry . . ."

Now Mum was crying, but she was smiling too. "That's what mothers do," she said.

"I'm sorry, Mum. I don't want to make you cry," said Bo. She turned the mixer back on. "I'm supposed to be the one who makes you feel better."

"Honey, you're not making me worry, or making me cry. I'm crying because I love you, I'm crying because I'm worried, because I'm happy that you're you, because I'm tired . . . and it's okay. I'm feeling my feelings right now, and you are allowed to do the same.

You have always been so responsible, taking care of so much. I so wanted you to relax in this new life of ours, feel free to be a kid."

Bo started adding the flour mixture and yogurt to the mixing bowl. "I feel like you don't need me anymore. You're always pushing me away."

Mum held Bo's shoulders. "It's not your job to take care of me, Bo. I need you because of who you are, not because of anything you do. You're my heart, little buddy. Always. And I *have* been pushing you, *to* your sisters. I wanted to give you the gift of sisterhood." She smiled a half smile. "Is it a little too much of a gift that keeps on giving?"

Bo sniffled and laughed. "Sometimes. But I don't know if it's okay to say that. I don't want you to be disappointed in me. And Sunday, Lil, and Lee, they think I'm so grown-up and organized, and I love them, I love"—she gestured around—"all this bigness in my life now! Even you guys," she said, glancing over toward the doorway where Mr. Bultitude and Mrs. Pilkington lay washing themselves defiantly just outside of the kitchen. "I don't want to mess up . . . or at least, I don't want anyone to know."

"You're a kid, honey, you're supposed to mess up. And I apologize. I haven't been practicing what I preach. I should have recognized that all this is overwhelming. I'm overwhelmed myself some days!"

"You are?"

Mum nodded. "I've been so busy wanting to make you live the perfect life that I haven't paid enough attention to how you

might *feel*—and I haven't given you the opportunity to tell me."
She rummaged through a drawer, took out a notebook and purple
pen, and held them out to Bo. "So now's your chance. Ready to
make a list? Two columns, pros and cons?"

Bo smiled. Mum still understood her. "But shouldn't I help
you finish this up?"

Mum smiled and pointed to the kitchen table. "Go ahead," she
said. "When you're ready, I'll be right here."

Bo started writing, and as she wrote down things like "swimming lessons," "living in a literal zoo," and "reader-response journals," she realized that she had a lot more things in the pros
column, like "making music together," "Table Talk," "fresh eggs,"
"Auntie Sunflower," and lots and lots of things about each of her
sisters.

"Oh, and one more thing," Bo wrote. "You make me happy. If
I forget to say that out loud at least once a week, give me a nudge,
okay?"

Mum got the cake into the oven and sat down at the kitchen
table. She looked hard at Bo. "So when you're feeling this way, can
you talk to me instead of running off like that?"

Bo nodded and thought back to her subway ride with Sunday.
"And . . . I can talk to my sisters." She breathed in the smell of
Sunshine Surprise Smilecake. "It smells really good, Mum. She'll
love it. We all will." It was okay that this cake wasn't all her own.
Bo knew for sure that she had more love in her life, not less. And
anyway, she hated cardamom.

Right on cue, Sunday returned. "I've got ginger turmeric and hibiscus," she said breathlessly. "And they're coming to the party with free samples!" She looked from Bo to Mum. "You know, Mum, I just wanted to tell you how much I've been bugging Bo to take me to meet Dougie, so it was really all my fault—"

Bo held up a hand. "It's okay," she said. "We're not in trouble."

"Oh, you're both still in trouble," said Mum. "There will be some extra chicken coop duty and kitchen cleanup happening for the next two weeks." Mrs. Pilkington meowed. "Oh, and the litter box. Every day for a month."

Bo and Sunday looked at each other and shrugged. "It could be worse," said Bo.

"Yeah, it could be way worse, like my dad's chili every day for a month or volunteer cleanup duty at the shelter or something," added Sunday.

"Don't give her ideas," Bo whispered.

"And, Bo, honey," said Mum. "If you want to go back to the way things used to be, don't do it alone, okay? Let's talk first."

Bo nodded. "Yes, Mum. Can we start now, by talking about swimming lessons?"

"Nope," said Mum, smiling. "Nonnegotiable."

"What about tennis? Freeschooling is all about following our passions, and I can definitely say that I don't have a passion for tennis."

Sunday gasped. "But I just got Serena Williams and Naomi Osaka posters for a joint project. See, I was thinking we could make a documentary about our road to tennis glory, combine my penchant for story flourishes with your down-to-earth attention to fact, and—" She stopped. "I was totally going to ask you first."

"If you're asking now, I love *watching* tennis," said Bo. "I just don't want to play. But a doc about other people playing sounds good as long as we get Venus Williams and Coco Gauff in there too. Nice use of *penchant,* by the way. So . . . how about it, Mum? Doing my own thing as part of the family? Following my own path to my passion?"

Mum sighed. "I won't force you on the tennis lessons anymore. But if you're doing a documentary project—"

"Ora Mae Washington, Althea Gibson, Zina Garrison, I'm on it, Mum. You know we'll talk history, legacy, all that stuff. It's what freeschooling's about," said Bo with a grin.

Sunday raised her eyebrows. "Hey, can we talk about volunteering at the animal shelter? Because that's really Lee's passion, and—"

"Don't push it," said Mum, laughing.

"Worth a try." Sunday grabbed Bo's hand and squeezed. "Should we get the Twins and practice? We do have a battle to prepare for, and I got about a million ideas on the way home."

"Battle?" Mum asked. "Do I want to know?"

"Nope," said Bo and Sunday in unison.

28

LIL CLICKED ON HER FLASHLIGHT and shone it at the wall of Sunday and Bo's bedroom. "You've really done a lot with the place," she said for the one hundredth time. "I had no idea this room was so big."

"We know, we know, and no it's not bigger than yours," said Sunday. "It's just more organized, and we're keeping it that way, right, Bo?"

Bo kept her eyes away from the pens and notebook on the floor near the closet. "We're working on it," she said. "Anyway, let's get down to business. We've only got a few days left before the party, and . . ."

". . . And we have no idea what we're doing," said Lee. "Why did we ever think we could battle Reese? We haven't been able to agree on one song. This is stressful—maybe we should work on a plan to turn the shelter animals into therapy animals instead! I've been working with Dwayne Wayne and Urkel, and—"

"It doesn't matter what we sing if we don't look good. If some-body would just take over my chores, I'd be able to finish our out-fits and at least we'd look cute," said Lil.

"Nice try, both of you," said Sunday. "Bo's got it all worked out. Bo, please continue."

Bo took out her notebook. "Actually," she said, "I don't have it all worked out."

"Ahhhh!" cried Sunday.

"Go to bed!" yelled the Parents from downstairs.

After a few minutes, Sunday turned her penlight on. "What do you mean, you don't have it worked out?" she whispered. "That's your thing, remember? I'm the zany one, Lee's the wacky animal lover, and Lil's the sore loser."

"Hey!" said the Twins at the same time.

"Oh, cool, you guys almost never do that," said Sunday. "Also, I was just kidding. Lil cheats too much to lose." An immediate almost-silent pillow fight ensued; even Bo joined in. The cats, who had been curled up by the closet door, left in disgust.

Bo grabbed her sticks and tapped out a half-time groove on her notebook. "Guys! We're going to get busted, and trust me, we're skating on pretty thin ice as it is."

"Thanks to you two," said Lil. "Still haven't forgiven you for going on an adventure without us. I want to meet Dougie!"

"You will, at the party, if we can get it together," said Bo.

Sunday insisted that a "retro disco jazz groove" would be a surefire win over whatever "generic pop blandness" Gloss had in store. Lee, still feeling "itchy" about singing lead, was in favor of anything that involved extensive background vocals, and Lil reminded them of her essay on the history of pop music and the genius of Johanna Jackson. "There's a way to do pop music that's flavored with soul," she said. "That song 'Brixton Bop'? It's like chocolate Rice Krispie treats."

"What does that even mean?" asked Bo.

Lil shrugged. "I don't know. It sounded good, and I'm hungry."

Giggling, they shushed each other repeatedly, and they were completely silent and still by the time the Parents arrived at the bedroom door.

Over the next five days, Pop served chili four times (he tried to pretend the fourth was a "spicy shepherd's pie," but no one was fooled) and offered to make a tub of it for the party. All four girls agreed to launch a group appeal to keep *that* from happening. Bo helped Sunday create a chart of all of the neighbors who'd promised to bring food, and they discreetly double-checked while they made the round to collect RSVPs.

"I've been working on my act," said Ms. Tyler one day as they were headed to the bookstore. "What's first prize?" The girls, who were walking Rubia, looked at each other.

"We were thinking that this is more like a community-building thing," Bo said. "You know, bonding. Togetherness."

Ms. Tyler rolled her eyes. "I heard y'all were competing with that Cruz girl and her friends. Doesn't sound like togetherness to me."

"That's different," said Lil. "Some neighbors need to be destroyed."

"Lil!" said Bo, Sunday, and Lee.

"She didn't mean that," said Lee.

Ms. Tyler laughed. "You're the feisty one, huh? I like that. Did you make that dress? Looks like you might know a thing or two about a needle and thread."

"I did," said Lil. "And I do. It's actually a skort dress. See, these are trick pleats. . . ." Lil and Ms. Tyler jumped into a conversation about things like sergers and fabric grain, until Rubia barked that it was time to get going.

"That dog is too big," grumbled Ms. Tyler, but Bo could tell she didn't mean it. That was how she found herself talking to or about the animals these days. She'd even almost laughed when Mr. Bultitude had knocked over an entire quart of full sours from the Pickle Guys, and vowed to do a research paper on Why Must Cats Knock Things Down in the fall.

People in the neighborhood said hello to them as they walked. A little girl coming out of Grandma's Place toy and book store jumped up and down and waved, like the sisters were celebrities. A trio of elders sitting on a stoop in matching orange T-shirts that said *227 Crew* even mentioned the party, and Lee happily pointed out that nobody was making "the scrunchy I-hate-dogs face." Amy informed them that she had assigned herself the job of garden security. On their way back home, they bumped into Sunflower, who had made another run to the hardware store.

"You all have the block buzzing," she said. "Need anything?"

"Prayers," said Lee, and Auntie Sunflower laughed.

They stopped by the bookstore, where Bill was in good spirits. "I have great news," he said.

"Are people shopping?" asked Sunday. "Ordering hardcovers?"

Bill smiled. "I got an email from the day care center around the corner from us. They want to hire your band to do some . . . gigs? For the kids at their center. It sounded like it could be a regular job!"

The girls looked at each other and cheered. "This is only the beginning," said Sunday. "Today day care, tomorrow Radio City Music Hall!"

"Actually, how about tomorrow Bill's Bookshop?" asked Bill. "Your first customers are looking to return. And a Mrs. Clayton came in to say that her daughters Renée and Tameka told her they wanted to be looked after by the 'amazing musical babysitters' that 'live' in my store. Word is spreading!"

More cheering, and then the sisters began to hatch a plan for their next session at the store.

"Lee, you have that Ella Jenkins vibe," said Sunday. "You can sit them in a circle for a bunch of call and response."

"Abiyoyo will be fully trained by then. Who's going to manage the dog story corner?" Lee asked.

"More importantly," Bo said to Bill. "Is it okay? If we babysit here again?"

"I'll be honored to have you and, of course, provide a little light supervision."

"I'm happy to join," came a voice from the doorway. "Since I'll be here and all." Bo turned; Mum was standing with a big platter of cookies. Confused, the girls looked from Mum to Bo. "I'll be launching Lola's Cookies from right here in the shop!"

"It's a way to boost business for us both, and having the family in the shop as much as possible is a dream come true," said Bill. And Bo realized that it was a dream she'd never had before, but now it sounded perfect, and new, and she liked that. A lot.

"I have an idea," she said. "Sort of an idea and an announcement."

"You sound like me!" said Sunday. "And I love it!"

Bo took in a deep breath. "I need help. With the cupcakes. There are a lot of them. Can we bake them together"—she looked at Mum—"here?"

Mum tilted her head toward Bill.

Bo took a deep breath. "What do you think . . . um, Pop?"

"We thought you'd never ask!" yelled her sisters. Group hugging ensued.

Pop took another bow. "Again, honored. And happy to be your apprentice . . . or not." He pointed to the wheels on his chair. "And if you all need a backup dancer or a hype man, I can get my spoke lights on, break out the whistle," he said, snapping his fingers and doing the Snake. "Ask your sisters—I can get my Club Quarantine groove on anytime!" Sunday, Lil, and Lee groaned loudly.

Mum pulled Bo aside. "I know you were disappointed about our trip, really disappointed, and I have a gift for you. It's not Black Paris or Lagos, but . . ."

"Is it Queens?" asked Bo. "Because we can get a taste of both just by riding the 7 train."

Mum laughed. "True. But this involves a plane. A trip to Auntie Fola's cottage in Savannah, Georgia."

"Savannah is dripping with mystery!" said Sunday. "So many stories! Uh . . . not that we're going with you this time, but could you take good notes?" Everyone laughed, and Bo hugged her mum, hard.

29

IN A BOOK, Bo thought as they surveyed the garden on the morning of the party, this day would be perfect. The sun would be shining. The garden would be blooming, the birds would be singing . . .

Just then Barbara and Shirley clucked. Loudly. Bo was snapped back to reality, where the hens needed feeding, the garden looked clean but unfinished, they were exhausted, and the clouds looked a little heavy. The Parents had made lights-out an hour earlier every night—instead of, Bo complained, canceling swimming, "domestic arts and sciences" (chores), and reading journals.

"This isn't exactly how I imagined," said Lil.

"But it's awesome," said Sunday firmly. "Different, but awesome."

"Is this the performers' entrance?" said Marcus. He and Kareem were standing at the garden gate.

"It will be in, like, three hours," said Lil. "You're early."

"We're here to help," said Kareem. "Do you need any?"

Bo looked at her sisters. "Yep!"

Amy, Papa Charles, and Mama Hope came out early too, laying out tablecloths, setting up activity centers, and organizing the food buffet area. Dougie and Mrs. Dougie carefully chalked out a dance floor on the sidewalk.

"There's gonna be so much Electric Slide," Lil muttered, shaking her head. "The Wobble, Cupid Shuffle, Cha Cha Slide . . . old people sliding all over the place."

"Elders," said Papa Charles. "And you're right," he added, as one of his favorite songs started playing on Bill's tablet. "Before I let gooooo—oo—whoa—ooo—whoa!" he sang, and started dancing himself. The Twins made identical faces.

Ms. Tyler marched in wearing a red cape and carrying a tray of deviled eggs. "My grandmother taught me this recipe," she said proudly, holding the tray high. "Uh-oh, come on, now. Is that 'Candy' I hear?" She twirled as Bill's "Cookout Classics" playlist continued. "This stuff is starting now!" She wiggled her hips.

"Elder central," loud-whispered Lee. Ms. Tyler shot her some side-eye.

Drip! Drip!

"Did you feel that?" asked Mama Hope.

"No," everyone answered quickly.

Drip! Drip!

Bo looked up at the clouds. It didn't look good.

Three hours later Ms. Tyler and Mrs. Atta and Mama Fatou from the West African grocery were chilling in beach chairs and trading Bible verses like cards. "'Weeping may endure for a night,'" said Ms. Tyler, winking at Bo, "'but joy cometh in the morning.'" The sun was, in Amy's words, "high and dry in the sky," DJ Kendolyn was playing an Afrobeat set that had everyone dancing outside the chalk lines, and Mama Hope was showing off her double Dutch skills. Bo and her sisters cheered when the legendary 40+ Double Dutch Club clapped and invited Mama Hope to join them. Mama Yemisi's suya was grilling, and Pop's Brooklyn crew was managing the book table and providing hilarious commentary on the impromptu hat fashion show. Bo could almost say that the garden party was a resounding success.

Sunday said it. "This is a resounding success," she said as she ran past Bo in the middle of a game of hide-and-tag with the Bullock children, which looked confusing but fun enough that no one cared. Ms. Yolanda and her Dorothy Maynor Singers from Harlem School of the Arts were gearing up to sing the Black Lives Matter song that Bo and Sunday had written, and Mama Vy's Sing Harlem Choir would be taking the stage for a highly anticipated gospel medley that Mum said was sure to spark some auntie praise dancing. "And the community came through with the eats. We even got lobster fries from The Lighthouse *and* those fried shrimp from Famous Fish Market!" She winked at Bo. "I saved us a plate. Or two." They dapped each other up.

"This is beautiful, honey," said Mum, who was wearing a flowy yellow dress and a headwrap set that Lil had designed for the occasion. The sisters had gone to the Malcolm Shabazz Market to pick out the fabric together. Gold bracelets ringed her arms, but it was her smile that made her shine. "Thank you so, so much."

"You look amazing, Mum," said Bo.

"So do you," said Mum. "You girls look like real superstars. Is this all Lil's work?"

"We did it together," Bo said. "I know how to sew in a zipper now!" Lil wanted to set up an online business like one of her sewing idols, Mimi G., so she'd been filming herself giving her sisters lessons. Bo enjoyed it, even though Lil said they had to keep smiling at the camera and say "Lilly D, you are an outstanding instructor!" every five minutes.

Bo wasn't sure if any adoptions had happened, but Dwayne Wayne, in his summer hat, was the star of the animal corner, where Lee had placed him next to the Madagascar cockroaches. As Mrs. Dougie prepared to go onstage as the emcee for the talent show, Pop came over. "Hey, it turns out that I know Dawn's cousin Craig. He was a producer on *Video Music Box*. Legendary show."

"Dawn?" Bo asked.

"Sorry—Dougie's mom," Pop said. "Little Dougie's got bars too." He looked around. "I'm thinking of doing a weekly talent night at the shop."

Bo smiled. "That's a good idea," she said. "I'll help . . . and I have some more ideas, Pop, if you want."

"How about we talk over tea tomorrow?" asked Pop. "The three of us?" Bo nodded.

Rubia was staring longingly at a beagle leaping around the open fire hydrant near the end of the block. "Go play," said Bo, nodding toward the water spray. But Rubia stayed put and looked back at Bo as if to say "That's cute, but obviously Beneath Me." The talent show was about to start, and Gloss was nowhere to be found.

"You think they chickened out?" said Sunday. "I knew it!"

"Nah, they're going to make an entrance, watch," said Lil.

"Whatever they do doesn't matter," said Bo firmly. "We do our thing." She opened her arms wide. She looked around at her neighbors, old and new, plates piled high with food. It was like a book, or a TV show, but it was real life. Her life was new and different, not one thing or the other, and she wasn't sure what would happen next.

"Thanks again for helping me with the cupcakes," said Bo. "I couldn't have done that without you, no matter how much I might have wanted to prove that I could."

"Why are you thanking us?" asked Sunday. "It was fun to do together! And the reward is going to be delicious."

"It is," said Lil. "It really is."

"Lil!" Lee looked shocked and shook her head, turning to Bo and Sunday, who looked away. "Wait a minute, you had some too?!"

"Here," said Bo, holding a piece of cupcake out. Lee held her frown for another second, then she grabbed it out of Bo's hand.

DJ Kendolyn started playing "Jerusalema," and everyone with a plate of food in their hands started doing the line dance.

"What did I tell you?" said Lil, but then she jumped in beside Auntie Sunflower.

Bo took a few moments alone to survey the garden. It truly wasn't much yet, but she could see its potential. Mum's friend Mama Tanya had come down from the Bronx to check it out; she was a community garden expert and was going to help them work on more crops and a possible community fridge setup. There was a lot of summer ahead for everything to grow.

Sunday came up next to her. "Okay for me to join you?" she asked. And because Bo knew that she could say it wasn't, it was. They wondered aloud how long it would take for the sunflowers to grow tall, and if stray cats were ever going to use the Cat Clubhouse. The lavender in the herb garden was giving Bo ideas; maybe a lemon-lavender loaf?

Sunday nudged Bo and pointed to the garden gate. Gloss stood there, looking around like they were expecting to be asked for autographs. And then as the Twins joined Bo and Sunday, a little girl did ask Reese for her autograph, and Lil fake vomited.

Marcus and Kareem came over. "Are you ready to see our moves?" asked Marcus, striking a pose. "Check out the fit— Dapper Dan hooked us up."

"For real?" asked Lil.

"Well, we saw a video of his fashion show at Howard

Homecoming, so . . . it's kind of inspired by that." Marcus shrugged and posed again.

"What's your act again?" asked Bo. "I don't think you ever actually said."

"It's a medley," said Marcus.

"A mélange," said Kareem.

"Sounds like a mess," muttered Lil. "But . . . break a leg."

"Thank you," said Marcus. "You guys too."

Kareem smiled. "This is a pretty awesome party. You guys really went off. Thanks for inviting us." The sisters looked at each other in surprise as the two boys went off to grab some cornbread from the Red Rooster table.

"Are we . . . actually friends with them?" asked Sunday.

"Oooh, I'm scared," Lee said as Gloss started warming up, complete with dramatic vocal runs.

Mrs. Dougie kicked off the talent show with a freestyle tribute to Biz Markie from Dougie, and the sisters took the opportunity to help Lee take deep breaths in front of Abiyoyo's kennel at Dr. Coleman's shelter pop-up. By the time Gloss went on, people on the sidewalk were crowding around the garden to watch the show.

"Welp, they're still good," said Lil as Gloss took their bows.

"So are we," said Bo and Sunday at the same time.

"Whatever happens, we have fun," said Bo. "And then we have cupcakes."

"Coming to the stage," said Mrs. Dougie, "is . . . is . . ." She paused and ran over to the sisters. "What's your group name?" she asked.

Lee looked at her sisters and said, "We're a well-oiled machine."

"A thing"—Lil waved her arm with a flourish—"of beauty."

"A pretty complex operation," added Sunday.

"Operation Sisterhood," said Bo, as they got into position. "Operation Sisterhood! We're Operation Sisterhood!"

The crowd cheered, and the sisters smiled at each other until Bo heard a familiar *tcha* sound as Ms. Tyler sucked her teeth. "Well, come on, then," said Ms. Tyler. "Show us what you're working with."

Bo started a sixteenth-note groove and looked at Sunday. "Let's GOOOOOOOOOOOO!" they yelled together.

Author's Note

Hello, Bookish Friend!

In a lot of ways, *Operation Sisterhood* has been around since I was a kid. Not long ago, I found a few typed-on-an-old-school-typewriter pages that were part of its beginnings—mini stories about some of the at-home adventures that my sister and I had in our many backyards and neighborhood playgrounds and behind plastic-covered couches on boring visits to Aunties before they inevitably made us play the dusty piano or organ and gave us mints and hard candies.

Over the years, we also had some of our best times with another pair of sisters, especially creating the many "shows" that we subjected our poor moms to. (We quickly learned to write "NO REFUNDS" on their tickets.) We loved music—to dance, sing, and play—and it didn't matter to us how good (or not so good) we were. We started a band called GLOSS and never got much further than designing a graffiti-inspired bubble-letter logo.

I loved stories about big, happy, creative families, like the Melendys and All-of-a-Kind Family, and had a special place in my heart for Noel Streatfeild's books because they were full of the arts. I'd imagine myself into those stories and write and rewrite my own Black versions because I wanted to see the Black love and joy that I knew in life reflected on the page.

My own family was big in its way, across the African diaspora, but very spread out. We had a few large gatherings on holidays and special occasions when our travels allowed. I longed to be constantly squeezed together around the piano, singing and laughing, devouring rice and peas and plantains, and just eating the icing off black cake. My parents were immigrants from Jamaica and Nigeria; we moved a lot throughout my childhood. I rarely had the big family-gathering experiences that I read about or the matching T-shirt family-reunion cookout extravaganzas that were part of the lives of so many of my friends in the United States. While I had a perfectly good little sister (I guess), there were a number of years when I asked my parents to "get" us "twins" for Christmas. Sure, a little sister was fun to boss around and force to watch my "cooking show" when I made dinner, be a student in my "dance school," and ask our parents for things they had already said no to, but I thought: How magical would it be to have a sister exactly my age, and *two* little sisters exactly the same age who could do *double* the things I wanted them to do? It seemed genius to me, and I convinced my sister that it was. Unfortunately, our parents never saw it that way.

Fortunately, they *did* see that nothing could replace the magic of New York City. No matter where we lived, we spent so much of our time in the city where I was born (big ups to the Bronx), the city of my heart, with frequent trips to the theater and to street fairs, museums, and parks. My mom taught us how to take advantage of all the free-of-charge magic that NYC has to offer. I spent hours every weekend exploring the Village, the Lower East Side, and Tribeca. There was the Harlem of Rosa Guy, Walter Dean Myers, James Baldwin, and Alice Childress; I booed during

Amateur Night at the Apollo and marveled at the treasures in the Schomburg. I cheered Nelson Mandela on 125th Street; I marched with Ben & Jerry when they opened their Harlem store. I visited all the places that I read about in books, from Harriet the Spy's Carl Schurz Park on the Upper East Side to the pickle barrels and penny candy shops of the All-of-a-Kind Family's Lower East Side. I figured out how to get to Sesame Street and brought my skates to Central Park—then just watched the real skaters do their thing. I took subway rides to whole new worlds just a few stops away—or sometimes to the ends of the line (shout-out to the A train).

Operation Sisterhood is a celebration of all the wonderful galaxies New York City contains. Now I use those long subway rides for writing and thinking through stories. I scribble on park benches and by the Hudson River. I write in the libraries, where I can have tea and biscuit breaks at Seward Park, meet a therapy dog at George Bruce, and sort books for a book sale in Clinton Hill. I'm grateful for and inspired by community gardens like the vibrant Joseph Daniel Wilson Memorial Garden in Harlem that welcomes a variety of neighbors, grumpy feline friends included. There are still some skaters in Central Park—I smile and stroll past. It's one of my greatest joys to walk this city of wonderers, wanderers, music lovers, movers, readers, shakers, believers, and dreamers.

Finally, *Operation Sisterhood* is a love letter to my daughter, and all Black girls who long for the room to be, to discover and rediscover themselves, to laugh until they fall on the floor, to cry and be vulnerable, to be righteously angry. To the ones who need a quiet corner now and then, and the ones who claim center stage.

The creative, brilliant, beautiful, and powerful girls who look for themselves in stories, who love meeting new friends on the page, who read to ask questions, who write to answer and ask again. To all of you, who deserve our loving care, our listening ears, our grace, tears, cheers, and to be *seen*, just as you are.

OLUGBEMISOLA RHUDAY-PERKOVICH

Bo's Sunshine Surprise Smilecake

INGREDIENTS

CAKE

1 ½ cups sugar (I like raw cane sugar or turbinado sugar. I've also used dark brown sugar in this recipe. Basically: sugar, get into it. But not too much, because, you know, it's sugar.)

½ cup softened salted butter or margarine

2 large eggs (Barbara and Shirley have shown me the joys of super-fresh eggs. If you know someone with hens, maybe you can make a swap. Or if there's a farmers market in your area, check it out!)

2 ½ cups flour

3 teaspoons baking powder

¼ teaspoon salt

1 cup whole-milk PLAIN yogurt (Trust me, it'll be sweet enough once you frost it. I won't let you down! I use Ronnybrook Farm yogurt.)

pinch of ground ginger (A pinch can be up to a teaspoon sometimes for me! I was inspired to add ginger to this recipe by my sisters, Lil and Lee, who told me a very funny story about the first time they went "back home" to Jamaica.)

zest and juice of three lemons

1 teaspoon vanilla extract

RASPBERRY FROSTING

8 ounces cream cheese, room-temperature

1 stick salted butter

3 ½ cups confectioner's sugar

About 1 cup freeze-dried raspberries (or strawberries for strawberry frosting!)—if you don't have those, a plain cream cheese frosting (just the cream cheese, confectioner's sugar, and butter) or a lemon cream cheese frosting (swap in the juice and the zest of a large lemon for the freeze-dried fruit) works fine!

DIRECTIONS

CAKE

+ Put on an apron or T-shirt to cover your outfit (especially if your sister Lil reminds you of how much time it took to make said outfit), and wash your hands thoroughly. Preheat the oven to 350° F. Spray a 9-inch cake pan with baking spray; the sprays that also contain flour are great. (Or you can grease the pan with butter and sprinkle it with flour. This just keeps it from sticking, but if it sticks, no big deal—that happens to Sunday a lot; she likes to think of that as a bonus "scrape-n-taste" opportunity.)

+ In a mixing bowl, combine the sugar and butter. Beat on medium speed with an electric mixer until well mixed. Add the eggs and beat until combined.

+ Combine the flour, baking powder, ginger, and salt in a bowl with a whisk.

+ With the mixer running, alternately add the flour mixture and yogurt, mixing until blended after each addition. Stir in the vanilla, lemon zest, and lemon juice.

+ Pour the batter into the prepared pan. Place in the oven and bake at 350°F for 20 to 25 minutes, or until an inserted knife comes out clean. Remember that one oven's 350 might be another's 375—ovens can vary, so I like to check after 20 minutes. (We had a whole history and science unit on cooking with heat that was both delicious and fun!)

+ Turn off the oven. Wearing oven mitts or gloves, remove the cake pan from the oven and let cool for 5 to 10 minutes, then remove the cake from the pan and let it cool completely. I usually just flip it onto a plate, but Mum has an official wire rack thing.

+ Now frost that baby like it's going to be in a frosting fashion show! And I mean go for it—lay it on thick! See below for frosting recipe ideas.

- Store the cake in an airtight container at room temperature for a day or two. But if you still have cake after a day, I'm like WHAT.

FROSTING

- You can blend the freeze-dried berries with the other ingredients if you want something like "candy" bits in your frosting. If not, first pulverize the freeze-dried fruit in a food processor or with a mortar and pestle, if you're old school like that, which is pretty cool.

- Blend the cream cheese and butter together.

- Slowly add the confectioner's sugar, blending it in.

- Add the freeze-dried fruit. Blend until you've got the frosting consistency you want. Sometimes you might want a little more confectioner's sugar for a thicker frosting—go slowly and add it little by little, as needed.

Acknowledgments

To all my sisters, biological and by choice, who know how I am and bear with me anyway.

To the brilliant and large-hearted Marietta Zacker, who knows more than a thing or two about true sisterhood.

Infinite gratitude to Phoebe Yeh, for your trust and support and genius—you "got" this story from the moment we first talked about it and carried me through ever since.

Many thanks to Brittney Bond for the beautiful and vibrant art—it is EVERYTHING.

Most of all, thank you to the readers of all ages who open their hearts to my characters and their lives. Thank you for inspiring and motivating me, and reminding me to honor the enduring magic of childhood.

ABOUT THE AUTHOR

Kikelomo Amusa-Shonubi

OLUGBEMISOLA RHUDAY-PERKOVICH is the author of *8th Grade Superzero*, the nonfiction books *Above and Beyond: NASA's Journey to Tomorrow* and *Someday Is Now: Clara Luper and the 1958 Oklahoma City Sit-Ins*, and the upcoming *Mae Makes a Way* and *Saving Earth: The Climate Crisis and the Fight for Our Future*. She is the coauthor of the middle-grade novel *Two Naomis*, which was nominated for an NAACP Image Award, and its sequel, *Naomis Too*. Inspired by some of her favorite family stories and the city she loves, *Operation Sisterhood* is a celebration of the sweetness and spice of sisterhood.

Olugbemisola is a member of The Brown Bookshelf and a former board member of We Need Diverse Books. She lives with her family in New York City, where she writes, makes things, and needs to get more sleep. You can find her online at **olugbemisolabooks.com**.